On the BLUE TRAIN

KRISTEL THORNELL

ALLEN&UNWIN
SYDNEY • MELBOURNE • AUCKLAND • LONDON

First published in 2016

Australian Government

Allen & Unwin
83 Alexander Street
Crows Nest NSW 2065
Australia
Phone: (61 2) 8425 0100
Email: info@allenandunwin.com
Web: www.allenandunwin.com

Cataloguing-in-Publication details are available
from the National Library of Australia
www.trove.nla.gov.au

ISBN 978 1 76029 310 9

Set in 12.5/20 pt Adobe Garamond Pro by Bookhouse, Sydney
Printed and bound in Australia by Griffin Press

10 9 8 7 6 5 4 3 2

1

SECOND DAY, 4 DECEMBER 1926

Harrods like the *Titanic* on a grey sea of winter daylight and nothing for it but to go aboard. Only she couldn't budge, couldn't even recall what she needed to purchase. The last hours had been simple. Now she was emptied and dopey again, her limbs dull, everything woolly. A woolly gentleman was holding open the door. Had he noticed her soiled shoes?

A lady brushed past Agatha, all polish and ease. She was slim, dark-haired and piquant in an uncommonly well-tailored magenta dress.

A foppish young man at her side drawled, 'Teresa, darling, I'll see you in half an hour.' It was clear that he wasn't her husband.

Teresa wasn't terribly young, Agatha thought, but she had not surrendered to age. She gave him a farewell peck and was so magnetic, heading for the open door, that Agatha with relief was able to follow her through it. And she continued to trail Teresa, the two women sauntering among covetable merchandise, Agatha pausing when the other paused and even, after a while, trying some of her gestures, which were wonderfully collected and free of anxiety. They stroked pairs of kid gloves, eyed hats with chin tilted. The gap between them was closing.

Until at last—they were each holding a copy of the same white silk shawl specked with silver—their eyes met. They didn't smile but regarded one another candidly before turning away.

It wouldn't have been seemly to go on following Teresa, so Agatha rested her bags from the Army and Navy Stores on the floor and fished in her handbag as if for a shopping list. She chanced on the ring with the loose setting that an age ago she'd meant to have fixed. Surely this wasn't the purpose of her visit to Harrods? It wasn't a pressing task, though there was always a sense of rightness about seeing to repairs. When she looked up, Teresa with her magenta glamour was gone.

Not entirely, for Agatha discovered traces of the other woman in her own stance and walk, which remained light and fluid as she retrieved her bags, straightened her spine aristocratically and proceeded on to the jewellery department.

She wavered only when the jeweller was examining her ring. So thoroughly, his touch delicate and humane, that she wanted to cry. *She is all right*. Saying it might make it so.

He reassured her that the mending would be a straight-forward matter. 'It'll be as good as new,' he avowed.

She swallowed. 'Good, excellent.' Her voice still wanted practice.

'Where shall we deliver it to, miss?'

He must have studied her ring finger, a region that was his professional territory. She was taking a holiday from her wedding ring.

'Where?'

'Yes, miss, to what address?'

She hesitated. She was determined to get herself to Yorkshire, where she and her husband had intended to go for a little getaway, before. 'To Harrogate.' She remembered an advertisement she had seen. 'The Harrogate Hydro.'

'Very good, miss. And to what name?'

Behind her a voice exclaimed, 'Cracking!'

'Teresa,' she said firmly. 'Teresa . . . *Neele*. Mrs.' He would find this odd, given her bare finger.

She made her way shortly after to King's Cross, with the stealth of a spy, of a magician with his vanishing trick. For then it was all as light and silky as breathing in another's breath.

2

SECOND DAY, EVENING

It was almost seven o'clock when the stone edifice appeared finally in the taxicab's headlamps. The Harrogate Hydro was a dignified hotel, congenially discreet behind scrawls of ivy. The driver's conversation had limited itself to the unlikeliness of snow in the coming days but she had remained indifferent to the weather throughout her long journey. She climbed out, requiring no assistance with her eccentrically meagre luggage, and stood before the entrance. She was acutely thirsty. Could this place be the very thing?

Indoors, she found a hospitable fire burning, inviting armchairs, a fine grandfather clock. The lulling promise of the setting was mighty, though like tea-leaves it would take time to infuse and unfurl.

'Good evening, madam,' a woman of a certain age greeted

her, solidly but well made and preserved, with a stolid air and a head of intricately braided dark red hair.

Concentrating, she introduced herself and declared interest in a room.

'How long do you plan to stop with us, Mrs Neele?'

The question might have been put in a language she once knew. 'I'm not sure yet,' she said, at length. 'That will depend. I'm awaiting word from friends.'

'Very good, Mrs Neele. Your luggage . . . ?'

'Just this. You see, I've not long arrived. From . . . Cape Town. My things will be sent along.'

She signed the visitors' book dutifully, *Teresa Neele*. A wavy signature, light and silky.

Redhead now revealed herself as the proprietress and too professional for chitchat or cross-examining. Teresa was thankful. A chambermaid accompanied her in the electric elevator, one floor up.

The room and its robust, unflinching furnishings would do well. She'd be at her ease here, wouldn't she? The maid got a fire underway, and went to see about tea.

The window gave onto the drive and the road the taxi had taken, with its line of smart stone houses. The North. She had been living on the numb side of amazement, but she felt then a remote shiver of adventure. She divested herself of the barely recognisable coat purchased in London that morning—just that morning?—at the Army and Navy Stores, along with the small case, a nightdress and a hot-water bottle. The maid returned, and departed.

Solitude and tea! Oh yes. The flames started to give off heat. She had only the clothes she wore and it was tiresome not to be able to change, yet she determined to go down to dinner like any traveller. Her memory for food was usually as faithful as her memory for conversation, but she struggled to call her last meal to mind. Something at King's Cross? Egg-and-cress sandwiches? She avoided the looking-glass on the dresser, reckoning on fatigue's shabby treatment of her face. And she'd postpone a letter to her husband until after dinner.

As she lay back into the animal contentment of a hot bath, she noted a twinge of lumbago, and quite a severe pain in her right shoulder or the side of her neck. Though these began to fade and she saw the view from the train again. The winter fields all lilac drifts of spindly trees and dark mists of hedges in the advancing night.

•

The only other tardy diners, she observed from a small table in an expansive, gracious room, were an elderly couple appearing to wear age rather pertly and a man who, while seated at their table, maintained a certain apartness. Dark brown hair, barely silvered. Eyes set deeply in a face between thin and gaunt.

The younger man, likely a year or two older than she was, that was to say, than Teresa, negotiated what seemed to be a vast pudding carelessly. He was also reading a newspaper—a stratagem for independence—with a studious but unstuffy aspect. Then he raised his eyes and nodded to Teresa so gravely and minimally that, had there not been a fugitive smile for confirmation, she'd have doubted having seen it. Her dormant hunger was roused. She ate a rabbit pie and two helpings of bread and sublime butter with relish. It was tasty, well-prepared country food, and she congratulated herself once more on having reached the Hydro. She only wished she had a book to hand. She toyed with the idea of taking some alcoholic drink—quite unlike her, a loather of the flavour of the stuff. She wasn't particularly fond of the drinker's bonhomie, either, which could be somehow eerily self-pleasing. But she'd sometimes regretted her aversion and it might have been a notion of ceremony or play-acting that was attractive that evening. Still, her travels had left her in enough of a stupor as it was, so she contented herself with water.

The elderly couple stopped by her table as she was relinquishing knife and fork. 'Good evening,' said the woman, amiably formal. 'I am Mrs Jackman. And this is my husband. We were adjourning to the drawing room. I don't suppose you'd care to join us there for coffee?'

Mrs Jackman conferred on Teresa that radiant, almost beatific smile that some older women possess, while Mr Jackman nodded chivalrously. Teresa wondered how to express her intention to retire to bed with diplomacy. However, she had noticed their vain efforts to persuade the younger man to accompany them to the drawing room, their eagerness for company only too plain. She herself had gone a long time without it, and maybe this fact too swayed her resolve.

'I'm a widow,' she said once they were seated, as if to clarify her position.

'Oh, I'm so sorry.' The good lady blinked in stately sympathy. Her husband rearranged his serviette on his knee. 'I hope you don't mind my asking,' ventured Mrs Jackman tremulously, as if constrained to put the question, 'whether you have any children?'

Feeling a touch in jeopardy, Teresa studied the pretty white flowers in the vase on the chimneypiece. She might have stood and left them with a vague excuse, but it was in her character to be socially meek. She sipped her coffee.

'My baby girl also died.'

'No!' exclaimed Mrs Jackman, spellbound. Her husband's leather armchair creaked as though communicating in its old, softly world-weary way a pity he could not formulate.

Mrs Jackman: 'Illness?'

'Accident.'

The older woman asked no more. She would imagine—vividly, judging from her brightening, suddenly ageless eyes. Treacherous flight of stairs, unfortunate motorcar, rebellious horse. Mr Jackman's despondent effort at a smile suggested he'd had experience of grief. It was commonly observed that men wouldn't speak of emotional suffering. Indeed, it could be as if they *had* no words for it. They were still waiting on the arrival of that particular script. In fairness, Teresa too had come to distrust words, since Mummy had gone. What did anyone have to say about pain? What could be said?

This was their annual *cure* at the Hydro, Mrs Jackman explained, taking the burden of the conversation onto her own capable shoulders. She elaborated that they did not approve of diet meals and eschewed them. All three relaxed a little. The Jackmans wanted to know if this was Teresa's first visit, and assured her she'd enjoy Harrogate. It was so restful, and beneficial for rheumatism. There was excellent exercise to be taken, many charming hours' occupation to be found in Valley Gardens and on the moor. The healthy air made you ravenous and devoted patrons of Bettys Café Tea Rooms. They were mad for the Royal Baths. So well appointed. The firelight endowed their cheeks with a renewed rosy youth.

'We try it all,' stated Mr Jackman.

'There's the nicest Turkish bath suite you've ever seen,' his wife emphasised. 'You come out as fresh and bewildered as a babe. We *must* go together.'

'I'd like that.'

The prospect of receiving curative treatments, of some self-indulgence, was not unappealing. Such a lovely word, *convalescence*: susurrating, dove-grey, respectable but steeped in sanatorium romance. Oh, to lounge and be coddled.

'It's decided. And you'll be taking the water?'

'I think I will.'

'Pretty strong flavour,' offered Mr Jackman. 'Like old eggs. Or gunpowder. Not that I've tasted gunpowder.'

'Salty. But you grit your teeth, you get used to it. There's no question about it,' Mrs Jackman ended, 'it's rather nice to be taken care of.'

A short while later, Teresa approached the foot of the staircase, about to retire to her room. The solitary man from dinner was passing in through the hotel's entrance with a slow thoughtfulness, as if concluding a leisurely stroll. Was he given to reverie? It could be a mistake to assume a poetic spirit in a man, and to trust him, of course. But she lifted her hand, more a reflex than a conscious action. He returned her wave quite naturally. He had the face of someone you might have met before, with those deep-set eyes that appeared to be brown. Meeting them, she had to reach abruptly for the banister. It was the exhaustion, slinking up on her.

•

Without further delay, she would write to her husband.

Who was very much alive, contrary to what she'd said. Even if it wasn't often owned to, it was reasonable to conceal aspects of oneself. Imitating the great icebergs was a prudent modus operandi—only the tiniest portion exposed and the rest of your leviathan self gliding beneath the waterline.

She seized the pen with a pang. How she longed to again be juggling sentences like so many flashing knives. Busy at that, she was always in her right mind. Like a child perhaps, being bold, but prettily, for the most part, and so quite getting away with it. However, this was a different business altogether. Peter was *not* at his usual station beneath her writing table: no gentle aroma on the air of wire-haired terrier, no torpid barrel of him warming the hollows of her feet. The pen was poised like a person, just beyond the threshold of a room, who has forgotten the task they came there to complete. For hours she'd been scrabbling aridly in her mind to compose a letter. Now she was compelled to test its possible parts sotto voce before she could risk entrusting them to paper.

Darling.

Do forgive me for my last rushed note. I was in something of a state. You know I haven't been myself. A cure will be just what the doctor ordered, then I'll be as good as new. The idea of our reunion sustains me. Know that, darling.

None of it was right. Her pen had been thoroughly infected by the ugly inadequacy that had stalled her Wretched Book.

•

Sleep refused to snuff her out in a nice bed in the north of England. Her brain hummed on. She had difficulty taking deep breaths, something she'd learned to recognise as the presage of a bad night, that and the crouching sense of catastrophe. A brutal malediction, a brain not able to rest when it most needed to, resisting comfort. If it were to be so, there would be no mercy, no place to hide at all.

3

THIRD DAY

'I beg your pardon, ma'am,' the maid said, quietly but decidedly. 'I've woken you. Shall I draw the curtains and have a fire going?'

'Oh, please. Is it late?' She rose onto her elbows, narrowing her eyes at brusque daylight. Teresa had slept—solidly. Astonished, she observed the springy mind that lifts from true rest. Recalling last night's unease, she felt washed clean, hugely improved.

'Ten o'clock, ma'am.'

A *grasse matinée*! The nightdress she'd broken in had a scent of pristine flannel. This and the regenerative sleep gave things a hopeful Christmassy aura.

Without being pretty exactly, the maid was youthfully willowy, her darkish blonde hair captive beneath a bonnet. At this age she could get away with violet depressions under the eyes, fatigue for now a touch of spice. Those eyes did not look at Teresa quite directly, yet they paid attention. They were keen. An observant eye wasn't necessarily ideal in a servant. One rather preferred them less alert, at times.

'Would you care for a newspaper, ma'am?'

Was there something strained in her tone? Teresa wasn't ready for the wide world. 'No. I don't think so. Thank you.'

'Your breakfast, ma'am—will you be having it downstairs, or wanting it here?'

She pictured the lazy curiosity of a gathering of recently woken hotel guests. 'Here. I'll take it here.' Her imagination wandered to sausages, black pudding, a gay breakfast. However, her eating having been off, and after the previous night's good meal, she ought to be cautious. 'Something light?'

'The slimming diet? Split toast and grapefruit, ma'am?'

Reluctantly, she accepted.

She ate in bed, blank-headed, then lingered over a make-shift toilette. She dared to peek into the glass and wasn't unhappy with its cool truths. Genuine sleep had given her a cleansed, peaceful look. She thought of a pale river stone, of the River Dart—this pleasure disturbed by a flicker of disgust at having to wear the same old green jumper, grey stockinette skirt, grey cardigan and velour hat. How abject, one's own mustiness. She'd *have* to see about new clothes. And books! But it was Sunday, so patience.

On the point of departure, she noticed the sheets of stationery left out on the writing table and remembered the letter that was still unwritten. She searched for an acceptable phrase, standing at the window.

Darling . . .

Abandoning the effort, she consigned the empty pages to the glowing end of the fire and assured their combustion with the poker. There'd be time to write when she'd settled, wouldn't there? The pain in her shoulder she'd been forewarned of the night before was now radiating irrefutably, nagging. Neuritis?

•

The sober, comely stone terrace houses were mesmerising, and Teresa fancied that the air, nippy but so fresh-tasting, purified her lungs. Gentle sunshine in a cerulean sky. Benign clouds that might have drifted from an illustration in a children's storybook. Harrogate was a salubrious, superior place, time itself seeming to progress smoothly there, coasting. She was judging herself not far from Bettys Tea Rooms when she passed an uncompromising-looking church, its doors the deep red of new blood.

A gargoyle sprang out at her like a jack-in-the-box. A haughty boyish figure fixing her with an ignoble, insolent stare. Leering.

Or so it seemed. She was stock-still, her idiotic heart hovering in fright. The sun had lost itself in cloud, the holy edifice engulfed in a stagnant cold. Red doors pulsing with the cadence of a migraine. It would be all right, Teresa was all right.

There was a beech tree nearby, and after a moment she went and braced herself against it. This jolt, this reaction to what was naturally nothing but carved stone, completely harmless, was preposterous. The only explanation she could furnish was that gargoyles had always unsettled her. Their stunted fiendish bodies appeared set on bursting into freedom and swooping voraciously down on the nervous like crazed birds of prey. She was grateful for the tree, which reminded her of the beech in the garden at Ashfield.

The clouds opened, a young woman passed with a skipping step, swinging a sparkling silver lamé handbag—vestige or foreshadowing of a festive evening—and everything slipped back into the sponginess of unrestricted time in a place where she was unknown.

She said aloud, experimentally, 'Swanning around, fancy-free.'

Just ahead of her, a lordly man in exquisite riding apparel turned at the sound of her words, his eyebrows raised.

Bettys was pervaded by an exceedingly English decorum. The lunch hour over, it was quiet. Almost steady again, Teresa requested a table for one. Her waiter, an enormously thin fellow, was as unobtrusively attentive as she could wish.

The pianist, less adroit or inclined to dissemble, played a deflated charleston.

Sipping superb tea, river-brown in sheer white china, she lunched on calming pumpkin soup and a most respectable roast beef sandwich. A book would have been secured between the weighty silver knife and the edge of the plate, and she sorely regretted not having one. Also, the servings were on the modest side and embarking on a course she foresaw its end, asking herself what would follow. She wrangled a little with her instincts, but ultimately undertook a scone studded with candied fruits. If she always needed treats, then this wasn't the time to deny herself. And hadn't she lost a considerable amount of weight? The coffee she ordered in conclusion set her heart scuttering.

•

The Royal Baths were lavish. The palatial premises boasted a cupola, turrets, winged lions for guards. She passed in, drawing her shoulders back.

A woman in a hypnotic white uniform, thick features, babyish blonde curls, expounded on the correct proceedings, Teresa only retaining that she should avoid the cold plunge bath if she'd just eaten. There was the hint of a scolding here, of the gruff head nurse keeping in check a wayward patient. Teresa swore gravely to steer clear of the plunge bath. She had zero desire to expose herself to another shock.

The close wooden walls of the chamber she was assigned along the ladies' dressing hall recalled a confessional. Inside it, she might have been years distant from the streets beyond. Where was she, exactly? She was apprehensive, then, as if something were awaiting her, looming. Was it only the residue of that featherbrained nonsense with the gargoyle? The strong coffee?

Wound in just a towel, she forced herself to sally forth into what might have been a luxurious little corner of the Orient. A civilised cavern, Moorish vaults and a mosaic of tiles underfoot. It was a hothouse in which female bodies were like voluptuous waxen jungle flowers somehow uprooted and moistly thriving. There was a naturalness to being hardly clothed like that, and she hadn't experienced it in . . . so long.

She ventured into a Hot Room—the Caldarium, or was it the Laconium? The settling of heavy red velvet drapes behind her gave the illusion of coming onto a stage. But there was a lone matron in a state of undress dozing there on a deckchair, so it resembled more the wings of a theatre, the matron an unlikely actress, ageing and relegated to shrill comic turns, stealing a nap between speeches.

Growing stupid under the single-minded influence of heat, Teresa wandered between warm and warmer rooms. Post-lunch somnolence was stalking her. She had grown accustomed to being in great need of sleep while unable to achieve it, and having to fend it off was a sly twist.

There persisted, too, that hunch that something was waiting for her, impending. However, in the scented mists of the Russian Vapour Room, she had to sit and could not fight any longer.

Oblivion like a hand pulling her through her own resistance.

•

The drawing room at Ashfield, a party afoot. Agatha in a decorative white muslin dress. Her pale hair is long enough to sit on, as it has not been in years, floating, lustrous. She is somewhere between child and woman, and perfectly happy.

Overhearing a guest she does not recognise exclaim that she is miraculously lovely, it dawns on her that the cause of this—she does feel unusually radiant—is the beverage she has been absently sipping. Mummy (who is not comfortable at social gatherings and will be dying for these festivities to end) had pushed it into her hand some time before. The glass has a kind of aureole. She understands that what she has taken for her favourite drink, half milk, half cream, is in fact a rare elixir whose brilliance has been seeping into her and illuminating her from within. She mustn't spill any.

Auntie-Grannie is there, as steadfastly cynical as ever (*You haven't left your handbag anywhere the servants can get at it, have you?*), and yet so sound, an unsinkable ship. And dear agreeable Father sits universally adored and unsuspecting on a Chippendale chair.

A man is leaning over him whispering something. A friend of the family, presumably, but she can't place him.

All at once tired and thirsting for aloneness, she slips out into the garden. Wind is coming off the sea, the air salty and sweet, perfume that always seems the clue to an ancient secret. She realises she's been missing it horribly as soon as she is offered it again.

She finds herself at the bottom of the garden's slope. Sensing she is not truly alone, she turns.

It is the man who was whispering to Father.

He faces her, but his features are masked with shadow. She is now less certain that she is indeed looking at a man. Such a thorough obscurity clings to the individual's whole figure that it could be a woman disguised in men's clothing.

What she can discern is the gun being pointed in her direction. Not with any evident malice. The gesture is almost offhanded, even vaguely genial. And this is the worst of it: that this person should have passed himself off as a friend, working his way surreptitiously into their cheerful family circle, into their confidence, only to turn and so blithely reveal his cunning.

The shadows about him shift as he proceeds towards her. It *is* a man's face, pleasant, quite handsome, and unthreatening—except for the eyes.

The menace is in the eyes. Here you see he is a bad lot, downright evil. Despite the half-light, she has the conviction they are a preternatural blue. Terribly clear. A colour that should mean innocence and is its opposite. Horror. An appalling Trojan horse of a gaze turned upon her in her childhood refuge . . .

•

'Mrs Neele!'

Through rolls of swirling vapour a figure advanced on her. She recognised the infantile golden curls and attitude of determined disapproval. Grouchy Nurse. It was clear she'd failed the lesson.

'I haven't set foot in the plunge bath,' Teresa protested.

Her recurring childhood nightmare, featuring the slippery impostor she had christened the Gun Man, had returned of late in the measly helpings of shut-eye she had been served, and it was around her still like a dark scent. Why had it always had such power over her?

'Your colour is very high, ma'am.' Nurse clicked her tongue, apparently discombobulated. 'We'll get you into a cool shower.'

Dizzy, Teresa leaned heavily on her strapping guide as she was assisted to the showers. It was nice to be handled with stern solicitude and positioned on a marble bench beneath falling water. If only the refreshing flow would never end, would purge her of the Gun Man for good, make her truly new and serene. She saw the River Dart again, then the tide coming in to Beacon Cove. 'There's nothing like water,' she said, 'to give you a fresh outlook. Growing up by water teaches you that, I suppose.'

'Pardon, ma'am?'

Teresa straightened up, head a little unwieldy but better. 'Water's wonderful.'

Nurse studied her. 'We're improving. Can I ask, ma'am, what complaints you have?'

The music of that northern speech was pleasurable. 'Complaints? Oh, some lumbago, and neuritis in my shoulder, I think, pretty sharp.'

'The massage douche would be of help there, I'll warrant. And bathing in the thermal water.' She unfolded a towel, looking to one side. 'Which is good for nervous tension, too.'

•

Teresa wafted out of the baths in a daze. The sunset was of a pink so tender it brought tears to her eyes. The Gun Man aside, it hadn't been a bad day, considering, had it? It had been all right. She hushed herself by picturing a jaunty stone cottage in some sweet isolated country, a life involving a dog, a kindly hammering typewriter, liberal meals. Walks, sky-gazing. Two dogs, at least. A remote, quiet existence. Could there be such a shelter? Mightn't she one day have the right to live without nightmares?

4

IN THE WINTER
GARDEN BALLROOM

Accompanied by the agreeable if fragile voice of the Lady Entertainer, the Hydro Boys were abandoning themselves to 'The Sheik of Araby' when Harry ambled into the Winter Garden Ballroom after dinner. It was his habit to take an evening tipple there. He appreciated that incongruous air of the summerhouse, with a winter night pressing against the glass walls. He was glad of the music's jolly vim. The six-piece band didn't usually play on Sundays. An anomaly, he gathered, in celebration of someone's birthday.

The new arrival was there, at a table far back from the stage. She was alone again and appeared to be solving a crossword puzzle. Her colour now was much higher than yesterday's pallor. She was dressed not in evening wear but the same green jumper, grey cardigan and grey skirt she'd worn the day before—yet she had the slightly stupefied look of one sporting new clothes. Had her luggage been lost?

He acknowledged the prominent-eared saxophonist, who was smiling fraternally at him, and sat after a moment's hedging at the table adjacent to hers. A young couple rose to dance, rather poorly but with evident mutual goodwill. An older couple joined them, these more controlled. Several songs exhausted themselves without any communication passing between Harry and the new guest. He suspected she preferred not to be engaged in conversation. She seemed bent on going unnoticed—risible, a woman of such majestic carriage—and somehow swollen with silence, battened down. Why was she there?

He'd heard the Jackmans refer to her as Mrs Neele. The name pleased and perturbed him a little, offering a picture of her genuflecting. The previous night, when he'd come in from his stroll and seen her at the foot of the stairs, and she'd turned and given him a faint involuntary-seeming wave, she'd struck him, indeed, as a woman kneeling, as both debased and distinguished. A vanquished queen.

The young dancing couple were more and more absorbed by one another. The girl was considerably taller and unembarrassed. It dawned on him that the two had to be lovers. The pockmarked waiter stopped by Mrs Neele. Harry had missed her signal to him. Her newspaper had been closed and folded. She ordered more coffee, and after the waiter departed, Harry addressed her with the clumsy fatality of one tripping. 'You know Balzac ruined his health with coffee? I think it was Balzac.'

Calmly, possibly interested, she asked, 'Did he?'

'I gather. Drank it constantly—I imagine to keep himself going.' He wondered how old she could be. Thirty-two? Twenty-eight? Thirty-eight? Forty-one? He was usually pretty spot-on at picking ages.

'Even good things can be overdone.'

'Well, yes, and the problem is realising when something is turning into poison. Balzac didn't, or didn't care enough to stop.'

'Or he simply couldn't do without his coffee. I guess writing like he did would have been very trying. Like climbing mountain after mountain every day.'

Her grey eyes—no, blue, but anaemic, almost ashen—were uncommonly evasive.

'Forgive me, I haven't introduced myself. Harry McKenna.'

'Teresa Neele.' Her eyes went to a potted palm. 'Pleased to meet you.'

'The pleasure is mine. Are you literary yourself?'

'Oh no.' Her tone was appalled. She had reached over to touch a leaf of the palm. 'You?'

'Heavens, no.'

In fact, in his youth, and also after he was old enough to know better, he'd let himself believe—as you indulge in believing certain things in youth, things so implausible, gossamery, seductive—he'd turn out a writer. He convinced Valeria he was *working* on a book, adoring her for sustaining the illusion. Over years of supposed toil he'd amassed maybe two dozen passable pages (those that didn't make him altogether *ill* with shame), kept under lock and key in the drawer of a bureau. The alleged book really became an alibi for when he was in a foul blue funk. A sort of moan: *I have to settle down to the book*. And she'd compose her face and withdraw with that stealth she mastered like a solemn dance, leaving him to his own sad devices. It was also convenient for excusing his absence from dinner parties and bridge or mahjong soirees. But they were dingy times, when he slaved at the book. At better moments, they spoke, Valeria—nearly—achieving affectionate humour and he savage irony, of his magnum opus. His life's work. Poor Valeria. How badly he had let her down.

Mrs Neele's coffee arrived. Stirring in sugar, she commented, 'How many cups, I wonder, would you need to drink each day, and over how long a period, for it to prove lethal?' It was as if there were a drag in the movement of her thoughts. Her voice was placid again, viscous.

'A slow method for doing away with yourself, wouldn't you say? You'd need such doggedness.'

'Yes.' Her gaze was skittery, then languorous, always distant. 'It would take place in plain view, yet be invisible—because so ordinary. But you're right, it'd take forever and I suppose be rather dull.'

She was an oddity. 'One prefers a more colourful suicide?' He was suddenly a little bilious.

'Well, less tedious.'

'You're going to risk another cup, then?'

'Yes, but I proceed with my eyes open.'

He smiled and noted, slightly aghast, how unusual this arrangement of his physiognomy felt when it was spontaneous. The other occupants of the ballroom would be watching them, beginning to speculate as to the whys and wherefores of their conversation. Soon, if it hadn't been already, the lack of a husband at her side would be remarked upon and subjected to deductions. As occurred in any small community somewhat removed from the wider world, gossip was a kind of drug among the sojourners at Harrogate, depended on to pass and variegate the time. Oh, it was handled with casual sophistication. The health spa's shifting population was naturally or unnaturally considerably more cosmopolitan than that of the average smallish town, its members less prone to being scandalised and adept at cultured discretion. Most were champions of tactfully managed and—as necessary—incognito convalescence and leisure. Still, gossip was an indispensable diversion. No matter how worldly and refined a person, his own ailments and concerns will become so stale as to threaten to asphyxiate him. And he must turn elsewhere.

The conversation petering out, Harry sensed Teresa preparing to take her leave and decided on detaining her. This was not typical of him. Despite his loneliness, he generally gave a wide berth to most of the hotel guests. 'Will you be staying long at the Hydro? I've been here two weeks and plan to stay on another few.' His plans were rarely very clear, Valeria's legacy permitting him the luxury of being whimsical.

'I'm not sure yet.' She inspected her coffee as if it might delicately metamorphose. 'What complaints bring you here?' There was an interval while he was contriving a reply into which she hastily added, 'I'm sorry. I didn't mean to intrude. It's just that today someone asked me what *my* complaints were. One doesn't necessarily come here for one's health, of course.'

He found this fluster fetching and remembered again the wispy little wave she'd accorded him the night before. 'Intrude by all means.'

He should have let her be. He'd learned how wrong it was to see a woman as a conundrum that could be resolved. He tried to focus on the infatuated lovers, who were the only remaining dancers. The others must have realised how they paled in comparison.

He had an urge to be honest and succumbed. 'The official answer would be a hernia.' He took an ample sip of brandy. Endeavouring not to sound doleful, he continued, 'The real, hopelessly unmanly answer is that I sometimes lose my nerve. I get quite—dispirited. When I'm like that I need a break.'

She opened her mouth partially and closed it again. He thought he saw panic in her expression, as if honesty stipulated honesty in return. 'Yes,' she said finally. 'Breaks are important. There are times when it's wiser to get away.' She cleared her throat softly. 'From it all. The Jackmans aren't here? I'm assuming you know them.'

Over one temple, a glint of silver in her reddish hair. Thirty-four or -five, surely. At least.

'You were right to assume. I believe they had a dinner engagement. Fine people.'

'Yes, very. I wanted to tell them I'd been to the Royal Baths on their recommendation.'

'I'm a habitué myself. Addicted. Nothing like a Turkish bath to clear out the cobwebs. Enjoy it?'

'Rather. I may almost have fainted, at one stage.'

Harry couldn't have said just why but he began to ask himself whether they mightn't have something in common. Was Teresa Neele in her reused green and grey outfit somehow lost? In that slow voice, camouflaged, could there have been ruin?

The lovers were waltzing. The girl laughed gleefully and then gave a little yelp and a grimace, probably at the boy standing on her toes. *One, two, three*, she was chanting secretively when they passed his table. Teresa Neele moved her spoon and sipped from her second cup of mortal coffee. He laboured to suppress the vision of her kneeling, along with the vague strife in his stomach. Belatedly, he considered her ring finger. A kind of internal shudder. Bare of wedding ring. And the *Mrs* Neele? She wore only one band—platinum, by the look of it, a setting with a small diamond—that sat loosely on her thin finger.

'The Jackmans told me you're from South Africa.'

'That's right.' Her eyes on the gentle chaos of the waltz.

'It must be a fascinating country,' he persevered. 'I've never been there.'

'Yes, indeed.'

She continued to pay painstaking attention to the dancers, and it got into his head that perhaps she'd never been there either. Harry was disconcerted and somewhat thrilled to think she might be lying. It was as if they stood on either side of a screen through which he could only make out her shadow. Was she (and he was in all likelihood being *too imaginative*, his mother's words echoing through hollowed years) a woman who didn't know how to be honest—not out of deceitfulness but because she took human affairs as a quagmire about which precious little could be said with any exactness? Was she extremely sad?

He was asking, 'Where have you been happiest in your life until now?'

Her gaze jumped. A perverse, too-intimate question.

He forged on. 'Try not to think about it. Just say the first place that comes to you. Me, I suppose London. Or Trieste. I'm Australian and, don't get me wrong, my native country . . .' He'd lost his momentum.

'I'd never have suspected your origins. Your English is truly admirable.'

Such comments always annoyed and somehow vindicated him. 'Well, it *is* our mother tongue, you know.'

'Of course, yes. It's just that the Australian accent usually tends to be—forgive me for saying so—noticeable.'

'To an English ear? So you're familiar with it?' His instinct would have been to respond peevishly to the assumptions now compelling her to recast him as a colonial, but tonight he was disinclined to. It was the persistent image of her on her knees, perhaps, or her oddly opaque attitude—that screen between them. 'I do seem to pick up accents easily. Well, the French. And the English, as you kindly observe. My wife, my late wife, was Italian. I speak little Italian, and badly, but Valeria used to say my accent was deceptively good. I can't detect any trace of South Africa in *your* accent, by the way.' Her accent was, in fact, phenomenally plummy. The speech of the English Quality often sounded to him like a caricature, both repellent and intriguing.

She took a slow sip of coffee. 'I'm so sorry to hear that your wife has passed on.' A drawn-out silence. Her long hands, sculpturally narrow-fingered and pale, were curved around her coffee cup for warmth or to convey composure. At last, she said, 'You must be nostalgic for Australia. I hear it's lovely.' She smiled uncertainly. 'I'm always thinking of Devon, where I was born. My early childhood was spent there. Then we moved to South Africa—I suppose my accent was already well established. But Mummy and I were so happy in Devon.'

This sat before him. A green field nudging the sea. Teresa Neele in little-girl form, tentative, near translucent like Dresden bone china. Her face flushed with the self-importance of grave play. A breeze lifting her silky hair—blonde, beginning to melt into brown. A proud woman standing a carefully monitored distance away, looking on with hawkish Victorian eyes, oracular. Both woman and child with regal bearing and considering the closeness of their alliance eternal. Mummy should have known better, that everything would always be changing.

'I was wildly happy as a child.' After a moment's pause, she returned to the lagging, limp rhythm to which he realised he'd become acclimated. 'There are different sorts of happiness, though, aren't there? The city of Nice comes to mind. Being in Paris was wonderful also, in its way, but I was at finishing school there and studying quite a lot. In Nice I distinctly recall looking at the *light* and understanding I was free.'

He was about to proffer something flippant—which he didn't, however, consider false—about the difficulty, if not impossibility, of bringing together an anchored kind of happiness with a more unbound, when he thought to say, 'Funny you should mention that. A coincidence. I felt rather free in Nice, too.'

'Oh?'

'I spent some months there once, before the war.'

'Mimosas. Balconies looking out onto transparent blue water.'

He rallied. 'I almost felt guilty there, to be leading such a comfortable, simple life. Some afternoons, I'd doze off on a great rock by the sea.'

'The French know that meals are Events. Starting with your morning *café au lait* and croissants—how I loved the almond ones, with orange blossom water in them.'

'God, yes.'

'And those preserves. So solid with crystallised fruit you can't spread them in the usual way.'

'They stand to attention. So you're a voluptuary, Mrs Neele?'

'With food, at least. And flowers.'

He raised his eyebrows. To slay a silence that, despite their stillness, he experienced as squirmy, he said, 'And here we are in the grey north of England.'

They laughed ruefully.

She cocked her head. 'I love England too. *Vous parlez aussi bien le français que l'anglais?*' Her French wasn't in the same league as Harry's, but it was reasonably nimble, the Englishness in it hardly stiff, really quite sweet and affecting.

'Je fais de mon mieux.'

'You do well when you're doing your best. I was going to be a professional musician, back then.'

His stomach muscles were loosening their grip and he was savouring her company. 'One was going to be many things. What sort?'

'A pianist, or an opera singer.'

'Hence the study in Paris? And what happened?'

'I had famous teachers. I worked hard at the piano, practised an awful lot. I wasn't bad at it. Performance was the problem. I didn't have the right temperament. That's what my Austrian teacher concluded.'

'And the singing?'

'*That* I could do in public, for some reason. I wanted to be an opera singer very much. To sing Isolde . . . But later an American friend of my family, who knew people at the Metropolitan Opera House, listened to me and told me, compassionately but honestly, that I didn't have sufficient voice. I'd only make a concert singer. And that didn't interest me. The end of a dream.' Her tone was mild.

'What was wrong with concert halls?'

'That would have been . . . a compromise. Maybe I was a snob. I really should be retiring. I've sleep to catch up on.'

She appeared uneasy at having spoken of herself. She stood to leave, her height rather overwhelming, as the band commenced a charleston.

He emptied his glass and lurched to his feet. 'It's been pleasant, chatting like this. Oh, "Yes! We Have No Bananas". What does that mean, anyway?'

He thought a ripple of hilarity, even hysteria, passed over her face.

'I haven't the faintest.'

Unable to resign himself to her going, he plunged. 'Perhaps we could dance?'

'Oh, I couldn't. I'm not even in evening clothes.' Thin fingers patting at the green jumper to prove it.

'We won't let that stop us.'

They looked at one another. To his astonishment, he saw that she would let herself be persuaded.

'It *is* quite a merry song.'

Actually, it wasn't a question of her deferring to his impulse. There was a playful tremor in her smile. Something insubordinate. They drifted to the dance floor to take their place beside the indefatigable lovers. He was relieved to note that the boy's footwork continued to leave much to be desired, and wondered optimistically if the chap could possibly be an inferior dancer to himself. Harry was lousy at the charleston and found it somewhat irritating. But dance music sometimes buoyed him, even if his body didn't easily fall in with its caprices. He was forty years old. Fortunately, with age, his monumental physical shyness had lessened. The evening seemed to be obeying some unorthodox logic.

'Don't worry, Mrs Neele. They shall not intimidate us.'

'Teresa,' she said as they came closer together. 'Please call me Teresa.'

'Teresa.' Out of the corner of his eye, the blurry continent of her cheek. Soap. Faint, sour-warm feminine perspiration. Dear Lord. His heart was as keyed up as if he'd been about to deliver a long-anticipated lecture to a priggish learned society. They clasped hands and his free hand found her back, hers coming to rest hotly on his shoulder. Their knees knocked together as they began, and she quickly retracted hers. 'Forgive me,' Harry apologised. 'I'm terribly out of practice.'

'So am I.'

'No, you dance very well.'

'I was better when I was younger.'

Their fellow dancers nodded to them conspiratorially.

'The birthday girl, I believe,' Teresa said.

The next time their knees collided, there was no rapid retraction and no apology. He might have been trying hard not to laugh, or not to fall. They avoided noticing whether they were being watched. At one point, Harry caught the saxophonist's eye, but he was poker-faced.

By song's end, they were breathing heavily. Smiling, they separated, though he continued to feel the phantasmal pressure of her hand on his shoulder and a suggestion of the contour of her spine against the palm of his hand.

'I must be going.'

'Mrs Neele—Teresa,' he said quickly, 'would you care to come for a walk with me tomorrow in Valley Gardens? That is, if you're not engaged.'

'A walk?' She hesitated. 'Tomorrow . . . I'm not sure about tomorrow. Maybe . . .'

As she was turning away, he entreated her clownishly, 'Beware of coffee. And don't forget Nice.'

Her smile was sheer but not unfriendly. Harry remained in the ballroom, witnessing her retreat. He sat back down at his table. Aloneness pooled around him, while the Hydro Boys terminated the evening with the customary Blue Danube, to which the young lovers waltzed. The waiter insinuated that Harry might like another brandy. He acquiesced. He thought the saxophonist was observing him, though he tried not to meet the man's eye again. It appeared to Harry that the bandsmen only made a display of indulgence towards their audience, knowing the guests comfortably classified them as provincial and of lower orders than their own. Whereas maybe it was the other way around—the audience the performance, some curious combination of well-to-do and poorly, for the musicians' supercilious enjoyment. The music subsided and he applauded profusely, staring past the glass glossing over the night.

5

TORMENT ME NO MORE

Back in his room on the second floor, Harry considered the decor, somewhat at a loss. Objects hinting at a lone man's appreciation of easeful hours. Roll-top writing desk at which instructive, affectionate epistles could have been penned. A bottle of tawny port and another of Dry Oloroso sherry, a carafe of virtuous spring water, two clean, inverted glasses, all neatly aligned on a small table. On another table, a gramophone. A residual fire, coals crimson and orange—the colours of passion, or hell. Tartan dressing-gown slung over the homely wingback chair. Single bed, readied and fat with its duvet. It was sadly comical, and no doubt so predictably, contemptibly human, that when Valeria was alive, for all that Harry had loved her, he'd often secretly suspected himself of being a bachelor at heart. And now with her gone, he tended to feel like a would-be married man on whom the manacles of solitude have been imposed.

With his foot, he pushed his suitcase further under the bed to smother its whisperings of transience. He removed his shoes and served a little sherry. He quite fancied himself as a drinker, though he wasn't much of one. Even for that, he might have needed a sturdier personality. He took just enough liquor to smudge the edges, to bring it all into a slight blur, and only of an evening when his brain was at its most overwrought. He'd not reached the desired point tonight, not quite, not yet. He sipped.

It was true, what he'd said to Teresa (he liked her first name—like a sibilance of wind in trees—as much as her last) about having been dispirited. The past two years had been, no two ways about it, vile. After Valeria's passing, he'd no longer required the pretence of literary efforts. His blue funks had changed, assuming a midnight hue. Become so frequent, he'd stopped remarking when one ended and the next began. Furthermore, he'd hardly minded.

Until six months before, when he found himself in a particularly bad state. Rather, it was his landlord, Mr Vaughan, who discovered him. Later, the good man would explain he'd taken the liberty of entering Harry's flat because the postman had complained that letters would no longer pass through the clogged mail slot and bottles of milk were multiplying at the door, rancid and despoiled by birds.

Mr Vaughan had knocked awhile, and waited, and knocked again. He called out. Then, with his spare latchkey, he cautiously turned the lock. Slow to open, that door. It swelled with humidity, sullenly intent on refusing any passage in or out. He gave it an insistent tug that provoked a harrowing wail.

From inside the flat, Harry heard this too. In fact, it was aeons since he'd heard anything so clearly. Peculiar—but recognisable, intimate. It had something of the strange purity of an infant's squeal. Stirred into lucidity, he registered that it must have been Flash, Valeria's cat. He still never thought of the beast as his. They shared a tolerably tranquil mutual annoyance.

No sooner did Mr Vaughan have the door ajar than the cat sprang through it, with the reflex savagery of a powerful spring released, and that shriek, so eloquent, of famished rage. Mr Vaughan thought to pursue the cat and persuade her back, but when he turned to go after her she was already streaking around a corner, absolutely ungovernable.

'Mr McKenna?' he called once more through the open door, as proper as ever.

This time Harry deciphered his voice. He even pictured Mr Vaughan wiping his shoes on the mat before stepping with regretful dignity into the hall. 'In the living room,' Harry's own enfeebled or just horribly bored voice informed him. The front door closing, and footsteps. Then the final door between them opened, the long, dark shape of the man appearing against dim light. He half turned back, maybe towards the glass panels of the front door, which allowed that trickle of radiance. The ringbarked light of hallways. He coughed.

'Mr Vaughan,' Harry saluted him casually, as if he were arriving fifteen minutes late for a regular rendezvous.

'Mr McKenna, I'm afraid we may have seen the last of your cat.'

'Valeria's cat. Flash.'

'Oh.' He cautiously penetrated the gloom Harry inhabited.

'*Micio* means "puss". In Italian. That's how you call a cat—*micio, micio.* Puss, puss.'

'Ah, right.'

'I'm more of a dog man.'

Full daylight struck Harry a low blow. Mr Vaughan had drawn the curtains. Becoming painfully accustomed to this befuddling violence, Harry saw that his landlord was attired in the usual loose-fitting suit on a frame so slender and protracted as to seem desiccated, a vanilla pod. Ironic that deliverance should have arrived in this form, for though Mr Vaughan was a subtly spruce individual, his handsome sunken cheeks were rather sepulchral, belonging more to the Reaper than the angel. Harry wouldn't have been excessively surprised to see him equipped with cape and scythe. Nothing would have surprised Harry very much right then. From his prior dealings with Mr Vaughan he'd gained the impression of a man who gave things measured consideration but not undue weight. This seemed such an awe-inspiring balance that, while Harry knew very little of him, he respected him (not the most common sentiment to harbour for a landlord). He even wondered whether Mr Vaughan wasn't something of a clandestine sage. There was a movement of air, a window having apparently been opened, too.

As Mr Vaughan wasn't one for superfluous words, when he declared dryly, 'Good God, man,' Harry understood this was warranted. It occurred to him later that his landlord must have anticipated coming face to face with a cadaver.

•

How had it come to this? A part of him, rational and indifferent, hard and cool, had observed what was taking place, without having the energy required to avert it or any particular interest in resistance. Looking back on his first year without Valeria, searching for a clue that would have helped him to avoid arriving at such an impasse again, his memories were a boggy terrain. He confused the careless condition he'd been in with the despised room that had housed all those awful, stagnant hours. As if at some treacherous instant his rented living room and his mind had become reflections of one another. Something had gone awry in that familiar space occupied by him peacefully enough in the past. Was it the arrangement of the furniture? What angle, what detail was badly amiss? Something unobtrusive but crucial. And the door had locked behind him. He was reduced to that room, to its unfortunate convergence of brown sofa, brown curtains, green rug, floral-print armchair (quite late in the game he began to ask himself whether the design, in perky mauve and acidic lemon, could be a poor approximation of ranunculi), detritus of reproachful unopened books and clotted dust. He found the sofa especially noxious, reeking as it did of Valeria's wronged cat—or of his own decrepitude. It seemed to remind him of a sin he had committed.

At the furthest outposts of his awareness had sailed the possibility that he might have performed a rearrangement, as it were, of those unsavoury furnishings, some simple adjustment that would have set everything to rights. But how would he have gathered himself to proceed with it? He couldn't breathe deeply enough for that.

•

His travels began not long after the flight of Flash. It was Mr Vaughan's idea, actually: another proof of his wisdom. Soon after pitilessly opening the curtains, he made Harry a cup of tea and ordered him to drink it, watching for the first reluctant sip. The aggressive sweetness of the beverage caused a fluttering in Harry.

'Don't take umbrage,' Mr Vaughan said, possibly after a prolonged interval. 'You've been a good tenant till now. I've had no complaints. But it might be time for you to move on, so to speak. Change of scene and all that. You do see my point.'

Harry struggled to organise his thoughts. He did, of course. Most definitely, he could not remain there. They both recognised that Mr Vaughan had after a fashion come face to face with the cadaver of the Harry who had lived in his flat. That life was no more. The notion of going on living there made his flesh creep, like the prospect of wearing a dead man's woollen suit to a funeral on a day in high summer.

'Could you go to relatives for a time?' Mr Vaughan suggested with some hope.

Harry shook his head, seeing the veranda of his parents' farmhouse in Young as he had at sixteen, looking back at it on a cool morning, bound for Sydney. He hadn't even scratched one last time behind their blond mutt's ears, the gesture already of the past, a rite he'd teach himself to forgo. Having taken off her apron to lend the occasion formality, his mother was nonetheless in one of her businesslike poses that made him curious about the time before her marriage, almost never alluded to, when she had been in domestic service. His father appeared resigned and somehow sympathetic. A man who assured his control of their household by allowing himself to utter—not necessarily every day, nor even every week—underhandedly or plainly vicious words. Harry had often wondered whether it mightn't have been simpler if he and his mother had been able to rely on cruelty, or even suffer bodily knocks that would have been more irrefutable than twisty, slippy speech. The sky above the roof had been so open, cobalt blue, marbled with soft, silvered cloud.

'Hardly.'

'Drink your tea. A health spa?'

Harry almost laughed, extraordinarily, sugar in his sinuses.

Mr Vaughan went on, 'I myself was once at Bath, for a liver problem. I benefited from it, I did.' He studied Harry's continuing groggy silence. 'You'll have to go somewhere—and better somewhere they'll look after you a bit. Drink.'

Everything was desultory, ludicrous. See-through. Every inch of that horrendous charade of a room, the pigheaded sunlight, any word Harry might voice. The daft uneasy cage of his body. And yet more intolerable pen of his mind. Notwithstanding, Mr Vaughan had planted a seed. A visit to a health spa, in spite of—no, *because* of—the quaint futility of it, the folly, the farcical self-indulgence, just might have fitted his unworthiness. It was an idea, at least. What else would he do? He had no better plan.

•

First, aided and abetted not a little by Mr Vaughan, he moved from Lincoln's Inn Fields to new lodgings in Chelsea. His next landlord was of unexceptional height, stout and sardonic, a joyless joker. Harry was not in the least impressed by his sagacity and couldn't seem to trouble himself to recall the gentleman's name. His new rooms, though, were smart and blank (the sofa a hygienic shade of rose), and he never stayed in them too long. If they started to look a little *off,* if he caught himself turning a less than benign gaze upon them, he'd expeditiously pack a case and away. Head for some small hotel somewhere in the British Isles or on the Continent, often in a spa town. And there he'd stay until he'd had enough or he was moved to visit another place. Or it appeared safe to return experimentally *home.* He was a transient for much of the year in the hope that time, broken into these shards, wouldn't congeal again as it had in the flat in which he'd failed Valeria. Harry considered himself very much an invalid.

He had a thought occasionally for the cat, Flash, wondering if she had survived. He imagined she had. She flourished in a sleek new coat beneath which her heart beat smug and strong. Her iridescent eyes remained as contemptuous of cowardice as ever.

•

He and Valeria had lived well though carefully, without any pomp, in their little flat in Lincoln's Inn Fields. Neither of them had received a bean from their family. Harry had been the private secretary of a wealthy businessman, Mr Ainsworth.

Valeria had announced one day early in their marriage that she would become the assistant of an elderly lady she had just met in an A.B.C. tea shop. Though he assured her that his salary was sufficient for them, she'd insisted that it would hardly be work (and wouldn't pay much, anyway), more a device for providing a few hours of company each afternoon to a lonely widow with poor eyesight but personality, who only wanted to be read to and taken for walks around Bloomsbury, where she resided. Her husband having been a diplomat often posted abroad, Mrs Mortlake had far-ranging international interests and was a proficient conversationalist in three languages. Valeria had claimed, furthermore, that since she'd given up painting she needed something to occupy her mind and shape her days. And her association with Anne Mortlake had indeed been a happy one—for the first seven years. Then Mrs Mortlake had grown good-naturedly senile before lapsing into a rather long and cantankerous decline. Valeria remained a steadfast friend to her till the end, even seeming in the most testing times to have a flair for nursing. Harry understood that Mrs Mortlake had bequeathed his wife a token sum in her will. When Valeria herself died, he was shocked to discover that Mrs Mortlake had made her, in fact, an heiress of some stature.

Why had she not let on? Why keep it from him? The money might have made their life together much more breezy. Very puzzling, especially as in her own will Valeria left the entirety of the startling amount to him. He became a man of not insignificant means, able to take an early retirement at thirty-eight. And after Mr Vaughan's intervention he began to behave like a man of leisure. It may seldom have felt so, but he was freakishly fortunate. Had he lacked such resources, he'd no doubt have died.

The System, as he thought of his new itinerant life, was working, though he was aware it could break down at any moment. He had himself in hand for now, but a lesson of a period such as the one he'd lived through was that control is an illusion. Once everything has gone see-through on you, it can again. You know that perfectly well. If only your head were to be tilted once more in that way . . . He hadn't been saved so much as granted a reprieve.

Another lesson learned, as modest and obvious as it might have seemed, was the importance of having his mind and body engaged. To this end, he made a concerted effort to take an interest in the newspapers, he read a little and listened to music, he became a compulsive walker, frequented Turkish baths and submitted to massages and other treatments. Sometimes he became fixated on women. The latter was a mild distraction he never mistook for love. (He was certain that after Valeria he was incapable of falling in love, of anything so grand and strenuous.) He'd simply cultivate an interest in some lady or other, someone unaccompanied and, if possible, travel-wearied, a little frayed and tending to the antisocial. Work to convince himself he was bewitched. The aim was to clear his head and ideally—did he really believe in this possibility?—to achieve a sensation like the one you could have at the sea's edge of being gently thrilled, washed clean. In reality, nothing had ever gone far beyond tame flirtation. No doubt the women could smell despair on him, like the dankness of an alleyway that may have a certain shady allure but into which, after a hesitation, you would not venture.

Teresa Neele was alone and apparently reclusive, and maybe wilted. However, she wasn't like the women he usually chose or who chose him. She was singular in a way he couldn't identify. He strongly intuited it would be a mistake to concern himself with her. Sipping sherry and undressing distractedly amid the pretence of hotel furnishings, he relived their conversation. Then said to himself, Music. At the gramophone, he dithered before deciding on Monteverdi's *Lamento della ninfa*. Perhaps it was a suggestion of the music, but as that exquisite woe unrolled itself, he wondered if he'd really glimpsed in Teresa Neele's eyes what he'd once or twice thought he might have. He couldn't let go of the impression that she was suffering, or endangered. It quickened his heart. He pulled on his tartan dressing-gown, the wool softly aggravating. He was suddenly startled to remember that so little space separated them. On what floor was her room? Was she already in bed?

He saw the gestures she would make as she took off the pearls he'd noticed. Her head dropping forward, heavy all at once, the back of her neck revealed, and her long thin fingers fumbling at the clasp. How many times had he watched Valeria make those gestures, grappling with fatigue until she eventually asked in the tones of a child for help? Countless. No, they had indeed been counted. That was all over and done with. Concluded.

Teresa Neele (*Please call me Teresa*) was taller than Valeria had been and, Harry thought, longer-necked. More statuesque. These comparisons, a dark reflex, pained him like a contemplated betrayal. But he'd only had one conversation and, for heaven's sake, danced the charleston with Teresa. Why was he taking the encounter to heart? How was this different to his other flimsy infatuations?

When the record finished, he set it playing a second time. He drained the dregs of his sherry. Almost there, the requisite haze. He slung his woollen dressing-gown once more over the chair, turned out the lights and climbed into the bed designed for a single sleeper. He was escorted into his lone slumber, into the ebb and flow of night proper, by a woman's satin distress. *Non mi tormenti più.* Torment me no more.

•

A female body in his arms, turned away from him.

But he knew the fine white skin of Valeria's back, which he worshipped. And all the more as time's poignant softening work made the bone rope less austere. He laid his hand against that bone sheathed with skin. Kissed it. How he'd revered her back, though the truth was he'd also forgotten it. For whole years he'd been neglectful of this pallid desert, the hidden, wordless side of his wife. He felt the kind of guilt it was possible to feel returning home to one who has been waiting too long. He kissed her again rapturously. No response.

That was why monks lived in monasteries, he mused. To hide from anything that might divide their attention, tease their minds away from the intricacies, the less obvious, more desolate expanses of their loved one. To offer love the labour of observation it demanded. In ordinary, worldly life it was hard to love with the wholeness of a holy man. Was this the great failing and disappointment? Fragmentary love? He could almost taste the salt scald of weeping.

'Darling, won't you turn around?' He wanted to see her face, apologise for his shoddy heart.

She gave a throaty, heedless laugh. Finally, unwillingly, his love turned.

It was *not her*. Not Valeria. A stranger in her place.

And an even more bizarre migration had occurred. For this woman was without life: a corpse.

A corpse, with Teresa Neele's face. The mystifying divide had just been crossed, and the body he felt along his own length was pliable and warm. The eyes were open, slate-coloured and prudent, even in death.

Just who had she been? Why did it seem he should know? To his confusion, amid his shock and disgust, he was overtaken by a sweeping attraction. He was hungry for information, true or even false, but greed was an error, for as he tried to hold her fast, to press secrets from her flesh, there was alarmingly no woman in his arms. No flesh at all, but the finest desert sand. White lunar dust escaping at speed through his clutching, futile hands.

6

FOURTH DAY

The *Daily Mail* claimed it was Monday, but how arbitrary being in an unfamiliar setting made time. Today she *had* to write the letter—indeed, she'd start the day by doing just that. Eager to be done with it, she sprang out of bed and winced. Her shoulder really was misbehaving. A piercing pain, as if originating from an injury. It went right down her arm, which felt weakish. *Was* it the neuritis back? What exertion had stirred it up? Funny how things came and went.

She ferreted out the laudanum in her handbag. The Torquay pharmacist's label was a prick of nostalgia. Sunlit-green Devon hills, Torbay seen from Barton Hill, pine scent. She took a dose, promising herself she'd make an appointment for a massage.

This time she wouldn't sit down and be cowed by stationery. First compose, pacing the room, then sit and efficiently transcribe. Like a fisherman caressing a trout into submission before slipping in the hook. She strode back and forth. *Darling . . .*

I've been thinking of the Empire Tour (she might say), *especially our month of heaven in Hawaii. Our escape from the folly. Bliss! It's probably the neuritis that has reminded me. It's returned, you see, and the first time it afflicted me was in Honolulu. Four years ago already. Staggering. Then it was all the royal bathing and surfing that did it. My right shoulder and arm were a shambles of pain, remember? But weren't we happy? Two fish. Rather indecently sunburned. The endless shedding of skin! I felt quite dashing in that skimpy emerald-green woollen bathing dress . . .* Or something about South Africa? Or Canada, maybe, or New Zealand? Australia? Mention having met an Australian in Harrogate? Who of course reminded her of Shy Thing, as she still called him to herself. Australia *was* the sort of place that caught in you like a tick. But her strongest memories of it weren't as gay and simple as the ones of Hawaii. And in them her husband didn't have a leading role.

Her husband. Mr Neele. He would remember inspecting various factories, doing the major's bidding. Meeting people who for the most part weren't really their sort. He wouldn't recall Sydney's overrunning light and the damp that surely contributed to those unpleasant hotel odours. Almost certainly not the fantastical riotous birds, or the trees she hadn't been able to describe to Mummy, try as she might. Startling white trunks . . .

Thinking of Mummy at home, virtually alone and so curious, she'd wanted to share it all with her in letters. But she'd never really had the knack of capturing places. Not that she was unobservant—it was just that she concentrated on them in her own way. (Mummy hadn't taught her to be ashamed of dreaminess. *Might* she have? A high price to pay for being lazy about seeing reality.) Landscapes so subtly dour and secretive, not appearing to care whether you appreciated or understood them, hardly facilitated the task. Anything you might say about the downcast feelings they inspired, or the queer exhilaration, was unsatisfactory and only made you cross. Nor was the uncouth Australian voice mellifluous. Though Shy Thing's version of it was *not* grating—or was the harshness alleviated by his being so much her sort of person and her so at home with his family?

Harry had no trace of it she could hear, which was peculiar. Leaving you uncertain as to how to approach him. Unsure whether he might be your sort of person or not.

This attempt at the letter, too, was clearly aborted. Wrecked on the island of Australia. She didn't have long to be vexed, for here was the chambermaid come for her tray.

Teresa didn't want to be exposed to those intent eyes that put her on the qui vive. She tried not to show her face to the girl, by getting back into bed and fussing with covers. One shouldn't be obliged to show one's face in the morning before one's toilette, anyhow.

•

She had to keep herself in motion. Teresa dressed quickly, so sick of the green jumper, grey stockinette skirt, grey cardigan and velour hat she'd have jubilantly banished them from her life forever. But today she would at last acquire new clothes. Before leaving the Hydro, she made an appointment for a massage for three thirty that afternoon.

Much better to be outside, where the air was brisk, the light clear and soft. At a fruiterer's stall on Cold Bath Road she bought some apples and pears, making speedy work of a crisp, enlivening apple. Harrogate's high-class shops pleased her. She could have done some profligate spending here. Peter would have enjoyed all those people and fine trees and moorland air. Promenading, she once or twice almost sensed him at heel.

At the fashionable Marshalls she contemplated appealing furs, evening wraps and lambskin slippers. She had to be practical, though, so focused on dance and dinner gowns. When she turned before the glass in a salmon-hued georgette, she saw a tall, tastefully stylish Teresa, somewhat ageless, blank-slateish. She smiled faintly at her preening. No pain now in the shoulder or arm. The laudanum was working. She'd have the dress—fortunately she'd a reasonable quantity of money, having followed Auntie-Grannie's principle of always travelling with tidy folds of extra five-pound notes for anything unforeseen—and a frock for ordinary wear patterned with violets. Cheering to assemble the beginnings of a new wardrobe. She also tried and settled on a maroon jumper, a pair of black evening shoes, black gloves. Three pairs of stockings. She had the larger articles delivered to the Hydro.

She was anxious to go back to change, but there was more she needed. Further wanderings took her to a smart black cloche hat, with a pink stripe on the front of it, at the nicely named Ada Nettlefold. Then, at Taylor's Drug Company, she found face cream, *papier poudré*, *crème de lys* soap and rose eau de cologne, Mummy's love of the flower prompting this last choice. She continued to softly fancy that Peter accompanied her.

The solace of W.H. Smith! She became a member of the circulating library with alacrity, and borrowed several tomes, nothing heavy. With the books in her arms, an imbalance had righted itself. She looked forward to observing the stack of them on her bedside table, the little barricade. She only briefly contemplated purchasing letter pads and notepaper before finding herself back out on the street. It hit her that it was curious, given the array of temptations and the time of year, that she'd had no thought of Christmas shopping. Usually such a fun enterprise.

Finally, at a ladies' outfitter on the same street that was home to Bettys, Cambridge Crescent, she bought a tweed skirt, two blouses, a lavender dressing-gown and some woollen underwear. She hesitated here, wondering how many days to provision for. She didn't think many, and she could avail herself of the hotel's laundry service as necessary.

The exemplary young waiter was absent from Bettys, but this time the cutlery did serve for anchoring a book. She started a mystery story along with her roast beef. The title of the book, *The Phantom Train*, echoed in her mind. Towards the end of her luncheon, with a slight start, she realised that she herself was writing a book about a train, *le train bleu*. A wretched train wreck of a book. Even remoter than a phantom to her it was, for she was receiving no visitations from it whatsoever. Rather like a woman scheduled to soon give birth who has ceased to feel her baby moving. A wave of something not unlike nausea ran through her. She doubted it was on account of the very good charlotte russe, for which her digestion would be as grateful as it ever was for excellent dessert.

•

Harry was in the lounge when Teresa returned to the Hydro, galvanised by a sense of having begun to furnish her new existence in Harrogate, which (as long as she thought just a little) was feeling like a fresh chance. He was sitting in an armchair, perusing a newspaper.

His eyes lifted to her, with a look of both surprise and recognition. Oh. *You.*

She barely knew him. They'd had, what? One conversation?

'Mrs Neele. Teresa. I don't suppose you're free for that walk?'

She had not forgotten his invitation—she'd intended to decline it, if the need arose. But sometimes one had the illusion that a certain event had occurred before and would go on recurring, like an addictive unit of melody. That's how it was, coming back to find Harry reading and then looking up at her, though she barely knew him.

And so, instinctually, she accepted.

7

TWILIGHT SLEEP

He had fixated on the unlikely prospect of this all day. After Teresa had failed to appear in the dining room at breakfast, and again at lunch, he had lain in wait by the hotel entrance, increasingly despondent.

But she assented readily, only saying, 'Give me a moment to leave these books upstairs. You see, I've had absolutely nothing to read.'

When they reconvened, he felt for some reason like a boy who has been caught out daydreaming. He was glad that there was only an impassive-faced young woman at the reception desk, her eyes remaining lowered as they departed.

They went down Swan Road and crossed to Valley Gardens. The air had grown sharper. Her pale coat was edged with abundant fur at the neck, wrists and hem.

'We'll soon be warm,' he said. 'Walking.'

'I haven't really been feeling the cold,' she murmured. 'Is that the Pump Room?' She gestured at the domed edifice outside of which several well-dressed people were waiting with an air of relaxed purpose.

'Yes, it's the Old Sulphur Well. Strange to think of European royalty flocking here. To the queen of British watering-places.'

Her smile suggested that she liked the idea.

'The Jackmans are always there of a morning before breakfast, taking the cure the proper way. Turns in the gardens between doses and so on.'

'You don't go in for that type of thing?'

'Me? No. I guess I'm not all that disciplined. I take the water at the Hydro occasionally, and I've seen their physician a couple of times. I do admire people who look after themselves. That conviction they have. Dickens, incidentally, apparently found Harrogate an exceptionally queer place, full of queer people living queerly.'

'Oh? I wonder why.'

They entered the gardens. Bare trees grand and faintly dilapidated like aged beauties. Those surroundings seemed to gratify Teresa.

After a while, she nodded and said, 'Charming.'

'I suspected you'd like it here.' Presumptuous, knowing her so little.

An elderly couple accompanied by a stertorous corgi greeted them in passing. Teresa averted her face from the salute, though he saw her affording the corpulent, bright-eyed dog a look of almost pained appreciation. Harry had a burst of envy for the dog, and for the human pair—for what might have been the comfort of their shared habits. A sturdy conjoining of two lives.

He glanced at Teresa sidelong. 'Good day?'

'Very industrious. I've shopped. Procured books. Been to Bettys.'

Feeling affection for them, he noticed below her coat the green jumper and grey skirt she'd worn on three consecutive days. Surely, he reflected again, given her evident social standing, a sign that something was astray. Her black cloche hat, however, could have been new. She blinked as if following his reasoning. 'I've had to leave the bulk of my luggage with friends in Torquay, dear friends. I'm not quite sure how long I'll be staying in Harrogate, so instead of having it sent on right away, I decided it would be simpler for the time being to just buy a few things here—clothes and so on, I mean.' She changed the subject: 'It must be because of this air that one sleeps so deeply.'

'Sleeping well, are you?' The thought of her having disarranged his night, he was a little piqued.

'You forget how smashing it feels.'

'I seem to remember vaguely, from childhood.'

'So long ago?'

'I'm only exaggerating a little, I'm afraid.'

'It wasn't just . . . ?'

'After I lost Valeria that I started sleeping poorly?'

She nodded.

'No. That made it worse. A lot worse. But for me sleep had been—let's say "temperamental" before.'

'Being unable to fall asleep is distressing.' She did not elaborate. Beneath a show of sociability, she maintained the same reticence, the slight detachment she'd displayed the previous evening—except when they'd danced the charleston.

Three girls with tennis racquets were coming towards them, loose-limbed and boisterous. One smiled at Teresa, who did not reciprocate or even appear to notice. Harry nodded, and another giggled into her hand. The barely harnessed power of the young. Their vigorous voices receded as he and Teresa took the long rising pathway bordered by laurels. He was guiding her along his usual route to the place where Valley Gardens abutted the Pinewoods.

She chuckled, a self-deprecating sound. 'I'm not very fond of going up hills. In Torquay you're constantly going up steep, endless hills. Maybe I climbed enough there for a lifetime. Or feel I should only bother with one if I'll be rewarded with a view of the sea.'

'Shall we go another way?'

'No, it's good for me, no doubt,' she countered, still with a cloudy tone of self-reproach. 'I'm always vowing to take more exercise.'

He wondered whether to offer her his arm, but decided it might have been construed as too forward of him at this early stage of their acquaintance. 'I'm sorry. I've been hurrying. I'm so used to walking alone.' He slowed. *He* had developed a certain appetite for mounting hills, welcoming them as due punishment.

They didn't speak further until they had reached the wood. He often encountered other walkers here. Today there was no one else about, perhaps owing to the raw turn the weather had taken. Teresa gave no sign of minding the cold. He invited her to pass ahead of him.

She hesitated, her eyes flicking to his face. Harry supposed she was asking herself if a jaunt in the forest with a virtual stranger were advisable. If he could be trusted. Fair question, he thought. Can I be trusted? Some quality of this quick appraisal reinforced his idea of her as bewildered, off course—but, in the manner of a hunted animal, furtive and canny, too.

She preceded him, hastening past the wooden crucifix, a simple war memorial he'd once stopped to examine, the circular stone base of which proclaimed, *They died so that we might live.*

Teresa slowing down, he ambled in the rear. Awkward, walking at another's pace. He tried not to stare at her figure. She moved as one who luxuriates in country rambles does, at a somewhat impractical, aristocratic speed, possibly allowing the piney air to tease at her thoughts. It struck him that her new cloche hat had given her a slight swagger, and the childishness of this moved him. Her shoulders were narrow and sloping. She was slim but you imagined her plump, on account of a certain softness or of her ankles being little defined. He recalled her reflective ardour when discussing French jam.

To divert his mind, he said the first thing that came to him. 'So we've rejected eventual coffee poisoning as a method for doing away with ourselves. What would be your suggestion for a more interesting end to it all?' His voice and the macabre topic rang weirdly to him.

But she laughed. Filling with a frail elation, he looked up at the brawny green of the Scots pines and the holly scattered through bald birches, rowans and sycamores. He pictured it here in summer. He adored the deep shade of forests in this part of the world, which made you feel yourself among the lamp shadows of a great sylvan boudoir. Roaming such privacy.

'A one-dose poison would be neater,' she observed.

For a second or two, he was light-headed. 'Such as? A large quantity of sleeping powder?'

'For example. Certainly nothing that would be too gory or dramatic. Not strychnine, I wouldn't fancy the spasms.' So he could catch her words, she was obliged to turn her head, offering flashes of pale—rather Scandinavian—profile. 'Not mercury bichloride—painful,' she went on as if speaking to herself. 'Some opium preparation would be superior.'

Absent steps. Sway of hips.

'Laudanum?'

'Yes. Or morphine. I took some laudanum this morning, actually. For a spot of neuritis.'

'Oh, sorry to hear that. It's not still troubling you?'

'No. I'm not feeling it anymore.'

'I wouldn't have suggested a walk if I'd known. Shall we turn back?'

'No, let's carry on. Hyoscine would be another option.'

'Hyoscine?'

'It's used as an anaesthetic, with morphia. Women may be given it during childbirth. Creates an amnesic condition without their quite going under. Twilight sleep, it's known as.'

'Twilight sleep,' he repeated slowly. 'You're very informed.'

'Not really. Well—I once worked in a dispensary.'

'In South Africa?'

'Yes,' she said indistinctly, not turning back. She fell silent.

He felt he must continue speaking. 'What do you say to hanging oneself in a bell tower?'

'A bell tower?'

'Well, it seems a larger gesture than just dangling from the rafters of a barn. I thought you might approve of it as a less bland alternative.'

'Oh.' He couldn't tell if she was smiling. He would have liked to intercept a smile meant for herself alone.

The path widened to allow for two to walk abreast and he came up beside her as she proposed, 'It'd be preferable, though, not to leave behind a corpse at all. A corpse is so . . . untidy. Better to just disappear.'

'Untidy, yes. How, disappear?'

She mused. 'To some place—foreign, ideally—where no one knew you. Where it would make no difference to anybody whether you lived or not.'

'And you'd—what?—quietly take your deadly nightshade in a fine hotel, between fresh sheets, in starched pyjamas?' Catching her restive eye, he went on, 'After a good dinner? Flowers in a vase on the bedside table and your few possessions arranged just so?'

She was looking at the path again. 'Yes. That might do. Organise it properly. Try to have a lovely last day. There'd still be a corpse to think of, however, wouldn't there? Better would be to leave your hotel late one evening, on a hot night, when the air is finally cooling off and starting to move. Slip into the sea. Have something and then simply . . . swim away.'

Their talk seemed to have become trancelike, reminding him of the way he and Valeria had sometimes chatted in bed before falling asleep. Discomposed, he waited for her to go on, restraining his breathing. After a minute, he enquired, 'Do you envisage somewhere like Nice?'

'I think of Nice as happy.'

He had seen something perplexing once in that city. He had walked the length of the beach alongside the Promenade des Anglais, hypnotised by the torpid aquamarine waves and all the thin men and women of indeterminate age, artfully dressed and groomed, whose carnivorous eyes declared longing. The beach petering out, he ascended to the road and was rounding the end of the promontory with the idea of continuing his stroll along the port. He happened to look up and into an apartment or hotel suite. Not understanding what he saw, he stopped.

The view resolved itself, through open terrace doors. Beyond them, an oval looking-glass, apparently mounted on the door of a wardrobe left open. The room's inhabitant must have gone off in a hurry. And the bluish, softly stippled reflection in the glass was the sea's.

But the room's inhabitant hadn't rushed off. A woman entered the doorway, showing first her narrow profile and then her back. Her dress was undone, flapping open to reveal a bony shoulder. And next there were a man's arms, shirtsleeves rolled up, gesticulating at intervals, underlining the tetchiness of his guttural tones. Harry distinguished the odd words. *Two days . . . how can you be so . . . why?* The woman remained largely silent.

The man's voice ceased and he came into full view, elfin yet muscular, and careless as to whether they might be observed. He was at her side, forcing one hand into the opening in her dress and raising the other. She was unsteady, inebriated or terrified. The whiteness of her slip was visible.

She twisted away a little, her body blocking the mirror's sea view, her mouth agonised. She could not move far. He had her pinioned. His raised hand, which Harry had feared might strike a blow, lowered to her throat, encircling it—but not caressingly. His grip appeared to tighten. Just then the woman discovered the bystander, her eyes strangely blank.

Harry's heartbeat had gone light and harried. As the man's hand dropped from her neck to her hip, still clutching with brutish force, her dress fell quite from her shoulders. Her cheeks coloured and Harry averted his gaze. The briny fetor of the sea was in his nose, and a perfume—hers, probably—cloyingly floral and somehow low-slung. Looking back, gawking in spite of himself, he saw a shockingly white slip, a lustre of sweat at the start of the dip between her breasts, the olive shine of shoulders.

Should he intervene, call out curtly to the man? But what was he seeing? The woman's will was not clear to him. What if this were only the half-playful theatrics of lust? Harry's hesitation made him feel complicit, the brute's accomplice.

They were kissing now, if that were the word for an act so rough and blurred. Rabidly embracing, though *her* arms remained limp. Was she responding—or just lethargic, snared?

Harry had an uncomfortable, intimate sense of pelvises colliding, of the jutting ridges of hips.

When they withdrew back into the room (who leading or forcing whom?) and the rippled sea gently filled the glass once more, Harry walked on. Sickly, stimulated, alone. The uncertain spectacle had stirred him, he realised, dismayed at his own peculiar disturbance. A husky impetus had awoken in him at the sight of whatever passion or violence he had witnessed. It terrorised him to think that he could be his father's son, though he had travelled so far. That lodged deep in his nature there might have been the instincts of a bully.

'So you consider there to be a contradiction'—he was talking to Teresa jumpily—'between a happy place and a quiet end.'

'Casablanca?'

He noted her taste for the exotic. He tried to dissipate the mood the memory of Nice had induced in him with silliness. 'How about jumping off a mountain, or feeding yourself to a large jungle animal?'

'You'd want to be unconscious before it ate you.'

'Assuredly.'

Pasture now to one side of them, and beyond it dales with wooded patches. Lavish greens and placid blue-greys.

'Oh,' she remarked.

Nearby, a group of hardy cows. Further off, a speckling of sheep. The sky was very clear and cold. Shifting cows, the smell of livestock.

'What an inviting place,' she went on meditatively. 'But *is* it? The problem with describing a place is that an *idea* of the place interferes. Like wallpaper covering it over.'

It appeared to him there was something like self-loathing in these words. She had exposed herself, and it was important that he advance with extreme caution—not cause her to recoil. 'I suspect we're all blinded by ideas,' he began. 'So much for man's superior intelligence.' She looked quite bleak. 'Don't you think it advisable to have something between us and the world, anyhow? A buffer, some diversions? Dreams, I suppose. The real world tending to be boring, or troublesome and disagreeable.'

'But if we saw what was real, we might be happier, in the long run. Safer.'

'Ah. Happiness.' He was not the man to comment on that. 'What do you think those cows see, looking around?'

'They seem content.'

He couldn't deny it. 'Grass? Ideas of grass? Is there a difference?'

'But grass *is* their reality. People have fanciful ideas that get *in the way* of reality. Some more than others. Some are purblind.' She was gazing fiercely straight ahead. 'Which is really a kind of stupidity. Unforgivable.'

Harry didn't disagree here, either. He had lived blind or part-blind for a good number of years, enveloped in his own inconsequential drama that had prevented him from truly seeing Valeria. From cherishing her as she had deserved to be cherished. The wisdom he had to offer was null. Still, he wanted to be reassuring. 'Oh, but come, who sees clearly? Who is wise? And if we were all literal-minded, *would* life be better? God, imagine how monotonous it would be. Intolerable, I'm sure.' Her expression was uncertain. 'Who's to say that cows aren't great dreamers?'

'Wouldn't you like to be so docile?' she asked.

He didn't say what was in his mind: Docile until put to death.

She made an effort to pull herself together. 'This does seem a healthy place.'

They were quiet on the return journey. He wondered if her neuritis was niggling at her. He hoped she wouldn't regret her elliptical yet frank-seeming words and deny a bud of confidence the possibility of blooming. The afternoon was frigid and delicate.

As they entered the hotel, she said, 'I heard music last night, before I went to sleep.'

Lament of the Nymph? 'Did you like it?'

But they were distracted by the Hydro's proprietress, who announced, 'There is a package for you, Mrs Neele.'

'A letter?' Her voice betrayed hope.

'No, a parcel. Small one. From Harrods.'

'Harrods?'

'Yes, ma'am.'

'Of course. Thank you.' Teresa received the package—
disappointed, he thought, or a little lost, but concealing it well.

'Coming to hear the Hydro Boys again tonight after
dinner?' he enquired as she made for the stairs.

'Excuse me?'

'In the Winter Garden Ballroom?'

'Oh, perhaps,' she said. 'I've a massage appointment at
three thirty. I was almost forgetting.'

'Well, I hope to see you later. I enjoyed our walk.'

'So did I. Thank you. I think I'll take the lift up.'

She was looking pale again, indeed, rather washed out.
He climbed the stairs to the second floor, aware of her in the
lift's cage. He was jealous of the package she was holding,
a reminder of an existence that laid claim to her and of which
he knew nothing.

8

THE MISSING WOMAN

He rinsed his face at the basin in his room, and peered into the glass. Cheeks fringed with droplets of water, eyes glistening, he could have just dashed in from a storm. Well, what do you think you are doing? Harry asked this bedraggled specimen. He looked like he couldn't be trusted, couldn't trust himself. Prudence, he entreated the fool.

There was a tingling in his limbs and an ominous doubtfulness in his chest. This didn't feel like the other infatuations since Valeria, not at all. He was not faintly amused. He was fidgety, rather than slothful. Instead of feeling lascivious in a playful, mellow sort of way, he was painfully edgy. As if his skin had trouble deciding whether it was hot or cold. He considered and decided against changing into the woollen dressing-gown. He'd change his trousers for dinner, so it didn't matter how creased these became. Oh minor vanities, he reflected, paltry and essential for keeping us pinned to the social world, where we would otherwise flutter away into the yawning holes of solitary hours.

He hadn't feared a woman since the early days with Valeria. And then the fear had in large part been excitement at the prospect of pleasure. Wonderment at the discovery of tenderness and the dearly tedious bonds it forged.

Had he, however, finally happened on what he'd been seeking for months? Was this the sea's-edge sensation? If so, it wasn't refreshing in the way he'd imagined. His back to the toasty hearth, he shivered, remembering the dream in which Teresa had turned into sand. His anxiety as she escaped through his fingers, leaving behind her such craving.

Bed, chair, writing table, gramophone, slippers, and especially the bottles of fortified wine (faithful guides to the vapours of sleepiness), all appeared absurdly precious. Only yesterday he'd considered this decor an irritating *mise en scène*, and now it gave him a pang to think he might lose what it represented, the relative calm he had fashioned for himself, the hush of hotel dwelling, of absconding, being well-nigh erased. He too had come to see the value, as Teresa claimed she had, of docility, regardless of how bland and empty his days could be. In truth, he was incapable of picturing a life different from his present one. Admittedly a kind of halved life to match the half-lie of the hotel furnishings. For though all the leisure time he enjoyed, particularly his compulsive walking through wholesome surrounds, had made him quite physically tough, he had no illusions as to the fitness of his spirit. *It* remained convalescent, requiring cosseting.

He should have dined away from the Hydro that night and avoided the Winter Garden Ballroom. He would not, alas. But he had to be on his guard. At this very moment, she was preparing to lie down under the hands of a trained professional. How on earth was *he* to wade through the sluggish hours separating him from dinner?

He subsided into the wingback chair and snatched up the *Daily Mail* he hadn't had the patience for that morning. Some pages in he encountered a photograph of a woman. It was not a very sharp image, yet it caused him to pause. The woman resembled—rather a lot—Teresa Neele.

He inhaled raggedly. Look at the state you're in, he chided himself. Seeing her everywhere. The likeness, though, was considerable. He scrutinised the photograph until the grainy chiaroscuro visage was unmade into flecks of light and shade that nevertheless remained hauntingly feminine. Then he read the article. Three times.

He had overheard a little of this story from the conversations of other guests at the Hydro, without paying it much attention. A woman had gone missing from her home in Sunningdale, Berkshire, three days previously, on Friday evening. She happened to be a quite renowned author of mysteries. Her abandoned motor had been found in nearby countryside at eight o'clock on Saturday morning. It had lodged in some shrubbery at the edge of a chalk pit, possibly after having been purposely allowed to run down from a place called Newlands Corner. The police had spent the weekend scouring the North Downs. They had dredged something called the Silent Pool. No trace of the woman had been uncovered. She seemed simply to have vanished. 'A beautiful woman,' was how the newspaper referred to her.

Somehow, this observation offended him as voyeuristic. They spoke of her with a nasty mix of surgeon's impassibility and circus-goer's idle glee.

Her husband claimed . . .

Husband.

Her husband claimed she was undergoing a nervous collapse. He described her, furthermore, as 'a very nervous person'.

He would. He had to explain her desertion so that it did not reflect badly on him. Which naturally it did. What a cad, to tell the press such things about his own wife, even if he believed them to be true. The stark fact that she'd run away from him was screaming evidence that he had not been the husband he should have been. These thoughtless comments confirmed it.

What appeared to be her sadness surely did, too. If indeed she was the person Harry knew as Teresa Neele.

When he returned to the fuzzy photograph, it seemed to him that the eyes were hers. The very vagueness of the image was hers. The story began to bring this into focus, explaining her evasiveness and her unusual conversation—so careful, slow, and then queerly impromptu. Had he danced the charleston with a notorious woman? He'd suspected South Africa to be a lie. He hadn't suspected his dance partner had removed a wedding ring.

He had always thought Agatha, as the missing woman was called, such a lady's name. Just slightly wild, with grey trappings, something of moths' wings or mole fur. Or a prettyish fuzz of mould that would make your blood run a little cold.

Agatha's husband was a colonel. Oh yes. A small likeness of the man indicated an appearance that some would have considered handsome. In it, he clearly felt dashing and satisfied with himself. Harry thought him uninspiring and rather insubstantial in his military uniform, with his studiedly distant, thin gaze. (Harry was sometimes sensitive about not having served in the war on account of the examining officer, when he'd gone to enlist, discovering that his blood pressure was undesirably high and his hands trembled.) The Colonel had returned to Sunningdale on Saturday. So where was he on the Friday night of his wife's disappearance? Why hadn't he been at her side? She left a home that was empty of her spouse.

Harry looked again at the photograph. Could it really be Teresa, on whom he had become stuck? If it was, then this could hardly go well for him.

He went over to the window and hauled it up. A clever man would leave the Hydro at once. Cold air slithered over him. Swan Road. In the distance the Royal Pump Room was like a small, squat chapel. Wasn't it a kind of earthly church? No steeple gesturing to the heavens but a well leading down to underground waters promising their own form of salvation. The grey stone houses lining the street appeared especially earthbound, hunkered down, and he saw that the sun was already setting, one of those premature winter sunsets that instead of a gradual condensing of darkness seem a reneging of light. A childlike sense of being taken unawares. Muffled panic.

Was this one of those fatal last moments when there is still sufficient perspective to be sensible and keep from following a course that would be regretted? Had there been such a moment in his marriage, when he might have prevented disaster? When he realised he was allowing the blues to eclipse Valeria? Gazing out over nearly nocturnal roads, he couldn't recall. It was unlikely he'd ever had much perspective. Sucking in a final mouthful of cold air, he closed the window. Curtains drawn, he went back to the fire and squatted before it. He fed more coal to the flames, then sat hunched over the heat, muttering, This will not go well.

Later, he laughed because he'd discovered he scarcely cared.

He didn't care anywhere near enough.

Changing into a well-pressed navy-blue suit for dinner, he entertained himself with the idea that he was an insane chap dressing for the gallows, a smirk on his mad, sorry face.

9

FOURTH DAY, AFTERNOON

Hands at her waist. Briefly, she didn't understand what was occurring. Teresa laughed in confusion. 'You had me hypnotised.'

'I'm always putting people to sleep,' the masseuse said matter-of-factly.

She had seized Teresa's ankles and tugged her feet as if she would detach legs from body. There had been a slight pain, and then nothing.

'Your ring, ma'am. I left it here safe.' It had slipped off so easily, testimony to lost weight.

She drank down the glass of water the masseuse, a rounded, hale creature, handed her. Her surprised stomach lurched a tad. Potent. Reminiscent, indeed, both of aged egg and seawater.

•

The clothes just delivered were radiant. New clothes remained almost as exciting to her as they had been when Mummy took her to the dressmaker in Paris who'd make her first semi-evening dress. Pale grey crepe de Chine. It was such a heady adult costume. The transformative possibilities of style! The surreptitious power of chic!

She enjoyed bathing with the *crème de lys* soap, and was prodigal with face cream, *papier poudré* and eau de cologne, which she even rubbed into the crooks of her arms and backs of her knees. Quite the coquette, she considered herself in the glass and had to conclude that the georgette gown and Harrogate agreed with her.

'You were right, I adored the baths,' she told Mrs Jackman in the lounge. 'I'll go again tomorrow.'

'I *knew* you would. Our daughter adores them, and I think you and she might have similar tastes. Doesn't she remind you of Jane, my dear?'

'Now that you mention it, she does, rather.'

Conversational procedures weighed on you less when you hadn't practised them for a time. Teresa asked after Jane, hoping Mrs Jackman wasn't one of those tiring people who prattle on about their children out of some fervid compulsion.

'She's an interesting girl,' the latter said. 'Very bright. You'd understand each other.' She lowered her voice. 'Actually, poor

Jane had a tragedy not unlike yours.' She regarded Teresa softly. 'Her baby died.' Teresa looked down into her lap. 'Well, Jane lost her memory. Strange, isn't it? It was frightfully hard on Ned. First the baby, and then his wife not knowing him. It was hard on everyone. Jane didn't—she just seemed to go somewhere else, until things got easier to manage.'

'My word,' offered a woman Teresa did not recognise, who was affixing herself to their conversation, despite its discreet volume. Her droopy pistachio dress was covered with overexcited beadwork and her inquisitive expression rather dull.

Smiling at the intruder, Mrs Jackman commented, 'To be honest, she hasn't been the same since. She did eventually remember what had happened with the baby. After, I suppose, a couple of weeks, it all came back. And she was able to go on and live quite normally. She's philosophical, Jane.'

'Stalwart girl,' Mr Jackman said.

Mrs Jackman reiterated, 'She isn't entirely as she used to be. Her eyes are where you see it.'

'Because she loved her baby,' surmised the hanger-on, animated, 'she lost her memory.'

'Yes,' said Mrs Jackman.

'Intelligent ones suffer more,' the woman went on.

'Oh, do you think so?' Mr Jackman smiled forlornly.

They were saved from further vapid discourse by the appearance of Harry. Once again, the sight of him was more familiar than it should have been, given the newness of their friendship. Was it a friendship? She didn't think he was impervious to her georgette gown. He was looking at her differently, somehow.

Teresa and Harry hardly spoke during dinner. No mention was made of their walk. There was talk of bathhouses and of Cairo, where it turned out that the eager new addition to their party, whom Teresa found herself actively disliking, had spent a season at eighteen. Cairo as a place to come out was much cheaper than London and therefore a reasonable alternative for a family rather badly off but desiring to provide their daughter with appropriate opportunities. This was also a feature of Teresa's history, a result of the shift in fortune her family had suffered. The woman continued to be remarkably lacklustre right through to a last spoonful of meringue, when, realising she was having no great effect upon them, she sulkily announced she was pleased to be leaving the following morning for York. Teresa and Harry exchanged looks.

A relief to be freed to proceed to the ballroom. He was at her elbow as she entered it.

'Will you trust me, Teresa, after last time, with another dance?'

He made this gallant invitation a joke, and not. It might have been the tedium of the dinner conversation that had left her restless, with the coiled energy best spent in exercise.

They excused themselves. It was a little like her youthful days of Cairo soirees.

They danced more smoothly this time to quite a sprightly instrumental piece he identified as 'Rose Room'. But she sensed that something was wrong. He was gripping her hand tightly. Conversation had been fluent during their walk, but now silence mounted.

'Everything all right?'

'Oh yes,' he replied. He seemed to debate with himself, and then he said tensely, 'You didn't read today's *Daily Mail*?'

'The *Daily Mail*? I flicked through it. Why?' (The trick, a buried part of her knew, was to have her thoughts go on slipping against one another with the least possible resistance, as thin and slippery as silken underthings.) 'Did I miss some noteworthy disaster or scandal?'

'Nothing caught your attention?'

They glanced at one another in the oblique, staccato way which dancing requires. Scrutiny at such close range would be unbearable.

'Not particularly.' It suddenly occurred to Teresa to wonder if he could fancy he was falling in love with her. She'd lost the habit of such ideas. Did he have the barnyard-animal-feeling-poorly look? She smiled involuntarily. But surely not. She floundered for something to say and chanced on—she'd been doing this lately, like an old woman—the distant past. 'When I was a young girl, I used to read the newspapers to my grandmother, who was quite blind with cataracts. Sordid situations were a stimulant to her. It's often so for the elderly.'

'Newspapers can provide certain necessary shocks.'

She said nothing to this, and presently the song ended.

'Another?'

'Better not. I think I'm feeling the neuritis again. Probably need an early night. Some reading in bed.'

'What will you read? A mystery?'

'Yes, as a matter of fact.'

'That music you heard last night was *Lament of the Nymph*, on my gramophone. Monteverdi. I hope it didn't disturb you. Do you know it?'

'I don't think so.'

'A light opera about a woman with a broken heart.'

'Goodnight, Harry.' She turned to the door.

10

THE BLUE HOUR

He had been afraid she would breakfast alone in her room again. When she joined the table in the dining room occupied by the Jackmans and himself, she greeted them with a vacant little smile for general consumption. Her face surprised him, though. It was flushed. It might have been this that made her eyes seem so dynamic.

Mrs Jackman asked, 'How did you sleep, my dear?'

'Excellently. And you?'

'Endlessly. I only wish I could say the same of my husband.'

'Never mind,' Mr Jackman said and raised his glass of fetid, health-giving water. 'Here we go. Bottoms up—or, rather, *santé.*'

'*Santé,*' they echoed, lifting their glasses and trying to hurry the stuff down their throats, while grimacing neatly.

'Sweet elixir.' Harry coughed. 'Makes you feel like a child pressed to drink medicine.'

Teresa giggled. He didn't think her a natural giggler.

'Perhaps we *are* all children taking our medicine, if viewed from the right angle,' observed Mrs Jackman.

'Funny how you can get used to anything, almost anything,' offered Teresa.

Mrs Jackman added cream liberally to her coffee, and passed the jug. 'The line between what can be borne and what can't is different for different people. Or even the same person, at different times. I suppose I'm thinking of our Jane.'

Teresa received the cream and the heaped plate brought to her with apparent delectation. A glass of the water that was so good for one tended to dampen Harry's appetite, but she applied herself enthusiastically to eating. Mrs Jackman unwound a reminiscence about her girlhood, something about a dance master, Teresa nodding and paying great attention. Mr Jackman and Harry had achieved the sort of exemption from conversation that newspapers can secure.

Harry almost choked on the toast he was nibbling. He'd come to an article in the *Daily Mail* concerning the disappearance of the authoress. He glanced up at the woman tackling her second sausage across the table from him, apparently oblivious to all except her meal and Mrs Jackman's lilting narration. Nerves jangled, he returned to the article.

A man had presented himself to the police, claiming to have come across the missing woman at Newlands Corner. On first approaching her, he had heard her wailing. Clearly in some distress, she had practically fallen into him. When she requested it, he had started her motorcar. Then he had watched her drive away.

In the opinion of the superintendent directing the inquiry, her motor had accidentally gone off the road at Newlands Corner, whereupon she had jumped out of it and watched fearfully as it careened down a slope and collided with some bushes over a chalk pit. After that, she had somehow blundered off and become lost. He seemed to view her chances of survival darkly.

Meanwhile, her husband the Colonel was utterly baffled and half desperate, their little daughter his only consolation . . .

Agatha and the Colonel had a daughter. This must have been mentioned in the article Harry had seen the day before, but he'd read over that detail. A daughter was left behind, too.

Teresa was concentrating on her toast. There were several newspapers at nearby tables, but no one appeared to be casting suspicious glances in her direction. Could it be that no one else at the Hydro had noticed this article or yesterday's? Or that no one who'd seen them had found any coincidence between the unexplained disappearance attracting so much attention and the arrival of the elusive Mrs Neele? Was discretion so much the norm here that if anyone had paused to wonder, they'd have guarded against showing it? Had Harry simply gone mad?

'You didn't stay long in the ballroom last night, my dear,' Mrs Jackman reprimanded Teresa affectionately. 'I was going to ask your opinion on a crossword clue—you solve them so masterfully—and I couldn't find you.'

'I was sleepy. And anxious to get back to a book. But today I feel so full of energy. The ghastly water doing its witchcraft. Or this place. Harrogate is, I'm convinced of it, a tonic. And the shopping is delightful. Today I've decided that I need a shawl.'

He didn't presume to know Teresa. How could he, when she was barely an acquaintance—an acquaintance who was possibly lying to him, to everyone at the Hydro? But this talk was, he sensed, *wrong* coming from her. To his ears, it had a slightly manic flavour.

'Indeed? I might be able to advise you on shops,' Mrs Jackman offered timidly.

'I'd like that. What was the clue?'

'The clue? Oh. Typical, now I've forgotten it . . .'

Finding the situation unreal, he returned to his news-paper. A Mrs de Silva, described as a family friend, said that the missing woman was a kind, sweet person, devoted to her husband. She had been severely afflicted by the loss of her mother, who had recently died . . . This had left the authoress poorly and unable to write.

Plates were taken away and Teresa, pink-cheeked, pro-nounced, 'Delicious.'

Her eyes finally met Harry's and she smiled, just a quiver. In that moment, he was certain she was *her*. To be the only one who knew her true identity was electrifying. It created a curious subterranean intimacy between them. He smiled in return and suffered from an urge to reach across the table to touch her hand, which seemed stranded. He was also entertaining a fantasy of catching her alone somewhere, cornering her and obliging her to explain everything to him.

'I hear you have every kind of dangerous animal over there,' Mr Jackman was saying to him.

'Hm? Oh, in Australia? Well, I haven't been back in over a decade, but, yes, the last time I checked.'

'Harry grew up on a farm,' Mr Jackman explained to his wife. 'Livestock?'

'Fruit orchard.'

'Ah, what kind of fruit?'

'Cherries, mainly. And some plums. Stone fruit.'

'You have all that over there? I suppose you do. We're fanatical about cherries. And I gather you have snakes that will kill you?'

'Indeed.'

Harry was awarded a fascinated smile.

Mrs Jackman and Teresa left the dining room, bound in a tête à tête. Mr Jackman paused as the two men made to follow. 'One last question about the Australian wildlife. Is it true you have a spider that . . .'

'Yes, yes, it will all kill you.'

By the time they'd arrived at the foot of the stairs, the ladies were not to be seen.

•

He encountered another newspaper soon after. On Crescent Street, just outside the Royal Baths, a gentleman stood absorbed in a *Daily Express*. Harry halted. Staring right at him from the front page was Teresa.

It wasn't at all how he had grown used to seeing her, and once again the image was grainy and shadowy, yet in some way he thought it came closer to precision than the last photograph.

She was accompanied by a female child. Of six years or so, he guessed. Had to be her daughter. Very pretty child. Their faces alongside one another, the child was notably prettier than the mother, with features neater and finer. She was more attentive to the camera, too, though her demeanour was somewhat cold. They were both sombre, but the mother looked weary with it, and aware of looking weary. What a thin, deflated mouth. Eyes a little hooded. The long, strong nose verging on hooked. Roman? Next to her daughter, she was slumping morosely into middle age. He had to recognise it: into plainness. Was that what Teresa had run from? This diluted, defeated version of her face? He found that because half of her true name was her husband's, he was disinclined to stop thinking of her as Teresa Neele.

'Can I help you, sir?'

Harry gave a start. The gentleman had lowered the screen of his newspaper. He was elderly and moustachioed, and Harry had the sense that they were taking part in some comical turn in a music hall performance. 'Excuse me?'

'Lost, are you? Wanting directions?'

'Yes, thank you, yes. The Royal Baths. That's what I'm after.'

The gent grunted. 'Right under your nose.'

•

While lowering his body fatalistically into the frigid waters of the plunge bath, it came to him that not only were Teresa and Agatha likely one and the same, but the woman in question would *do something desperate*.

He gasped. Stood bolt upright, the shocking water at his waist, his lungs astonished. He remembered his negligent banter about desirable methods of taking one's life and the gentleness of her response. Her description of a lovely last day, of swimming off to meet the end. It hadn't occurred to him to carefully consider the consequence of her words—to ask himself, indeed, whether she could have designated the Hydro as the last hotel at which she would ever be a guest. Had she tried to put him off the trail by declaring she'd only countenance for such purposes an exotic locale like Casablanca?

'Excuse me,' said a very handsome young man, not apologising but merely confirming his right to the space

Harry had been occupying. He proceeded to plash and prance, undeterred by the iciness of the water, executing swimming strokes, then shaking water from himself like an unruly pup, laughing. Exuding health, athleticism and exuberance. 'Aren't you cold, standing still like that?' he thought to ask.

'I daresay I should be, but I'm quite resilient to the cold.' Harry barely kept his teeth from knocking against one another. He turned away and exited the pool that he'd hoped would brace his mind.

'Admirable—I mean, at your age,' the younger man opined.

He was possibly sincere. He didn't look subtle enough for irony. But Harry wasn't in a mood to take a generous view of the insolent Adonis. He secured a towel around his waist, his body wanting to quake from the cold. The boy was performing some lazy form of callisthenics that permitted him to show off an enviable musculature and sensuous grace. How many would lose their hearts to him? Poor silly dears.

'Age isn't my exclusive property,' Harry said, confronting him. 'Wait and more will come to you. You won't need much patience. Provided, of course, you don't meet with an accident before then, there's nothing on which you can rely more.'

And with this attempt at reinstating his honour he departed for the Caldarium, where he laid himself out on a deckchair like the sanatorium exhibit he was, one arm draped rather effetely over his eyes. He was chilled to the core.

Yes, it followed that Teresa spoke so readily of self-harm because this was at the forefront of her thoughts. It wasn't her earlier queer languid manner or maybe sadness that had tipped him off, nor even his discovery of the notoriety she was earning in her escape from her detestable husband (assuming she truly was Agatha), but her brightness that morning at breakfast. Her ebullience, her almost aggressive gaiety. It appeared to Harry that this *had* to be a mask. And possibly—was it plausible?—a decoy to distract observers not only from her identity but from her serious plans. If grief over her mother's death had left her ill and incapable of literary work, what role might this have played in the unusual measures she had taken? The loss of a loved one affected a person in unexpected ways. He had found her lucid, if erratic and novel—however, what if the illness mentioned had taken its toll on her mind? Should she have been laughing, eating with gusto in company and going about shopping when all the while the police and the press were after her, hunting her libidinously, and anyone at the Hydro who picked up a newspaper might have summed two and two, and known it?

His tension spurred him into a cold shower. What was Teresa planning? He was sickened to have arrived at her own death, that ultimate flight from any and all versions of one's face, as her probable next move.

•

He didn't return to the Hydro after the baths, because he didn't know how he would have deployed himself there. Had he run into Teresa, he could hardly have questioned her. If she'd been willing to accompany him on another walk, as he'd have been tempted to propose she do, pretending that he hadn't discovered her secret would have been difficult. The desire to plead, *Tell me why*, or, *Don't do it!* might have overpowered him. And speaking his mind could lose him her trust, even conceivably cause her to run away once more. So he wandered about.

On Parliament Street he came to W.H. Smith and entered. Three of her books were in their circulating library.

'Oh, she's the one that's gone missing.' The lady who found them for him was affected by a marked rounding of the upper back that did not prevent her from somehow moving harmoniously, horsey and courtly. 'She's surely dead, poor thing. Dreadful for the family. Everyone will be wanting these now. I warrant it'll make her reputation.'

Teresa's other name on the books' covers seemed an affront.

He proceeded to the Stray, where he began, while meandering along, to examine one of the novels. The cover was rather theatrical: a bear in a man's suit appeared to be removing—or was about to hide behind—a human mask, whey-faced, raffish, vaguely lecherous. Harry smiled over the first lines. And, surprisingly quickly, was ensconced within the story, where he spent some hours, by turns drifting on foot and sitting.

A dog bounding into him returned him to himself some time later. An eager, pure-faced terrier. Remembering Teresa's passionate glance at the corgi, he stooped to pat the animal, which became increasingly excited until his master, an indeterminate sort of man in a mackintosh, forcibly reclaimed him. It wasn't raining, though the opaque sky was threatening. This man would be at home in the rain, and not just because he had dressed for it. His features already appeared nebulous and forlorn. He bid Harry good evening with a woebegone, slightly reproachful tone. The terrier extended a reluctant farewell. It was chilly and Harry had rushed out without his coat. Had he left it at the baths? He was also, he found, half starved but inclined to continue with the novel.

He was installed at Bettys a handful of minutes later, reading as he awaited poached salmon, the intrigue rolling up around him like the light sheath of a stocking over a woman's leg.

•

He emerged into early evening, beneath a sky of that drastic heartfelt blue, the dawn of black, which had always seduced him. He purchased *The Times*. The column of interest was in the middle of the paper.

The Colonel hadn't received any news as to the whereabouts of his wife.

In their search for her, the police had dragged Albury Mill Pond.

Someone said he had seen Teresa at Milford railway station, a few miles south of Godalming.

This unfamiliar geography began to take on hazy contours in Harry's mind. He saw a grim sort of marshland, spectral with fog.

He was nearing the hotel and it seemed that Teresa was standing in front of it. At first he wondered whether the vision was a trick of his imagination. But no. Drawing closer, he saw that she was wrapped in a luminous white shawl, its fringe trembling. He stopped before she had seen him, and rapidly folded the newspaper around the books he was also carrying. Hers.

Why was risk exciting? Resisted, the drive that should cause a person to flee worked like an intoxicant. He came forward. Her slanted head suggested contemplation of the sky.

'Agreeable time of evening,' he said. 'My favourite time of day, in fact. The blue hour. Would you call that Prussian blue? Lapis lazuli?'

'Beautiful.' They considered the sky together. 'God, I don't know what I'd call it. Good day, Harry?'

'Quite tolerable.' He smiled. 'And yours, Teresa? I see you found a shawl. Very handsome,' he added awkwardly. 'It suits you.'

'Oh, this.'

Ducking his compliment, she was toying with the ends of the shawl, swirls of moonlight flashes. Really, how absolutely different she was here, tonight, from the woman in the *Daily Express* picture. Now she was glamorous, vital. He still thought there was a giddiness to her, something like euphoria—or was he only seeing his own?

She said, 'I've come out for some air, because a ridiculous thing just happened to me inside. I'd gone into the lounge. I thought I might see the Jackmans there, or you, but there was only an old man in an armchair by the fire. Elegant, with a cane. Quite magisterial. But he was so still—like a statue—I thought he was asleep. I approached and he didn't budge. I came closer. His eyes were open behind his glasses, though being so perfectly immobile he *had* to be sleeping or, it occurred to me, *dead*!' She laughed. 'Nothing stirred, the whole room seemed under an enchantment. As I was thinking of bending over and putting a little mirror under his nose, something in that vein, he lifted his eyebrows rather drolly. You should have seen me jump.

'"I assure you I'm with the living, if only just," he declared. I couldn't think of a word of excuse, I was so ashamed. I blurted a sorry and rushed out. You see how frightfully I lack social grace.' She laughed again.

Harry laughed too, disoriented. He hadn't heard so many words in a row from her since they'd met. 'Yes, strange when you think how slight the difference is between a man and a corpse.'

Her eyes were back on the darkening sky and she didn't appear in the mood to follow him down this philosophical avenue.

'Social grace is probably highly overrated,' he went on. 'And are you well, otherwise?'

'It's been a pleasant day.'

He'd begun to acquaint himself with her literary accomplishments. The tale he was reading was hardly Serious Literature. It wasn't the kind of thing he'd had the grandiose pretension as a young man to dream he might produce. But it didn't take itself for that. And it was clever. It ushered you in, as if into the reliably cheerful house of a spry rascally great-aunt. Teresa had to have a nimble, astute mind and considerable strength of character. Did he still think she could be plotting her own end? He found today's volubility zany and a tad brittle. But she did appear to be capable of amusement, and resilient, somehow. Someone who could enjoy herself. Even if she *was* horribly sad underneath all this, was he arrogant enough to presume he could do anything about it? He was suddenly impotent and tired. *His* mind repeatedly showed its limits. He was not astute or strong. He tottered in darkness.

Was he even so sure that he had before him the escaped authoress of the book he had been reading?

'What is it?' She had caught his change in spirits.

'I'm just rather exhausted. I had a long walk on the Stray.'

They were quite near to one another. He blinked and saw the photograph in which Agatha's lovely daughter so upstaged her. If Teresa were to fall towards him in this instant, as Agatha allegedly almost had into the man who'd come upon her by Newlands Corner, he would catch her. Say into her warm neck, What set you on the run? Confide in me.

He leaned forward slightly, recalling the feel of her in his arms when they'd danced. But had she recoiled? She'd reassumed that cordoned-off countenance, suggesting barred access to a space both desolate and charged.

'Will you be coming to dine?' she enquired.

'No. I had something at Bettys not long ago.'

'Ah. Good food. It impressed me. Self-respecting food.'

'Yes, rather.'

She looked towards the entrance of the hotel. 'Perhaps we'll see you in the Winter Garden Ballroom, later?'

He oughtn't to dance with her that night. He was weak, uncertain and susceptible. What he needed was the comforting canniness of the mystery novel he'd begun. Books could be so much more soothing than people. 'Don't think I'm really in the right frame of mind. But you will promise me a dance for tomorrow night?'

'I don't know that I should be making promises,' she said. 'It's getting cold.'

'It is.'

Were her words meaningful? Had he made her suspicious? Rain hadn't come. The dog walker's precautionary mackintosh a vain gesture. The sky by this time was onyx black, a thin shiver of moon upon it.

11

SIXTH DAY

The chambermaid's knock.

It was a romantic dream at the rudder of which a semi-waking awareness had sat for spells. Leaving it was like lolling in a pool of sun, then being ejected into cold.

Odd, to be waking once more with vibrant, detailed recollections of dreams. By nature she was a great dreamer, but in the past months any dreams (other than those starring the Gun Man) had been as shallow as barely unlikely digressions of thought. Inadequate pseudo-rest that left her brain grisly and aggrieved. Offended with the world and all the more so for the suspicion that she had in some manner sabotaged herself. In Harrogate, however, deep sleep was returning. She lay still, reluctant for that particular sweet dream to dissolve.

In came the chambermaid with tea and newspaper. A wedge between Teresa and the warmth she'd been forced from. She said she'd take breakfast in bed, resentful of the young woman's efficient movements and elastic spine. Yet there were dark dips still under her too-penetrating eyes. She might know what it was to be betrayed by sleep. She probably had a child, several, and must be an old intimate of fatigue. How had she kept her pleasing waist? Her days would involve a great deal of hard work, of course, and possibly letdowns that may or may not be blunter than suffering. The beauty not quite managed was receding, a treasured friend waving on the quay, a shimmer in the distance. Light hair discolouring, silver strands creeping in like minor but disruptive misunderstandings. When the husband's eye roamed, she'd know it. Teresa continued to take exception to her energetic gaze.

Once she had departed, Teresa could dress. No penance of the green jumper and grey stockinette skirt for her today! Horrid baggy knits as slovenly as old skin ... No, for her, hurrah, there was fresh tweed and a white blouse and a maroon jumper. Even new stockings and knickers.

Her shoulder seeming improved, the arm just a fraction weak, she gave a twirl and in the dizzy middle of it heard stately music—being played, she supposed, on Harry's gramophone—that she might have identified if it had been louder. He had been a little off the last times she'd seen him, ill at ease. (Better not to give this much consideration. She was keeping her thoughts silken, thin.) Last night he preferred not to dance with her. Though he *had* wanted to be near her while they stood in front of the hotel. She was certain of that as a woman is of such things.

She put her head out of the window to gain an idea of the northern day. Sleep appeared to be sharpening her senses. Wood smoke and the opalescent silver and cream flecks of slate roof tiles. Clean, pristine cold. Light so fleecy it might have been filtered by cloud, when in fact the sky was quite clear. Even the stone of houses had a plush look, as if it were actually some stiff velvet or moss. No seagulls here, of course. No sea tang.

Two young people were down on the drive. His way of turning to her and arranging the scarf around her neck declared they were lovers. The girl's shiny brown head rather towered over him. It was the dancers—from when? The night she and Harry danced. The boy gazed adoringly up at Birthday Girl, and then noticed Teresa.

She withdrew, vaguely panicked. She sat down at the writing table to see whether she could dispatch the postponed letter to Mr Neele. A quick note might be sufficient.

But no development, apparently, on that front. No cooperative phrases to be found, the right ones still skulking behind a sort of dental-surgery woolliness of perception. When she muttered the simplest line aloud to coax it along (*Darling, I think of you constantly*), it came out ironic and mocking. The very touch of the pen against her hand was irksome. Hateful. Would she have been able to get something out on a typewriter? The music she couldn't decipher went on and on. She wondered if it had somehow woven itself into her dream, as sounds sometimes intrude on sleep to reinvent themselves in a dream form. It might have been interesting to see Harry, but it was no doubt preferable to keep herself secluded this morning.

She needed an occupation, however. Not being able to write, nor even to think about writing in any diverting, strategic way, was so boring. And worse, more menacing, was the unkempt feeling it gave her, as if nothing could be taken charge of and made shipshape. If Peter were with her, she'd be less het up. Oh, for a piano! Yesterday, her spirits were high. Today the restlessness seemed fragile, and she didn't want to become agitated. What she could, should, do was go out to buy more clothes.

•

She achieved this, rather admirably, with a cardigan to show for it—mauve, her favourite colour—from Henry Moore's. And a black silk evening dress from Louis Copé, because she wouldn't be able to get away with just the georgette for long.

Then she carried on to Valley Gardens. She'd liked it there. Her ulterior motive may have been to see whether a saunter would help to raise the Wretched Book from its mortuary sleep. Walking had been the best approach to a vexatious literary problem before. She'd unearthed many a useful piece of a puzzle in so doing. In fact, she couldn't remember a time when she hadn't worked through adventures while wandering alone through nature. The habit became formal, as it were, on Dartmoor, thanks to Mummy's characteristically capital idea that she go for a fortnight's holiday there, to the Moorland Hotel, to finish her first novel. But she had spent the better part of her childhood strutting around the garden and little wood at Ashfield—threading through ashes whose sighs imitated the sea's, circling the wondrous beech—lost in a kind of disconnected but fervent conversation with . . . whomsoever she chose. Virtuous or more curious girls her own age, captivating adults, cheeky anthropomorphic animals. Quite entertaining, frankly. Though there had been none of that for forever, as the stubborn Wretched Book was denying her such company.

And launching, now, her brain back into thoughts of Shy Thing and the morning's dream.

•

She had lost her heart to him during the Empire Tour. Her husband, not an imaginer, wouldn't have suspected it. Shy Thing was the youngest of the Brood. She had been acquainted with them in Sydney and was invited to go and stay on their gargantuan Queensland cattle station while her husband and the major undertook a dull, arduous tour of country towns.

She was always insatiably greedy for fruit, but the varieties served in the Brood's homestead, at breakfast, for dessert, at any hour, made English fruit seem commonplace and rather flavourless. Their pineapples, oranges, grapes, sugar bananas and mangoes had a gaudy sweetness, almost candied. Given the chance, she'd have devoured mangoes like chocolate truffles, face running shamelessly with juice. She had to control herself. They were a frisky, warm, amusing family, the Brood, people who expected to enjoy themselves and therefore did. The three girls managed to be extremely attractive—each one more svelte than the last—and forceful. A dazzling combination. How did they pull it off? Teresa was also drawn to all four of the brothers, who treated her with an endearing reverence that had nothing to envy in the most gallant Englishman. The siblings evidently shared a great deal of affectionate mutual regard, and she was struck by how they continually showed it. Touching, giving and receiving kisses. She watched, beguiled.

Her true crush was the quieter, musical brother they called Shy Thing. They related to him as to a jolly idiosyncrasy. It turned out that he and Teresa had in common inferior riding skills, and this fact, which she'd confessed to him, caused him to plead for her to stay behind one afternoon at the homestead in his company instead of having to embark with the others on a strenuous horseback expedition across the scrub.

'She has promised to sing for me,' he told the Most Svelte One, who conceded but smiled with a hint of mischief.

When the bubbly party had gone, Shy Thing turned to Teresa in the growing quiet and said, 'Shall we?'

She approached the piano. He sat at it, lifted the lid, and drew back his broad shoulders. His seriousness usually made him appear almost middle-aged among his livelier, more physical siblings, and for the first time, though he was just as sober as ever, she *noticed* his youth. He was, after all, more than a decade her junior. Barely a man. Was it his concentrated energy as he prepared to play that was boyish? Or the reddish-brown hair falling into his eyes? Just that extreme undamaged pallor of the skin beneath a smattering of mahogany freckles? She was ordinarily much less nervous singing than playing the piano, but she had a flittering then of stage fright's elemental doubt, the sense of nearing a trapdoor in herself.

His hazel eyes on her, eyelashes quite golden. His dusky-rose lips were rather self-consciously set. It darted into her mind that he might be stimulated by *her* age, by her greater experience of the world. Even by her being a married woman.

Fixing her gaze on the gracious ceiling rose, she sang. His accompaniment was understated and confident. They'd agreed on a program, Purcell's 'Passing By' and Metcalf's 'Absent', to get her going, then Cherubini and Puccini, beginning with the aria from *Medea*, '*Dei tuoi figli la madre*'. Her voice wavered slightly initially but was, she hoped, tolerable. She couldn't tell. To be singing again like this, so excited, brought back her adolescent self in Paris, the one poised to become an opera singer enrapturing devoted crowds in the best theatres of Europe. It was as holy as ever. Jumping free of the mundane. She was half abandoned to the music, and aware of him beneath the melody, plumping her up. They performed many pieces to an audience of no one. She'd experimentally commenced the soprano's part from the finale of *La Bohème*, '*Sono andati? Fingevo di dormire*', when something made her pause.

The house was silent, with that rural silence that can seem timeless yet final. His widowed mother had gone to call on a neighbouring estate, and the servants gave no signs of life. It started to rain. A downpour arriving as if from nowhere. Stunning after the preceding lull, the sound frightening upon the corrugated-iron roof.

'Storms here are first rate,' he said, his usual modesty replaced by a kind of pride. 'Come, I'll show you.'

She followed him to a red sofa in a bay window, where they kneeled side by side on brocade cushions. The deluge was a vast gunmetal sheet stretching the entire length of the long field behind the house. Closing them off from any more distant landscape, it had a stupendously implacable appearance.

'Will they find shelter?' She meant his siblings, though she found it difficult at that moment to think of them.

'Oh, they'll be all right,' he said carelessly. 'They're used to being out in all weather.'

'You're quite a band.'

'Tell me about *your* brother and sister.'

During her singing, he'd seemed to listen to her, or to his own playing, with tremendous fixity. His voice now suggested this same scrutiny.

'My sister is brilliant,' she began awkwardly. 'What energy. A natural storyteller. Uproarious—screaming! She once dressed up as a Greek priest to meet someone off a train. And while in Paris being finished, she accepted a dare to leap from a window, which involved landing on a table at which ladies were taking tea. She can and will do anything. She's uncommonly intelligent.'

He raised his eyebrows. 'The Clever Sister. I have three of those.'

'The Clever Sister.' She smiled, emboldened. 'And then there's the Adventuring Brother. Just returned to England from Africa with a long-suffering native manservant. He'd had various schemes there for years. He's quite intransigent but mysteriously charming—hugely popular, actually. Very expensive tastes. A great hunter. He and Clever Sister are both originals, you might say. Personalities.' She paused. 'I was the *un*remarkable one. The painfully diffident simpleton without anything amusing to say.'

He shook his head incredulously but said, 'Me too. I'm the overshadowed child in my family. Receding into a corner with his books and his music. Oh, they love me, of course. Indulge me. They just don't take me overly seriously.'

She pictured him as a little boy, humming muffled tunes by the cool glass of windows. 'You appear to be such good playmates, though. *I* was practically an only child. Well, Clever Sister is ten years older than me and Adventuring Brother eight, so when I was growing up they were always away at school. I adored my nurse and my governess, but I played alone mostly.'

'Were you lonely?' In spite of the casual lightness with which he asked this, the question made her think he'd have climbed into her mind with a lamp, if he could have done, to investigate the dimmer regions of her character. There was a private flavour to their talk, and something of the interrogation.

An astounding crack of thunder intervened then, like an immense dry thing exploding, and incredibly the flood increased. The absolute opacity they gazed on reminded her of certain storms in Torbay. A rush of craving hit her, for Devon, she thought. They might have been sea voyagers in that house, so cut off were they from anything else.

She mumbled, 'I was glad to have Mummy to myself, I guess. And after my father died—I was only nine—she and I became closer still. We were everything to each other. Ashfield is, was, our world. In any case, I had fun on my own.'

'Ashfield is your family home?'

She nodded, looking around the long music room. 'This reminds me of what we called our schoolroom.'

'Your mother must dote on you.'

It had been such a long time since a man had made her feel her own significance, listening to her as if any detail of thought or memory she might value was consequential. After the early days of courting and especially once a married life went on for some years, one listened less fully to one's companion, on the whole. Perhaps it was less troublesome to view that familiar person as an eccentricity not requiring fathoming. Or as some lesson mastered long ago. This attentiveness was irresistible. 'Yes. Dear Mummy.'

He put a hand to the window, long fingers spread. She caught a young man's odour she recognised and was at the same time taken aback by. 'She loved your father very much?'

'Oh, utterly. She was his cousin by marriage, but they grew up in the same household, more or less as brother and sister, though he was much older and spent a lot of time away being a young gentleman in America and France. She'd worshipped him since she was a girl.'

The window glass had clouded from his heat, and when he took his hand away it left behind an exaggerated, wraithlike record of itself. Beyond this, torrential water glowed greyly.

She was much less sure of her charm than she had been at twenty. She was growing discomforted.

'Were you jealous of your father?'

'*Jealous?* No. I don't think so, no.' Too thoroughly affable a man, too well satisfied with everything that befell him to have been a threat. He had possessed a mental transparency, the complacency of one not disturbed by an unremitting imagination, perhaps—or trust, an earnest reliance on people that made his life peaceful. At least until the money and medical worries came along. He had thought, having never worked but only enjoyed himself, that fortune and health were an inexhaustible capital to the management of which he needn't pay active attention. She had known that Father and Mummy would not share such dreamy, unpredictable conversations as mother and daughter braided between them. 'I may have felt a little betrayed when he became ill. Isn't that like a child? Oblivious and selfish! When I think of how she must have suffered . . . I was always happy enough at Ashfield, of course.'

Nevertheless, even the house had been slightly changed, grown somewhat insecure. She had a sharp image of herself striding about the garden, unsure of how she would ever go about being one of life's dramatis personae, petulantly declaring, 'I will *not* be *bored*!'

Witnessing an Australian storm, she said, 'He was ill more and more. They were secretive about it. It seemed an adult, grim business. I saw that my mother was afraid and possessive of him. I don't know that I've said all of this to anyone before.'

Either he asked it very quietly or the rain was particularly loud at that moment. To understand him, she had to turn and study his lips. 'Not to your husband?' It was the first mention of *him*.   .

'Oh, he doesn't ask many questions.' She smiled, strained. 'Or much like hearing about feelings. He hates any talk of sadness or illness. Anything gloomy.'

'Ah.'

A silence formed, thickened by the rain enclosing it. The piping on the cushion was pressing through her skirt into her knees. She wondered if it would leave a branding, as a crumpled bedsheet will, a pattern that might take some time to fade. A clock sounded from afar. Count the chimes: it was three thirty—three-quarters of an hour after the expected return of the riding party. She remarked on this. Shy Thing appeared unconcerned.

'They'll have taken shelter somewhere.' The quick reiteration of his earlier assurance and something in his tone jarred. 'You have,' he said, just as fast, 'a very lovely soprano.'

Was it not the rain causing their lateness, but some agreement the Brood had come to? Would he be so unworried otherwise? She had been regarding him as deeply honest, youthfully innocent. But as he stretched and folded his arms, these gestures seemed calculated. Her heart beat more emphatically. Her attraction to him did not decrease. A proclivity for subterfuge in a shy person shouldn't have surprised her. Looking down with a kind of queasy churning, she saw her wedding ring and blushed.

In the years that followed, the sensation she had had that afternoon came back every so often in the teasing fashion of half-known melodies. She thought on it as if it might be got to the bottom of and laid to rest. It had no bottom. There were no conclusions to be drawn. There was only the strangeness of a foreign country. Had it been simply that: travel's manner of unsettling you with its visions of other lives? And certainly the circumstance of she and Shy Thing—but perhaps not so shy, after all—being isolated together on a fine country estate had played a part. She was easily won over by seclusion in a manor house.

The storm, too, had collaborated. Without that peculiar heavy atmosphere, would it all have had such richness? Without the possibility that they would come too near to one another, touch in a way not befitting her married state, without a kind of inching towards a threshold of wrongdoing or forsaken opportunity, would the pauses between words, the arrangement of bodies in space, the distance between the piano and the window, the fact that it was just going on four o'clock, would any of it have had the potency of a sign? Would any bit of that afternoon have shone, distinguishing itself from the background of life's morass of common detail, time's indifferent turning over?

She'd started at the clock striking four. Her left leg had gone to sleep. It felt bled of strength, half-dead, alien. With a strangled chortle, she announced, 'I have to stand. My leg.' The inevitable soreness flowed in. 'Ouch!' She tried to get to her feet.

He sprang up to assist her. While less solidly built than his brothers, he had their limberness. Impaired and somewhat ashamed, she leaned against his arm, her leg continuing to throb.

'I've never known anyone like you,' he said.

He saw her, she thought, as an older woman, as a writer, as English—and these qualities intrigued him. Since the *Aeneas* had docked in Adelaide, she had found the Australian voice disorienting and distasteful—exceedingly rough or at best laughable. As a guest in Queensland, she had begun to forget to wince and smile at it. But that afternoon Shy Thing's pronunciation and inflexion disarmed her. His oddly wrought vowels were remarkably *direct*. Speech that was quite nude, half bold and half abashed.

They were on the cusp of delicate words and dangerous actions. She let go of his arm, not wanting him to feel her trembling. 'Thank you, I can stand.'

'Shall we go out?' he proposed. 'The best thing about a storm is being outdoors and smelling it.'

It was the kind of romantic urge she herself would feel but had learned not to share with her husband, who classified such inclinations as childish whimsy. 'Yes!' she exclaimed, too loudly.

Stepping off the veranda, she almost stumbled. The rain was finally abating, a great curtain opening onto a view of soaked fields. The last drops were only slightly more chill than tears, the sky a moody marvel, undulating rolls of blackish grey. An unprecedented odour. Not like the rank salt perfume of marine storms, but as transcendental in its way. A pungent fullness. Of earth, wet, pasture and leaf. In Australia one was assailed by impressions as vivid as the flavours of the extravagant fruit. It was almost dissolute. She glanced sideways at Shy Thing. His head hanging back, he was breathing as if absorbing into himself the wonder of drenched fields.

It was his pose, so open. That appetite or striving. She realised that what drew her to him, more than his foreignness, was his familiarity. It wasn't exactly that he and she were alike: bookish, musical and overshadowed, timid and avid, outwardly conforming to the wishes of others. It wasn't just that. What she recognised wasn't a version of herself. Not quite.

It was a version of Mummy.

An attitude of ecstatic expectation that gave experience such power to transport or dissatisfy. A meticulous, fastidious curiosity. The requirement that life be a grand bridge between an inner and an outer world. She had, in a manner, come home. And she was not safe. Demonstrating this, she nearly slid over on a muddy patch. But caught herself.

'Be careful,' he said.

'You're a fine pianist. I meant to say so. We were distracted.'

'Yes, we were distracted.' He laughed, appearing to laugh at *words*—at how ludicrously approximate they were. 'Thank you.'

Somewhat drunkenly, they wandered further from the house. He spread his arms wide. She noticed, benevolently, mud on her skirt, and spread her own. There was a spare, perfect moment.

Next they were lurching into one another and hip to hip. She decided he initiated this, but could not be certain. Their spread arms had made the encircling of one another's waists artless. They took a staggering step in unison. Turning a little towards him, she was confounded by his closeness, greenish eyes, mahogany freckles over skin as white as the thickest, most unsullied mist. He watched her watching him. They were practically embracing.

It took a heartbeat or two to decipher the pummelling rhythm of hooves, and then the raised voices of the returning riding party. In something like panic, they remained thus a few instants longer. And stepped apart.

'Hello, you two,' the Most Svelte One greeted them. 'Did he do himself justice?' She grinned winsomely. 'On the piano.'

'Oh, very much so,' Teresa said.

The Most Svelte One dismounted fluidly in her breeches and her next smile, as she took them in, was positively delinquent. Teresa was struck once more by how slight and how tough she was. She ruffled her brother's hair and kissed him, quite near to the mouth. Teresa didn't know that she'd ever seen such self-assurance in a woman. Terrific. An ideal young lord of the manor, adorable and steely.

She and Shy Thing were never alone together after that. The only unusualness anyone studying them would have remarked on was how very little they spoke to one another, and the occasional ungainly colliding of their gazes at the dinner table under cover of others' conversations. She went on consuming immense quantities of preposterously sweet fruit, her throat tight to think she'd never feed so again.

She soon rejoined her husband.

She had not ceased to love her husband as she was becoming enamoured of Shy Thing. If you were to consider the mind as a train, you might say she had simply sat for a while in a different compartment to the one she normally occupied as a wife. Such adjustments happened more easily when one was away from home. They were natural and perhaps necessary for successful travel. To contentedly inhabit new surrounds, one had perforce to turn away from certain habits, preferences, affections, and so on. She was a good traveller, predisposed.

In the compartment in which she traversed an afternoon storm with Shy Thing it was disclosed to her that she had been missing something. Badly. For it was still possible, at thirty, to feel altogether alive in the company of a man, for her dreaming heart and her skin to lean together. The smallest gesture between two people could still have a reverberation that seemed part animal, part mythical. She was shocked to have nearly forgotten that.

In her marriage, yes, there had been a certain lack. She must have known. She knew that she and her husband had been awkward together at times during the Tour. That there was an increasing irritation or chafing, causing stray comments to curdle into tension, leaving tenderness sporadic. But while a Queensland storm played itself out, she took the measure of what had been absent. She took its measure, and then exited that compartment of her mind. The knowledge of it put aside. Some instinct intoning that it should not be handled. It might be rigged to detonate.

Had she confronted and acted upon what a young man had shown her during a storm, she might have prevented what in time came. Her husband had also felt a lack, of course. *Of course.* She would pay for it. Maybe she should have gone with him on that tour of country towns, should not have been so quick to pass from compartment to compartment.

•

In the dream the curtain of rain opened, as it had in life, but the riding party did not return. Then . . . No, don't think of it.

She emerged from Valley Gardens and crossed the road in shambolic fashion, making for the Pump Room. A motorcar was forced to come to a halt to let her pass. She hadn't noticed it and the driver swatted her with an uncharitable look. She turned into the lane behind the Pump Room, seeming to taste the sulphurous water she'd dutifully drunk before breakfast. Sure to do miracles.

She was sliding—like on the wet lawn with Shy Thing. This time, she did not catch herself. Legs going loose and light, a small cry shooting from her.

It felt like a long moment that she spent plunging through space, and next she was surprised to be sitting on cobblestones. She looked quickly around. No one appeared to be watching, thank heavens. Then she saw a gentleman headed towards her. Why was it so much worse to have one's humiliation seen by an onlooker? She began to stand.

The man reached her, and she identified him.

'Dear me,' said Mr Jackman.

'Hello.' Prey to a childish shame, she hoped he hadn't heard her cry. 'How clumsy of me!'

'Not at all. Are you all right, my dear? I nearly came over myself, earlier.' He gestured and she noted belatedly that here and there the stone was darkened with clots of decomposed leaves. 'Awfully slippery. That rain in the night has made the streets a hazard.'

Teresa brushed herself down as best she could. The generosity in Mr Jackman's concern was upsetting.

He must have observed this in her face. 'You've had a bit of a shock, my dear. Are you sure you're all right?'

This was worse. 'Oh, quite all right.' She stared at the slimy cobblestones. 'And thank you—thank you so much for coming to my rescue.' They smiled at one another.

'Will you go back to the hotel now?'

'I think so, yes. I've made a mess of myself.' Muddy smears across the palms of her gloves. Her back was complaining, too. It must have received some of the impact of the fall.

He smiled again, and proffered his arm. They started gently back towards Swan Road. Lightly supported by him, she observed that he was not tremulous or rickety, as men of his age could be, but quite sturdy. And there was a sort of subdued hopefulness to him that cheered her. She wondered about his marriage—if he was visited by romantic dreams from which he was sorry to wake.

'I didn't hear rain in the night.'

'No? Well, I suppose my sleep *is* light. I don't sleep all that much, actually. Oh, it's not so bad now as when I was a young man.' He glanced at her, as if checking that she was recovered from the fall and welcomed talk.

'Oh?'

'Yes. You know, it's a nice consolation that while some things deteriorate with age—your girth and the thickness of your hair and the colour of your skin, your joints, and a few things like that'—he scowled amiably—'others improve, curiously enough. That's how it was for me, for instance, with the insomnia. I used to suffer from it terribly. Still do, on and off. At times more on than off, but I've become less solemn about it and that makes a world of difference, let me tell you. I used to look sometimes at the sleeping faces of my wife and daughter, so peaceful. *Normal.* And I'd curse myself for being a freak of nature, some restless demon, so unworthy of them. You'll laugh.'

'No,' she said, giving his arm a slight squeeze. 'Not at all.'

'I took it very seriously, you see. Do you know what it is to barely sleep for several days running? And for this to repeat itself rather frequently?' She kept her eyes down. 'You feel . . . well, badly done by. It's not nice. When you might as well be squinting at everything through a soiled veil, you don't find too many reasons to be light-hearted.'

They were passing a house where, through the windows of what appeared to be a comfortable drawing room, a man was pouring himself tea. Unfortunately, the teapot was rather like the faithful old white one she had been accustomed to using every day, in another life. It brought to mind an occasion on which that familiar teapot had sailed through the air.

Thrown.

It had not struck her husband. He'd dodged it easily, sportsman that he was, looking hardly surprised. Though the lid did not come off, a little tea looped from the spout, aesthetically. She could not believe she was responsible for this, but there was no taking back the gesture, or the intention it clothed. No taking anything back.

He had muttered tight-mouthed to the maid, who must have heard the kerfuffle, 'We've had an accident, I'm afraid.'

It was an end to the pretence of civility. Such cowardice to call any of it an accident.

Teresa looked away from the man drinking tea and shook her head a little as Mr Jackman continued, 'I couldn't say what changed. Henrietta was always very patient. Knows how to take me with a pinch of salt when I get lugubrious.' She remembered that he was talking about his insomnia. 'But over the years, it stopped mattering quite so much. I bore it. Saw that I was bearing it. It wasn't killing me, was it? Because you do start to wonder whether it might. In a slow, degrading sort of way.' He laughed. 'It's one of nature's sneaky little tricks that if you mind less about sleeping, you sleep a sight more and better.'

'You're right. I was sleeping poorly, recently. And the worst thing is knowing how much you *need* rest. Really needing something makes you . . . weak. You're caught, because how can you go about suddenly being indifferent?' She thought he might question her if she stopped there. 'Harrogate is putting me right, though. My sleep here is thick and full of dreams.' She glanced at her muddied gloves. 'You *do* sleep better now, by and large?'

'By and large. And when I do, it's as if a great honour has been conferred upon me, a knighthood or something. I'm invincible. When I don't, it's not pleasant, but I take it like a man.' His lips twitched. 'I try to be gracious. Sometimes I even find it interesting.'

How much more loquacious he was without his wife, and impish. They had almost reached the grounds of the Hydro.

A hangdog smile, and he added, 'I've rather grown to fancy insomnia itself a mark of distinction, like some tolerable obscure illness. Anyway, it gives you an excuse to drink whisky in the evenings. Copiously enough so that you might have been beaten lightly about the head. One tends to black out beautifully that way. Here we are.'

'Thank you for chaperoning me. And for the words of wisdom. I wish I liked alcoholic beverages.'

'You don't? Not at all?'

'Afraid not. I've never been able to stand the taste.'

He looked crestfallen. 'I *am* sorry. My most sincere condolences.'

'You've been splendid.'

'It was my great pleasure. And, my dear, while I think of it, I don't suppose you've come across Harry today? I passed him last night on the stairs and he struck me as being a bit out of sorts.'

'Ah? He's not a great sleeper, either, from what I understand. Perhaps that could account for it? I haven't come across him.'

'Indeed? Well, poor sleep must be a common ailment, alas, in places such as these . . . He's not what you expect of an Australian, is he?'

'No,' she said. 'I might duck down for a needle bath.'

'Excellent idea.' He was considering her. 'We'll see you at dinner, then?'

12

SIXTH DAY, EVENING

Harry was not at dinner and, regretting this, Mrs Jackman asked, 'Will he be at Bettys? What a rose you have in your cheek, my dear. How steam advantages a lovely pale young complexion. Not to mention that black silk.' She nodded appreciatively at the new dress that was so light and smooth to wear. She appeared not to have been told of the silly tumble Teresa had taken.

'You're kind. Maybe Harry likes to keep to himself—isn't very social.'

'Even the quiet ones usually enjoy some company,' Mrs Jackman said. 'Especially of an evening. Between you and me, I do imagine he must be lonely. He lost his wife, you know, poor man. As you did your husband. Forgive me, my dear, for bringing it up.'

Golly, Teresa thought, is she matchmaking? 'I expect you're right. Isn't this soufflé wonderful? I'm so fond of a good soufflé.' The cheese soufflé was in fact very good.

As she was about to bid the Jackmans goodnight, a man came to their table and asked her to join a game of billiards. Russian accent, or something like it. He was not prepossessing, though he intimated a type of physical confidence that a good-looking man might have had.

She'd have declined, but Mrs Jackman exclaimed, 'Teresa, you must. You young people should have fun.' It was plainly her aim to lift the spirits of anyone in her orbit whose morale might be languishing.

The Russian and Teresa raised their eyebrows at being called young, and it was decided. She followed him out into the hall and to the staircase leading to the billiards room. His rolling walk was pure flirtation. She felt absent. Was Harry really alone at Bettys and under the weather? She recalled his stiff manner of the night before and his avoidance of the ballroom.

At the billiard table she was presented to the Russian's two friends, of Harrogate. It would be him and her against the locals. Her heart was still taking stock of the ascent of the stairs. The billiards room was warmer than the dining room and seemed imbued with the memory of male joshing and a limitless army of smoked cigars, which made her feel at the same time nervous and devil-may-care. She professed herself deplorable at games, and proceeded to play fairly well.

They won.

Buoyed by the fleeting triumph of such success, Teresa said, 'There is some precedent for this. My golf game is disgraceful, yet I once won a women's golf tournament.'

She wished she hadn't mentioned golf. Golfing greens had for so long divided her from her husband. How could fields prohibiting rambling and picnics not be corrupt?

'And where was that?'

Eyes on her. 'South Africa. I've lived in South Africa for many years.'

'Cape Town?' Her partner in victory might have been a clandestine prince escaped from the Bolsheviks, but she was not really in the mood for chitchat.

'Yes.'

'You must tell us about South Africa. I've always wanted to go. The lions . . .'

'Yes.'

Someone was asking, 'Does anyone sing? Will anyone sing?'

'They want someone to sing—to give the Hydro Boys and the Lady Entertainer a rest and, I suspect, the chance to go and quietly find something to drink. Will you volunteer?' He was amused.

'Absolutely not.' She wished Harry were there.

'You don't sing?'

'No. Yes—a little. But I wouldn't here.'

'Perhaps if I accompanied you? I play the piano, though I am also modest. We could make each other brave.' He held her gaze, immodestly proposing a song, and more.

'I don't think so.'

If she knew how to be fast, she could slip him a note—no, not even that would be necessary, a gesture would do—and later, after everyone was in bed, there would be a constrained knock at the door of her room. Or Teresa would go stealing along corridors, a dressing-gowned silhouette in the gloom. Being slimmer now, she might look rather sinuous. What was stopping her, after all, from going to a man's room? One could learn to do anything. There were so many men's rooms, along so many corridors, corridors radiating out around her like spokes from the centre of a wheel.

'I'm sure I can convince you,' he said.

They'd separated themselves from the table, but one of his friends, whose countenance had grown mean during the match, interpolated, 'Another game! We demand revenge.'

'No,' she said. 'I think it's wise for an amateur to stop while she's ahead.'

He was reluctant to accept this and hung by the Russian's elbow. 'That woman,' he went on in a disagreeable, teasing tone, 'who has disappeared—they say she sent a letter to her brother-in-law. Telling him she was coming to a spa in Yorkshire.'

'Who?' the Russian asked.

'The authoress. Who went missing.'

'Oh, there was something about that in *The Times*.'

'It was the *Daily Mail* I saw. What do you say, could she be here in Harrogate?'

'Unlikely.' The Russian clearly wanted to close the topic and return to a private conversation with Teresa. 'The police don't believe she is in Yorkshire, do they?'

'What's your opinion, Mrs Neele?' enquired his tenacious friend.

In that stuffy masculine air it was imperative that she keep her thoughts as slight and cool as sheets of silk. 'You know, I haven't been following the story.'

'No? It's interesting, though,' he insisted. 'I think her husband killed her.' He regarded her. 'Are you scandalised? Do husbands do such things in South Africa?'

A touch muzzy and incredulous, she replied, 'Excuse me. I've just decided to sing down in the ballroom.'

The Russian was surprised but not unpleased. 'Indeed.' From his smile, it was evident that he considered his other unspoken proposition accepted, too.

What a scenario. An age since she'd sung in public. Then suddenly a dream of singing, and this appeared to have conjured a real performance. She should have been mortified. But she was cavalier as they marched down the stairs and into the Winter Garden Ballroom.

The Russian wasn't required, because there was already a gentleman in position at the piano, with wispy fair hair and a mien both apologising for his presence and grateful. He was introduced to Teresa as Mr Bolitho. All this blurring by, and the gathered hotel guests merely a kind of stickiness she would not adhere to.

'Angels Ever Guard Thee.'

They were off.

Not at all as it was with Shy Thing. Yet the music did enter her and mercifully carry her somewhere. Restful and rather fun, the anonymity one could have singing, the flesh displaced by something fresher and less delimited, like spirit. The only interference came towards the end, when her attention caught a little, and then slid over—as silk might on a ragged fingernail—the figure of a man in the doorway. She no sooner noticed him than he withdrew from the room.

Harry.

The song over, the Russian's stance was assured and expectant. Teresa smiled coolly without meeting anyone's eyes.

•

She had stridden quickly from the ballroom and it was ten thirty by the grandfather clock as she took to the stairs. Reaching the first floor, feeling clammy, she saw Harry. He straightened himself and moved along the corridor towards her.

She realised she had half expected, or hoped, such a meeting would occur, even as she had been working to avoid one.

'I was just . . .' he began and shrugged. 'You sang.'

A seamlessness, as if they were continuing a conversation only briefly suspended.

'You heard? Had my usual dance partner been present at dinner, I might have danced instead.'

'Yesterday evening, if you recall, you did refuse to promise him a dance tonight. I'm sure you were better off without him, anyhow. Not much of a dancer, from what they say.'

'They're wrong.' The corridor was empty aside from the two of them. Singing was audible from downstairs, and the creaking of stairs or floorboards. 'The Jackmans feared you weren't feeling well. They didn't see you all day.'

He laughed bleakly. 'Whole days often go by without anyone seeing me.'

'That can be reposeful.'

'Yes. Or pathetic.' They glanced away from one another. 'I was at the baths. Lying low.' He brought a hand to his forehead wearily. 'I wanted to talk to you. You sang very beautifully, by the way.'

'Thank you—I don't know what I was thinking. You wanted to talk to me?'

Brusquely, he asked, 'What have you done to yourself?'

'What do you mean?'

He was indicating her wrist. She turned her hand, uncomprehending. The outer edge was darkly outlined. Blood. Dried blood. Queer. She had a moment of embarrassed confusion, before recalling her fall behind the Pump Room. She must have scraped her hand, coming down. She'd bathed before dinner and not noticed anything. Maybe playing billiards had exacerbated the cut. She could have been bleeding while she sang!

'Oh, I had another comical incident today. Slipped over on wet leaves. Mr Jackman was my knight in shining armour.'

He took a handkerchief from a pocket of his jacket. She accepted it, and dabbed once or twice ineffectually at the blood.

'It's funny that blood should be so . . . *scandalous*. Seeing it, I mean. When it's constantly running through us, the very thing that keeps us on our feet. And yet the slightest visible evidence of it is sensational. Gothic horror.'

'The red? And the fact of it being outside us, where it shouldn't be?' He held her eyes. 'That, I think, is what makes it an affront, a travesty.'

'If you see enough of it, though, you get quite blasé. That happened to me when I was a VAD.'

'You were a nurse during the war? Well, I'm sure being afraid of blood is related to a primeval and very reasonable survival instinct—survival is the key, isn't it?' There was a sternness to his manner, something flinty that came and went. It put her on edge. 'You were a VAD in England?'

She was looking at her hand. 'The same colour is beautiful, say, on an autumn leaf. Or a lovely dress.' If she were confusing Harry with his countryman, Shy Thing, could that have caused what was developing rapidly between them—this intimate tone, the pressure of the unsaid? Certainly, Harry was as attentive to her as the boy had been. But he didn't talk like an Australian. He was older, too, of course, and less handsome—at least in the common way. Perhaps he was also less desperately idealistic, less like Mummy. Less rapacious. More frugal.

'You can talk to me. I realise we haven't known one another long, but you can, if you need to. You remember our conversation on . . . coffee and Balzac? Methods for dying?'

'Of course.' Having taken it out of her handbag on the stairs, Teresa was holding the chain from which her room key dangled, oscillating slightly.

He came nearer. For a moment, they gazed at one another. She had not shared such a look with anyone in years. His brown eyes and overly lean face seemed anguished. They got at her. She wasn't sure of his intentions, but nor was she, for that matter, of her own. Here in Harrogate, what was rational action? And good, and bad?

'Teresa?'

She had the swaying feeling one could have becoming self-conscious about standing immobile. She was still a little larger than life from the performance downstairs, but that power was leaching away. She had not been so aware of her body in—how many years? She was both in it and marginally above. How very strange it was to have a body, so material, inescapable, and yet animated by energies that could not quite be grasped. She surveyed her room's brass doorknob, the pleasantly papered wall, with its border of vines, the electric light sconces, the lift's grille, the Turkey rug leading the padded crimson way along the hall. All looming as large and portentous as the furnishings of a hallucination.

'Your poor hand.' He stroked where she had hurt herself.

In her blood that was so dark when spilled and dried there was a great suspense. She only leaned a hair towards him. He crossed the remaining distance at once, but then hesitated. Teresa's lips came to rest against his. He accepted the kiss as if lost in thought, or willing himself sedate. She felt his chest expand as he inhaled, a set of fine bones adjacent to her own heart's cage. She drew back.

'Teresa.'

He touched the side of her face. His fingers at her temple, thumb behind her ear, warm palm cradling her jaw. Next their mouths were meeting again and they had given themselves to something fuller. It was like being borne on a wave in Torbay. Limpness and vigour.

Recovering herself somewhat, she half whispered, 'Going down a well? What do you say to that?'

'Hmm?'

'Drowning in a well.'

He seemed to shrink away. 'As a means of dying?'

'Yes. Harrogate should be the very place for such a method.'

Just then a pair of old ladies crested the stairs, tittering breathily as though at a mild impropriety.

'Well, goodnight, Harry,' Teresa exclaimed, stepping away from him. 'Thank you again for returning my book.'

They nodded to the ladies. One raised a waggish eyebrow and the other waved indecisively before passing Harry and Teresa.

He approached once more. She was cautious, now. She had not been afraid to kiss him, only conscious of her fretful blood. But she could almost have drawn a man she barely knew into her room! She could not trust the vacillating body being returned to her. Hotels distracted you from your usual life, offering that choice of corridors radiating out in a circle, breathing into your ear that you could take any one of them, be whomsoever you decided to be. 'I must to bed.'

'Teresa, please.' He came closer still. 'You're *her*, aren't you?'

She must have jumped. A different fear.

'No, please don't be frightened.'

She had turned and clumsily fitted the key into the lock. 'I don't know what you mean,' she said, as steadily as she could. 'Who?'

She had believed herself incognito here, smugly pleased with—indeed, half convinced by—the story of the elegant, capable widow vacationing alone. The freedom of it had gone to her head. She had exposed herself horrendously. Allowed a man to come near her and find her out.

'No,' he whispered. 'I wouldn't tell anyone. It's of no importance to me. None. That's not why . . .'

She was turning the key, opening the door.

'I'm sorry. Please! I just wanted you to know you could talk to me, if you wanted. Or not, of course.'

She was in the doorway of her room, inside at last, and she turned back, trying to smile. Her face was trembling. 'I've no idea what you're referring to.'

'I want to be your friend.' He looked distraught. 'Whether or not you confide in me.'

She lifted her hand and he attempted to take it.

'Trust me,' he insisted plangently.

Tugging free, Teresa folded her arms. 'Trust a man?' She managed more or less to chuckle. The bitterness was real enough. ''Night, Harry.'

'There are many sterling reasons not to trust men, I know.' His hand on the doorjamb as if he would prevent her from shutting him out—but he removed it quickly. 'Couldn't agree with you more there. Frankly, I myself have hardly represented my sex as well as I might have and should probably warn you away from me.' Curiosity stopped her from closing the door. 'However, I do believe I'd do anything to help you.' He paused, gazing up at the ceiling. 'Teresa, I'm falling in love with you.'

It was those you presumed you could trust who revealed themselves as Judases. Harry's eyes were brown, richly dark, and somehow deeply set in a face of hollows, but how not to remember the suave transparent blue of the Gun Man's stare? The temptation to believe him was insidious. One always *wants* to believe oneself loved, and is hasty to take this bait.

'I think it would be better if we didn't meet alone again. Goodnight.'

She shut the door, registering the vibration unleashed by this action in the building's walls and in herself, as if she were part of that structure of interconnected rooms and corridors.

•

She was walking back and forth, unnerved. Could Harry be a Gun Man? He knew who she was.

And claimed she could trust him, despite the fact that he had not behaved well in the past. Said he was falling in love with her.

Who exactly did he think he was falling in love *with*? Teresa Neele, whom he had known for a few days after she materialised from the blue at the Hydro, shared some chats with him, two dances and a walk? Was it love at first sight, then? Flattering to her vanity—but if he knew who she was, wasn't it more likely he was smitten with the idea of a Mysterious Woman? With notoriety, maybe, the dirty excitement cooked up by newspapers? She flinched. (Stay clear of all that, it will make you sick again.)

Who, furthermore, was *she* attracted to? Was she really so taken with Harry? Or was it the memory of Shy Thing and Australia? A romantic dream making a halfwit of her. She reflected, Will we never know just what we desire, and if this is *real*? All terrifyingly unreliable.

She was discovered.

She was shaking. Would Harry keep her secret? She realised she still had his handkerchief. She'd been wringing it in her hands as she paced and the thing was utterly twisted. Rusty flakes of blood upon it. She went to the basin and ran warm water over her hand. She soaped and studied the cut, which could barely be made out. She washed Harry's handkerchief, inhaling the lily scent of the soap, quaking.

An Australian had once reminded her of herself as a woman, and the past seemed to be repeating itself. How was it that one's erotic life came to be buried? She had never stopped admiring her handsome husband, but along the misty path of marriage much was obscured, and that certain lack had come about for which retribution was being exacted. Her sensual impulses, it appeared, had been diverted into a deep place, where they had bided their time. Lambent.

A question of fault? Of going cold and staid? Her husband had not known how, perhaps had not cared, to reach the deep place. This had so dispirited her, she had to admit, that she had made no sincere effort to guide him there. She'd grown resigned to making love as though with a clumsy understudy in place of the leading man. Her own attempt at leading lady was certainly second rate. Heart not entirely in it, body an interloper displaying counterfeit emotion. Physical love had often been a question of settling on a serviceable part to perform, and fumbling to pull it off.

The sodden handkerchief appeared bluish white and compromised. Oh God, Teresa had sung before an audience. She'd played—admirably at that—a merry game of billiards! These things all at once seemed almost as shamefully immodest as the kiss. It was like that shuddering point in a particular sort of dream where you abruptly observe, Dear me, I've just gone down the high street without a stitch on! She wrung the water from his handkerchief violently and hung it over the towel rail, smoothing it.

Take care of chores, at least. Remove the black silk evening dress. Brush teeth, wash face with the *crème de lys* soap. Apply face cream, drawing the excess down the neck. Change into welcoming flannel nightdress.

The night was clear, she saw from the window. That moon could have been fully swollen, houses and trees and the curve of the road were so absolutely defined. Inside the room, too, the furniture looked burnished by moonlight. The bed and the wardrobe, the humiliating writing table. The indispensable books on the bedside table. Beside those the bottle of sleeping draught she might yet need. Shivering, she went to the fire.

She'd told herself she was waiting to be found, awaiting her husband's arrival. The Russian's nasty friend was right: before her own journey, assuming this would do the job, she had sent a letter to her husband's brother advising him she was going to a Yorkshire spa. But the message she had believed clear had proved cryptic (things so upside down). Or her husband had not given the message as much attention as she had hoped. He had not come, anyhow. In the meantime, she had been found, yes, but by someone else.

Harry, whom she had kissed as Teresa—whose husband was dead—might kiss. Like a free woman, that is. Was she free?

She had run away.

Brought suspicion on her living husband. *Mr Neele.* Created rather a bad mess. Thrown a teapot. (Only because he refused to see reason, insisting he wanted a divorce. Hideous snake's hiss of a word, *divorce.*)

She was swaying on her feet again. The fire had almost burned itself out in the grate. She was *so* tired. *Extenuée,* one could say in French. Not the same in English but she was lessened and made thin, too. She brought her hands to her hips, not unpleased to be rediscovering their bony design.

She *must* think that her husband would come for her (what alternative was there?). Would see what he was doing (the barbarity of that hissing word). Should she send another message? It would have to be a message in a bottle, from this shipwreck. Train wreck. Until he arrived she would be careful, and *very* careful of Harry and his unbending brown gaze. Mightn't be too extreme to avoid him altogether. Remembering desire was confusing, that was all. It was something of a battle not to be carried by it, as by a wave on Babbacombe Beach, manhandled and made amenable, so free.

Collapsing into bed, she seized a book from the bedside table, already the third of the borrowed ones. They had been all right. Teresa would be all right. She read at speed till the story had her and her sangfroid began to return.

A little later, she noticed music in the background of her mind—the same music she'd heard that morning? Just beyond the reach of recognition, persistent. And she was scared all over again, because it wouldn't be easy now to be Teresa Neele. Harry would interfere with her pretending and forgetting, with the lightness of her thoughts. He would churn up the pieces of the past that she'd been keeping low and invisible. And they would ascend like fireflies, abruptly flashing on.

13

SAN CARLO WHARF

His intuition was corroborated: confirmation had been in her eyes and voice. He would go on calling her Teresa Neele, to maintain her cover, and out of respect. Didn't she wish to jettison the old name? There followed an awkward night, antsy, almost perfectly sleepless. He swung between exultation—replaying for himself their kisses and caresses—and despair to think that she regretted them and there would be no more. He listened to a quantity of Elgar on his gramophone and drank sherry until his mouth was sickly and an imprecise aching commenced behind his eyes. He reached the usual haze, surpassed it, swallowed by a veritable pea-souper, but his thoughts went on shining obstinately from within this like electric lamps. He had told her he was falling in love with her. And, oh Lord, he appeared to be. But surely there was no way for him and Teresa to be together. On the other hand, if he really was falling in love, then he was letting down Valeria. Once more. He had been convinced he could not, would never love any woman but his late wife. That there was some consolation and even belated honour in this. Now he came face to face with his inconstancy.

Worse still, the terror that he would lose Teresa as he'd lost Valeria. Unbearable.

The only thing that gave him comfort during the night, any feeling of keeping the train of his thought on secure tracks, was reading her. Having finished the first novel, he went on with, and far into, the second.

When the dawn coyly announced itself he rose to confront in the glass livid circles beneath his eyes and the impotent, haunted air of a consumptive. It was Thursday. His beard was sore and sulky against the razor, with the result that he cut himself rather a lot shaving. Brilliant drops of blood dappling the sink's white porcelain. (*It's funny*, he heard her saying, *that blood should be so . . . scandalous.*)

Harry was early to the dining room and offended by the roughness of voices there. The Jackmans studied him with covert concern. He kept looking up for her, his head feeling fragile, wobbly and ridiculous, but Teresa never arrived to take the meal with them. His eggs, undercooked, were slimy, and his toast quite burnt around the edges and cold so that the butter refusing to melt mixed queasily with the flavour of charcoal.

Eating quickly, he began to cough when he came to the photograph of her in the *Daily Mail*. He could not stop coughing. The Jackmans plied him with water, although he gestured that it was nothing. Mr Jackman was bracing himself to stand and intervene.

'Down the wrong way, I'm afraid,' Harry managed, just in time.

'Unpleasant sensation,' the good man commiserated.

Harry nodded and went back to the newspaper. A curiously disturbing thing, the photograph had apparently been prepared by some newspaper artist by merging two different portraits of her, and Harry found it not only a poor likeness but not altogether human. An oddly meek woman was shown side on to the impudent viewer, holding her handbag inexplicably out in front of her. In a long cardigan she was quite shapeless through the middle. Her unfortunate stooped posture and even her expression, slightly bemused or discontented, recalled a turtle emerging somnolently from its shell.

This wasn't his darling, whom he imagined upstairs in her room, staring at the same image in dismay. Was she keeping herself hidden, nervous the other guests would identify her from it? The photograph, at least, he didn't think was cause for worry. It didn't show the woman they had seen among them any more than the portrait of the novelist and her daughter did. He hated this aberration all the more for the thought that it might scare her from him further.

He was on the watch in an armchair by the reception desk when she came downstairs in a dress patterned with violets, carrying a newspaper. She did not look at him.

'I was hoping to find you,' Teresa said exuberantly to Mrs Jackman, who had just wandered in trailing her husband. 'Shall we go to the baths?' At which the other lady was delighted.

She only acknowledged him with, 'Oh, hello, Harry,' and the most perfunctory glance. He thought the Jackmans were disappointed by her coolness to him.

Harry appended himself to their party with the excuse that he was finally enthusiastic about trying a peat bath.

He and Mr Jackman followed the ladies down Swan Road and into Crescent Gardens. Teresa had donned her fur-trimmed coat and neat cloche hat.

At the baths, resigning himself to going without sight of her for hours, he shuffled like a truculent invalid into the men's dressing hall behind Mr Jackman. They made for their dressing-rooms.

He pulled off his clothes, feeling somewhat poorly. His breakfast wasn't sitting well. He still had in his mouth the gelatinous texture of egg white and the taste of charred bread. A glass of water might have helped, but not that wholesome kind, which would have turned his stomach even more.

A white-suited bath attendant led him to a tiled room equipped with small high windows and unfathomable tubes and fittings that seemed to belong to an elite hospital. All a little alarming, though there was satisfaction in submitting to the attendant's directions and ministrations, in disrobing and simply acquiescing. An abdication of responsibility, a giving-in. Harry had to convince himself that he had learned, or was learning, to be a better man than he had been before. But he wondered, lowering his body into the tub of dark Yorkshire peat, if what had happened with Valeria had really taught him anything that could help him now. The downy odour of earth.

·

It was hard to say when things had started on their frightful course. There had perhaps been certain transitions to which he might have been more sensitive. Valeria's talk of taking up painting again and her subsequent failure to do so (his scepticism towards his own creative efforts—his magnum opus!—may have prevented him from rallying to this cause avidly enough and later from consoling her as he should have done). Her staid aloofness after Mrs Mortlake passed away. A moment when he realised that she hadn't been to the theatre in a long time or, unless it was to shop for their domestic needs, gone for walks.

And there was the intensification of her habit of reading novels. This was always her favourite occupation, but suddenly it took possession of her days like an invading force. She read on the brown sofa, the cat complacent at her side. Arriving home in the evening, Harry would kiss her forehead and find it warm. Flash sometimes flicked her tail at his approach. 'Hello, darling,' Valeria said, and smiled. Or only pouted a little, while she shifted, curling into herself to better see her page. In those days the kitchen had an evacuated air. His wife was never a cook but he had been used to finding traces of her there: a plate on the sink, a knife, a constellation of crumbs. Now her lunch was the digestives on which she also breakfasted and sometimes, despite his protestations, dined. She kept them by the sofa like something private and guarded. They no longer shared.

But perhaps it was all going wrong already on the San Carlo Wharf, as early as the day they met. 'I have a proposal for you,' she had declared languorously. 'I need to end a love story. Will you help me?'

They were standing at the end of the jetty, not far from Trieste's main square. It was his first visit to that subtle city, and indeed to Austria. Outside of France, he had travelled little on the Continent, having just begun to make such trips to transact business for his new employer, Mr Ainsworth. Harry had come by train and boat and train from London, bringing with him documents it had been thought better to deliver in person to the head of a company that was to assist them in importing coffee beans from Brazil. He'd left his luggage at the Hotel Roma, which was by the station, and weaved through a number of streets in search of the water.

He found it remarkably still. He was reminded of the Mediterranean at Nice, though this was possibly even more unruffled. Most familiar with the Pacific Ocean, a fiercer animal, he was disoriented by these lapping seas, their waves nearly as tenuous as those of a lake. Only the gentlest breeze rose occasionally, causing rigging to knock against the masts of sailboats, a sound that made him shiver, imagining long sea voyages. He watched the distant bulk of a steamer progress infinitesimally but inexorably. He was distracted from this by a much nearer rowboat, its scullers looking smart and relaxed.

The blue hour was approaching. The sky and sea had grown identical in hue, the horizon become negligible, a needless distinction in a vastness of creamy azure. There was considerable activity behind him, perambulating couples, small groups of perhaps soon-to-be passengers gathered around a docked liner, stevedores proficiently unloading crates from a mercantile ship. But the voices that reached him were not raised or rowdy, and the only other souls at the end of the jetty were a young woman and a fisherman of advanced years, smoking peaceably. There was a sense of respite or suspension here, it seemed to him, resembling the letup that might precede a new turn in the weather. He thought it a wonderfully lulling place. For some reason, he hadn't expected to find Trieste so, yet something in him responded with deep pleasure and possibly relief. An inexplicable feeling of camaraderie prompted him to speak to the young stranger close by.

'Excuse me,' Harry addressed Valeria, whose name it would take him a little longer to discover. 'Do you speak English?'

Her nod was dismissive.

'I wonder, could you tell me what that is, over there on the shore?'

She looked across a distance of water to the white edifice he was pointing at. 'The Castle of Miramare,' she drawled as if she should not have had to bother herself stating the obvious.

'Oh, I see.'

They went on to establish that Harry was Australian. Her interest awaking at this flamboyant detail, she informed him that he spoke like an Englishman, and that she herself spoke English because she had had a tutor—from the Berlitz School—since she was a child. She claimed, when he enquired, not to know whether her first language was the *triestino* dialect (which he'd never heard of nor, for that matter, imagined existing) or Italian. Her father *believed* in the importance of speaking foreign languages. 'How else can you appreciate culture?' She shrugged, adding that she read a lot of English books. 'Every sort.'

Her use of Harry's mother tongue, adorned with light grammatical idiosyncrasies and a thick, pleasing accent, was able.

'French is the only other language I speak anything like decently, alas,' Harry said. 'But I believe in the need to learn foreign languages, too, I think. No one else in my family did. I started to teach myself French when I was about ten, with some old grammars we'd inherited from somewhere. Don't know why. It was so different from everything else in my life. As an adolescent I did a desultory year or two of it at school. Then I surprised myself by struggling through a whole novel in French. Gide. By the time I moved to Sydney I was reading so many French novels that I was thinking for snatches and even on occasion dreaming a little in the language. Beautifully improbable thing.' He watched her, seeing that she was finding all of this reasonable and waiting for more. It seemed he could say anything. 'I'd entered a hidden space by magic. Open sesame. Or I was flying—gauchely, but flying. Or, I don't know, I'd become my own shadow. Does that sound strange?'

'No,' she said.

They were silent for a moment. 'When I knew what it was to think in and breathe a foreign language, I understood that I'd have to live in other countries. I think there'd always been a hankering in me for travel. For . . . elsewhere.'

'You went to France?'

'Yes, at first. Paris. Then Nice. Tried to be a writer there for six months.' He was too embarrassed to say that by then the end of his savings was nearly upon him and he'd seen that, given his rate of progress, it would be years till he'd complete any book. 'But I happened to meet Mr Ainsworth at the Negresco Hotel, which had just opened.'

Harry had gone there in a spirit of melancholy reckless-ness for an aperitif he could scarcely afford. His life in Nice had been far more solitary, less festive and dissipated, than he'd dreamed.

'It was one of those bits of chance that fall from the sky. Mr Ainsworth invited me to share his bottle of champagne and we found we got along. He was marvellously well dressed, in spite of a rather obvious toupee. It transpired that he was a very successful businessman—importation and exportation, mainly—and was looking for a new private secretary. For my part, while I still intended becoming a writer, I was beginning to consider other options in the meantime. I'd been a clerical employee in a textile factory in Sydney—promoted in the end to private secretary—and I had two pretty fair references. He was impressed by my French and what he called my unobtrusive accent in English. There was another bottle of champagne, and that was that. Mr Ainsworth is quite serious when we're working, but never unkind, and truly gentle with a little drink in him. My duties aren't too bad, either, and it really won't be forever.' He smiled. 'It gives me opportunities like this. And, well, I love London. It's a world unto itself.'

'I would like to live in another place,' she said. 'I also thought of being a writer, but I've decided I'll be a better painter.'

'You paint? You'd love the picture galleries in London.'

The fisherman reeled in his catch matter-of-factly, and a hush followed, upholstered with the murmuring of water and a fishy, clouded sweetness. Then there was that peculiar rattling of rigging against masts again, and she made her proposition. A young man newly arrived in a foreign country, though startled, he was enticed.

The 'love story' that she wanted his assistance in bringing to a close had been going on for five years, since she was seventeen. The fellow was a teacher of classics, an acquaintance of her father's. Her father was a psychoanalyst. Harry nodded knowingly at everything, impressed by the intellectual allure of it, so wildly at odds with his memories of his own family life in rural Australia. Her beauty was dawning on him. Neither tall nor short, she was sleek. Her hair was what he thought of as Moorish black, as dark as liquorice, while her complexion was pale.

She took out a cigarette case and offered it. They smoked. The glowing tip of Valeria's cigarette kept leading him back through the escalating dark to the planes of her face. He was riveted by her presence at his side and by the indigo melding of sea and sky—the two were somehow of a piece. There was a vague dourness or cynicism to her that he took for mystery and urbanity, or simply for fashionable European coolness. Laying out her brief account, she used no superfluous words or gestures. But if Valeria was restrained, she appeared sure of her own mind.

He was flattered that she was asking for his participation. 'What could I do?'

'We'll tell him we're engaged.' The matter might already have been decided.

'That I'm your fiancé?' he clarified stupidly. 'And that will convince him to let you go?'

'It will help. We could *suggest . . . insinuate* that we have no choice.'

'No choice? Oh, I follow you.' He felt like a young yokel. Their eyes were on the nightfall. 'Couldn't you just tell him you don't, well, love him anymore?' *Did* she love him?

She shook her head slightly. 'It will be easier for him to accept if there's another man. Better for him.'

There was warm-heartedness in this, Harry thought. His appointment the next day was for the lunch hour, so most of his afternoon would be free. He was to leave Trieste by an evening service. Both exhilarated and strangely calm, he assented to the scheme. He was pleased to have a lark to fill his spare time with, and more of the company of this girl who was so spontaneously trusting—or using—him.

•

When the next day he saw her waiting as agreed by the fountain in Piazza Grande, she appeared tense, or remote, and the whole idea much less frolicsome. After the previous mild evening, it was a chill white-sunned day, with a wind of surprising strength that he would later be taught to call, in reverential tones, the *bora*.

He came up to her and she pulled the glove off her left hand. 'I borrowed this,' she whispered, although they were not in danger of being overheard. She waggled her fingers to show him the evidence of their engagement.

He hadn't reflected on the need for anything so concrete. He nodded. She slipped her glove back on and, fast and solemnly, kissed him on both cheeks in what he supposed was the Austrian or the Italian way, as if this intimate convention would make the lie of their love more authentic. Or had they become friends? It felt stilted, formal. Her face was cold. He examined the fountain's spouting fish and the rest of that rocky, ragtag monument apparently representing the different continents from which the marvels of trade streamed into Trieste. A clunky thing.

'So, you don't love him anymore? That's why you're breaking it off?' it occurred to him to confirm, at the last minute, as they hastened across the square to the rendezvous at the Caffè degli Specchi.

Her cheerless smile struck him as the most articulate expression he'd seen her features assume. 'I'm breaking it off because I'm not happy, of course.'

Giacomo Petri was at a table by one of the long windows giving on to the square. He rose, seeing her. They kissed as she and Harry had just kissed, and he continued to stand while Valeria removed her coat, gloves and scarf. A little behind her, Harry managed to disentangle himself from his own.

'This is my friend Harry,' she said in English.

Giacomo was confused and perhaps disappointed, but he nodded and politely extended his hand. 'Hello, pleased to meet you.' His English was uncertain.

Harry knew that he was much older than Valeria, married and the father of children. Still, he looked fairly young, credulous and defenceless. If physically nondescript, he was very well groomed, and his olive-skinned face gave an impression of softness and assiduous personal upkeep. Impossible to tell whether he suspected that something unfortunate was about to befall him.

They switched to Italian, but had hardly begun to converse when the waiter came to take the order. When he'd gone, Valeria gave a low, deliberate speech, Harry considering his knees. The coffee arrived. They did not touch it. Harry drank his rapidly: singularly good. Short bursts of questioning from Giacomo, one or two concise answers from her. A quiet, desperate-sounding appeal from him. Harry was sharply aware of the absurdity of his own position. Once he caught Giacomo staring at him in a manner that could have been challenging, imploring, or merely curious. Harry tried for a congenial, philosophical demeanour, but soon dropped his eyes. Some time after, he saw Giacomo move to take her hand—she refused to allow it. Only later did it cross Harry's mind that this gesture must have been a risk. They would have been accustomed, in public places, to dissimulating any signs of particular closeness.

The full force of Valeria's beauty became apparent as she was denying it to Giacomo, downing her espresso like a nip of liquor before standing to signal that it was all finished, as far as he was concerned. Her eyes as black as her hair, dignified in their determination. The exchange could have lasted fifteen minutes.

Giacomo stood too, very quickly, as if afraid of missing his chance to do so. She conceded his final ritual kisses and he suffered the farewell like a wooden mannequin, arms inert at his sides.

He didn't volunteer his hand again and Harry didn't blame him. Harry let himself look at Giacomo's face properly just once. His eyes were fixed and glossy but it was especially from his listless mouth that you guessed at how deeply he was affected. There was no show of anger.

They were quiet for some minutes after leaving the café. At the road running along the sea they turned right towards San Carlo Wharf where, bizarrely, they had met just the night before. A man with an air of the eternal student passed them, slowing to study Valeria approvingly.

Indeed, her eyes were still very vivid and she walked with prowling elegance. Her movements were like her beauty more generally: you could fail to notice them, and then *notice* them. Abruptly she came forward, as it were, from the background. Harry never knew whether she somehow operated such changes on purpose. Ignoring the admiring man, she looped her arm through Harry's. He glimpsed moisture on her cheek.

'Are you all right?'

'I told him I would go to London to be with you.'

'Won't he know, if you don't?'

'I've broken his heart, he says.'

He pictured Giacomo's emptied face. 'Poor chap.' He thought of the years during which they had been intimate. A nibble of jealousy. 'Can't dwell on that, though, can you?'

'Thank you. For helping me.'

'We're getting married and I know so little about you,' he said lightly. Mentioning their fictional engagement pleased him.

'What do you want to know?'

'Oh. Was your childhood happy? Sorry, silly question.'

Their pace grew dawdling, her child-thin arm holding him tightly, her hand virtually on his ribs, his arm brushing her compact body.

'Of course.'

'Oh? Well, could you tell me . . . some memory?'

She mused. 'When I was small'—staring at the sea, she appeared to be reciting—'for carnival we dressed up, and my mother brought us to Piazza Grande.'

'That sounds like fun.'

'One year I was a queen. My mother had made me a beautiful costume. It had a very long dress, red and gold, that almost touched the ground. She made me promise not to run. I was so proud. Then I ran. Maybe I forgot. I was running fast through all the streamers and the confetti, chasing someone—or they were chasing me, I can't remember—and I tripped. The dress was ruined. I looked down and it was *ruined*. Torn. Dirty. I could see my ankles through a big hole. My mother found me, and said, "What have you done?"'

'How sad.'

She pouted. 'Now you.'

'Me? You want one of *my* childhood memories? They're quite boring. We lived on an orchard. I moped around, when I could get out of working on it.' He reflected. 'I walked back and forth along the fence line, speaking French to myself. Highly adventurous, you see. I seemed to spend hours staring at the tops of some handsome old gum trees that grew in the valley below. I listened to magpies.'

'*Mag* . . . ?'

'Magpies. A kind of Australian bird.'

'They sing?'

'Oh yes.'

'How is it?'

'You'd have to hear them. Melodic, pitched lowish. It's a fluted warble, somehow watery, and it goes with the approach of dawn, or twilight. Sorry, it's indescribable—though lovely. Nearly human, I sometimes thought.'

'A nice memory.'

He laughed. 'Is it? I do miss that sound.' He was losing his heart to her.

'Will you go back to Australia?'

'To live? Oh, I don't think so.'

'London is a good place to live?'

'Yes—for me, anyway. There's always something interesting to look at. The people, all sorts of people. You can lose yourself in a crowd if you've a mind to. Hear foreign languages. Potter around in the parks. Excellent parks. Like the gardens of country estates, or open fields. Smashing old pubs, like homey sitting rooms. As fine, wayward cities do, it irks you, and then calls to you like a siren.'

Proceeding at a crawl along the jetty, they were almost at the spot where they had first spoken.

She said, her tone analytical, 'We're getting married and you've never kissed me.'

His breath caught in his chest. 'That's true, isn't it?'

'You're timid like an Englishman.'

'Yes.'

She released his arm and he was cold where the faint warmth of her had been.

'You might come to London, you know, to visit,' he said to cover his embarrassment. He was acting at being a man. He was a maladroit boy.

'To visit you?'

'Why not?'

She kissed him. In the whipping wind that made him want to latch on to her, Valeria's mouth was prime-coffee-scented, apathetic, and incongruously hot. The skin of her lips was slightly broken and this delicate abrasion hypnotised him. Her lazy laughter announced that it was over. Stunned, he tried to laugh too, bracing himself against another of the *bora*'s squalls.

Speeding that evening out of the Stazione di Trieste Centrale, he knew that the encounter with Valeria, while so accidental, had hit him hard. He had been only a pretend husband-to-be but somehow the role had not felt untrue. He was already embroiled.

More than a year later, after the war had begun, her family sent her to London. And she did seek him out, at the address on the piece of paper he'd pressed into her hand as they took their leave of one another.

In greeting, she said bluntly, 'Hello, husband,' to which he responded, with equal forthrightness, 'Hello, wife.'

She didn't visit her family again until peace was reinstated and Trieste had passed from Austrian to Italian dominion (Piazza Grande now renamed Piazza dell'Unità), and then just briefly. Long before that Valeria and Harry had made their own peaceful tumult of a married life as real as any. They were never engaged. It would have seemed redundant.

•

'A needle bath now, to get that off you.' He liked the painful sound of it, though how much could water prick? Not the same white-suited fellow as before, which was just as well, given how besmirched Harry was with mud. This one was bare-chested and clad in shorts, ready for the dripping prehistoric creature into which Harry had transformed, a visitant from a nightmare's murk. 'You should find the inflammation much reduced,' he affirmed in a rich Glaswegian accent.

Harry remembered mumbling some improvisation about being gouty to justify his interest in peat. 'I sincerely hope so,' he said.

The highly pressurised water did in fact come harder than you would have expected, stinging certain areas of the body when directed in the right way.

14

AUGUST 1926
Torquay

She couldn't simply drift down the hill to bathe in the sea, because there was too much to be done. She couldn't sleep. The only thing for it was to work, Mummy's possessions having to be sorted, stored, disposed of. A life in mementoes, one more suffocating than the last. The sprawling wreath of wax flowers preserved under a glass dome that was her grandfather's memorial! Not a gay object to contend with. What the deuce to do with that? Could she throw it away with a clear conscience?

In another of the endless boxes that had been closed up for years, a photograph of an ethereal blonde child in a garden.

Her child self. An earlier Agatha at Ashfield. Beautiful, with long, so-fair, delicately curled hair. Solemn pre-Raphaelite nymph. She smiled, and ceased smiling. There was something about that face.

She straightened her stooped and tender back, nearly knocking over the saucepan she'd put out to catch drips last night when the rain started. Peter sneezed and she bent again to pat him. The overcrowded room suddenly seemed impossibly oppressive, fusty with all that past she'd never slog through. She beat the dust from her hands and, followed by her companion-saviour, took the photograph downstairs to the conservatory. The light was better there, but Peter was disturbed by the wicker sofa's suppressed screeching when she sat, and not liking being woefully regarded by tiers of wilted ferns, she sprang up and went out into the garden.

Along with Peter, her only bit of succour. The garden, with its sea breezes. Nothing better for scrubbing out your mind than salt air. It positively murdered her spirit to think that Ashfield might have to be sold, because it was still an oasis, even in its current dilapidation, all the delightful greenery a little overblown and readying to ferment. Lack of money for a proper gardener had obliged Mummy to adopt a laissez-faire approach, and the small park had taken on an almost sexual dishevelment as the weather ripened. The Alba roses, at their lightest pink, sweetly fragrant best (the waste of Mummy not able to breathe them in), appeared tousled and harassed by the enduring sultriness. The creepers still gamely climbing the villa were limp. Distorted seasons they had been, alien spring and mildewy summer.

The real child, her voice coming now from the open window of the schoolroom, where the servant was occupying her, couldn't understand any of it. Six years old—very nearly seven. She didn't even realise that the cataclysm of her birth had taken place here, that her father had kissed her mother hours beforehand under that beech.

Why couldn't he make it down—just for a weekend? The flummoxing answer was golf.

Peter licking her ankle, she considered the photograph. The unmoved mouth. The shadows like bruising beneath already hooded, strikingly serious eyes. Aged. A face not looking out but in.

She wrested a handful of petals from one of Mummy's beloved roses, releasing frenzied scent and the longing to rage. Such was that unhinged summer that this urge was somehow misplaced. It was days after that her husband finally came down from London, an energetic, youthful blue-eyed man to her ruined phantom.

Saying, 'Look, see, I want a divorce. I've fallen in love with someone.'

And she didn't scream (she would another day, and hurl a white teapot). Instead, she observed that it was only as quicksand swallowed your feet that you had its number.

15

A VERY ELUSIVE PERSON

Following his rise from the mud, Harry crossed paths with Mr Jackman in the dressing hall.

'Well?' Mr Jackman was robed, glowing.

'Seem to have survived,' Harry reported.

'Jolly good. Me too. I've stewed in sulphur foam.' He grinned. 'Feel fortified, rejuvenated. Starving like a boy of fourteen. I'm off now for a massage. You should have one, too, you know. You look a little rundown, if you don't mind my saying so.'

'I don't. But later, perhaps. I was just going for a turn in the Winter Garden, to see if the orchestra's up to anything.' Harry felt guilty for always snubbing the affable fellow, but he was too oppressed by his own thoughts to be sociable. 'Might see you after.'

He did not go to the Winter Garden. He sneaked out of the baths and loitered in Crescent Gardens, smoking, in the hope of spying Teresa leaving.

An hour or so passed, and the Jackmans emerged. They waited a few moments, he guessed for Teresa, but presently gave up and set out in the direction of the Hydro. He concluded that she must have already returned to the hotel, maybe via a side exit or the Winter Garden.

He concealed himself from the Jackmans behind the covered Promenade Walk, and then followed at a distance.

At the Hydro he waited for lunch to be well underway before furtively surveying the dining room from the doorway. No Teresa.

Too restless to eat in company, he stalked the corridors, on the lookout. He even went up to the mezzanine to see if she could be in the billiard room with the Russian and his cohort. Of course there was no one there and, coming back downstairs, he discovered the Winter Garden Ballroom likewise empty. Melancholy business, a deserted ballroom. He entered and found himself at the table where she had sat during their first conversation. He rested his hand on it briefly. The room grew cooler close to the glass walls. He looked out at the grounds and up at the muted winter sunlight falling in through the glass ceiling. With his head tipped back, he suddenly felt the effects of his broken night: an odd weight, or weightlessness, and an idea that his own outlines were smudged. He must have slept on his feet for a second or two.

With a start, he flung out a hand to steady himself against the wall. A climbing plant would throw out an arm—more slowly—to the radiance of a window with a similar instinct for self-preservation. At the Hydro the guests weren't unlike plants living out their lives confined to a delicate semblance of the wider world.

He resumed his patrolling of the hallways. Despite his recent familiarity with accommodations such as these, he couldn't say he was at home in them. His presence there continued to seem a sort of joke at which he was laughing soundlessly and without mirth. The irony might have been entertaining if he'd had any real appetite for amusement. He was an impostor in this curative pleasantness. He was doing his best impersonation of one who was footloose, but he could resort to watering-places for aimless sojourns only thanks to an unearned wealth that sat uncouthly on him.

Taking the electric elevator to the first floor, *her* floor, he reflected that to be an effective member of the Quality you must be born one, or become one before you've achieved full awareness of yourself and your position in life. Otherwise you won't have the sense—the reflex—to take luxury and repose as your due. While doing your best to find it natural, you'll suspect you're befouling a key moral precept. The Jackmans and Teresa knew no qualms of this type. For them, there was nothing more normal than living among first-class comforts, nothing strange or ironical in being a hothouse plant. Was he attracted to these people because he wanted them to teach him to be satisfied with comfort? To slough off guilt? He was a great one for guilt.

After a circumspect examination of the first-floor hallway, he stood close to Teresa's door and listened. Nothing. Where was she? Still at the baths? Out walking?

Back to his pacing. Was it because he belonged to the servants' caste that he could not feel at home here? His mother had been a maid before her marriage and his father had worked as a modest farmer. Granted, Harry hadn't known what it was to go wanting but nor had he known surplus. Which rather rendered the sensation of enough dubious, haloing it with insufficiency, a certain lack. In his own working life he'd been an assistant to a rich man. Proximity to money gives you some understanding of its ways but not an inbred instinct for them. He'd maintained a household successfully, with infrequent worries. Though he'd had to live knowing that he provided Valeria with a simple London flat inferior to the fine bourgeois villa in which she'd been raised. She'd even had to take on employment of her own. Perhaps he'd not made anything of himself as a writer because he'd been too afraid to try his luck at earning their living that way only to realise that he couldn't.

Harry's fraudulent feeling came in part, yes, from his failure to spend Mrs Mortlake's fortune with nonchalance, but also from his being such an unconvincing spa visitor. He was not exactly a pleasure holiday-maker, and nor did he possess any well-defined malady or interest in being cured. He fancied he'd have rather enjoyed some tangible complaints, dramatic anaemia, something to make him bedridden—or mobile only in a bath chair. During his walks in Valley Gardens, observing the fine silhouette of the Bath Hospital against the sky, he'd sometimes nurtured a fantasy of being an inmate there. *That* would have been more the spot for him. Or, better still, the Home for Incurables a little further along Cornwall Road. In such an establishment it would be virtually de rigueur to feel blackly sorry for yourself. Hopelessness would be logical and self-evident. He imagined being grimly uplifted by this.

Thus he spent the afternoon, feeling a misfit, and somehow betrayed—by his birth or character. He returned to his room eventually, consigned Wagner to the gramophone, *Tristan und Isolde*, and threw himself onto the bed. This was his fate, was it? These hotels his purgatory? He'd proven himself to be incapable and undeserving of normal life, and places dedicated to health or amusement in which he didn't truly believe had become the limbo he was destined to inhabit. He struggled to sense Valeria lying beside him, their hands interlaced. His guilt was still shocking. The stain of it that would not be cleansed by all the bathhouse cures of Arabia.

•

Harry was at table with the Jackmans when Teresa entered the dining room, the Russian at her elbow. He was hovering like an insect around sweetness, but you could tell even from a distance that she was being offhand with him. Also that he was a seductive personage, despite there being nothing particularly imposing in his face or physique. Where did that come from? Was she really insensible to it? The Russian gestured to the table where his friends sat. Harry distinctly saw Teresa shake her head and glance at Mrs Jackman, who waved. Her eyes only hopped over his.

A long moment later she was settling herself at Mrs Jackman's side, with a smiling though inscrutable look.

'We've chosen the French menu,' Mr Jackman informed her. 'Will you be our accomplice?'

'Certainly,' she said, all diffident courtesy.

'I lost you at the baths,' Mrs Jackman lamented. 'After my first dip in the plunge bath I couldn't find you.'

'I lost this chap here, too,' Mr Jackman said.

'I was ages in the Hot Rooms,' Teresa explained. 'You forget yourself in those.'

'You haven't braved the plunge bath yet?' Mr Jackman wanted to know. 'I submerge myself fully, head included, five or six times during a Turkish visit. Swear by it.'

'And look at his beautiful skin,' remarked his wife earnestly. 'You'd say he wasn't a day over forty.'

'Indeed.' Teresa was straight-faced.

Was she thinking what Harry was? They are old and love each other, still find each other beautiful. A success of a marriage. How is that done? She flushed slightly, looked down.

From the other side of the room the Russian was trying to catch her eye. Harry would have liked to pass him a surreptitious message: Desist from your designs. He noted the disagreeableness of his own disgruntled manhood.

Lobster bisque. Harry took to the chablis with a vengeance. Teresa was sipping only water, and he asked himself, Does she *never* drink?

'She never drinks,' Mr Jackman said. 'Poor thing. Nice chablis, don't you find?'

'I do.'

'Perhaps you can help us decide on an outing for tomorrow,' his wife proposed. 'Ramble to Birk Crag or motor ride to Ripon Cathedral with the Lady Entertainer?'

'We usually steer clear of such people, on principle,' Mr Jackman added, with a hint of being wicked. 'We've no interest in being *entertained*, and most definitely not with bridge or whist. One rather goes on holiday to get away from all that. But Yorkshire beauty spots are a different kettle of fish and we're considering it.'

'Actually,' Mrs Jackman interjected, 'we'd be thrilled if you'd come. Both of you.'

'Birk Crag is the more woodsy choice,' her husband supposed.

'Yes,' she said, 'but everyone raves about Ripon. Can't think why we've never gone before.'

They were savouring their ambivalence, and life generally, in which there were so many pleasurable things to choose between. What effortless enjoyment.

'Thank you, but I don't think I *can* tomorrow,' Teresa said. 'Massage appointment, you know.'

'Nor I, I'm afraid. I also have an engagement.'

Teresa and Harry had let them down. They were all on to the *boeuf.*

Mrs Jackman rallied. 'I'm worried something terrible has happened to the lady novelist. I just have this sense of dread about it.' She dabbed at her lips with a serviette. 'Don't you, Teresa? You saw the piece in *The Times*?'

Teresa swallowed, and said in a contracted voice, 'I really wouldn't know. I'm rather lazy with newspapers. It's more the crossword puzzles I take them for.'

'But what can have happened to her? I'll lend you my newspaper if you like.'

'I did *glance* at the article. She must be a very elusive person.'

'That's my feeling,' Mr Jackman said. 'Elusive. But who isn't?'

'You aren't,' his wife said, smiling. 'Not to me. No, but I'm afraid she must have been quite desperate, to drive off at night like that. Why would you do such a thing?'

'She might be—desperate.' Teresa was cutting fervently into her beef.

•

She was the first to finish eating. Her blancmange had been dealt with when the rest of them were barely beginning dessert. She laid down her spoon. 'I'm drooping. Think I'll go straight up to bed.'

Harry tried to concoct an excuse for leaving the table after her, but Mr Jackman detained him. In an undertone: 'I saw the physician this morning, and he mentioned you'd missed your weekly appointment. Asked how you were.'

By the time Harry had promised to fix another appointment and made his escape, she wasn't in the lounge, on the stairs, or in the first-floor corridor. She was still loath to have a tête à tête with him. She felt remorse—disgust?—at what had passed between them. He was bothered and hurt.

He lacked the courage to knock on her door. He left a request with the night hall porter, a discreet round-faced man of about fifty, for the *Daily Mail* to be brought to him the following morning with his tea. He envisaged relying heavily on sherry and Teresa's novels to get himself through another night in limbo.

16

BRAIN FAG AND DEBILITY

But after only two sizable glasses of sherry and a generous dose of Teresa's fiction, the uneasiness that had haunted Harry's day dulled, was quelled, and he was gifted a run of hours' sleep. Consequently, he woke on Friday feeling stronger and much more solid. Almost proud of some achievement in which the merit was his. You see, you're not in as bad a state as all that, my boy. You're a machine that functions. He was roused, not by the door opening—strange, given the usual sensitivity of his sleep—but by tea and newspaper being deposited by his bed. He thanked the ruddy-cheeked, mannerly lad, who got a fire going while Harry arranged pillows and ordered bedclothes so he could sit up comfortably.

He was hardly thinking of Teresa this morning—only softly, obliquely. It was possible after sleep of the better kind for the mind to be so freshened it appeared to have wrested back control of itself from alien agencies. It merely existed for itself again, at its own leisurely rhythms, naturally and philosophically. What was the problem, again? Anticipating disaster was melodramatic. Things would find some satisfactory resolution, or not, which was the nature of life, wasn't it? All the energy one expended fretting! He wondered whether he'd only *imagined* himself in love with Teresa. Wanting to see Valeria in her, wanting to revive the past. He'd always been prone to hyperbole . . . If this placid condition could be bottled and sold as a tonic, what a mad success it would be!

Once the fire was going, he was left alone. He downed half a cup of tea—properly brewed, hydrating, renewing— complimenting himself on being rather a sane man, everything considered. A sip more, and he unfolded the newspaper. He perused idly.

And came to it.

Five hundred police had gone looking for her. Photographs of the search. People striding across fields in woollens and high-minded expressions.

Comments from the Colonel. They had *not* rowed. (Why say this? Why be defensive?) He'd have no tolerance for tittle-tattle. (What was he worried would be said?) His wife was self-willed, capable, and had on occasion mentioned the possibility of disappearing. She was wont to discuss poisons.

When they had taken her little dog to the site of her vanishing, he had run straight down the hill.

Harry's fears returned. And his emotion for her. He saw her pale eyes, recalled the warmth of her kisses. With searches of this magnitude and such insistence from the press, it couldn't be long until someone here was on to Teresa Neele. He didn't know how, but he had to protect her from that.

Poisons? She'd spoken of poisons to him, too. Though that could have been related to her literary interests, or her experience as a nurse, couldn't it? Or did she also have to be protected from herself, after all?

He leaped out of bed and dressed hectically, not troubling with a shave.

He rushed down the flight of stairs separating them, almost tripping before he reached the bottom. No one in the corridor. On, down to the ground floor. She wasn't in the dining room. Up again to the first floor.

Fist poised to knock on her door, he stepped back. It was early. He didn't wish to wake her. He retreated to the lounge, where he went to stand before the fire.

After a while, hearing the Jackmans' voices as if the couple were emerging from the reading room, he hurried back up the stairs to the first floor. Down the corridor, finally, and to her room. He was sweating. It was eight thirty.

Before he could knock, the door opened. He drew back. A chambermaid.

'Oh,' he said, feigning casualness, while no doubt sounding

and looking horribly suspicious. 'Mrs Neele is awake? I have a message to convey to her.'

'She's gone out, sir.'

'What!' He stared. The girl was somewhat startled to see him so shaken. He enquired more docilely, 'Ah, really?'

'She said she was going to do some shopping and she'd be back tonight.'

'It's just that I thought she was feeling poorly, you see. That's why I didn't expect she'd be going out today. Seemed quite well, did she?'

The girl turned side on and resettled the pile of linen in her arms. He suspected this of being a contrivance, a delaying move to help her settle on an answer. 'When I brought her tea this morning, she said she'd have her breakfast in bed, because she was going out early.'

He nodded. The girl hesitated.

He endeavoured to coax her. 'So she was quite well, then?'

'She didn't say, sir. She didn't mention being poorly.'

He could see there was something else that she might have afforded him. She battled with herself. He respected her discretion even as he sought to breach it. He wondered if she were weary, at such an hour perhaps already having worked for some time. 'However . . . ?'

Her eyes lifted to him, and for a moment their training in blank servility was perforated. She found Teresa Neele curious. She hadn't guessed her true identity, had she? Could she read? Had she read the newspaper before delivering it and become watchful? He prayed not.

'Yesterday she was very cheerful, and today she wasn't. I didn't know she was poorly. When I brought her breakfast in . . .'

'Yes?'

'Her manner . . .'

'Her manner was . . . ?'

'Odd, sir.'

'Ah?'

'A bit odd.'

'I see. Thank you.' He nodded. 'Perhaps she's not entirely improved, but still felt well enough to go out. I'm glad.'

'Did you want to leave the message for her?'

'That won't be necessary. It'll wait.'

He didn't know how to read this. Had Teresa run? Gone somewhere . . . to . . . Was shopping a code word for ultimate nothingness? Or, at best, her departure from Harry's life forever? He mustn't even think these things. He waited for her return, unsure if she really would be back. Cruel process.

•

He lunched late and reluctantly. The Jackmans were away on their pleasure tour, so he wasn't obliged to talk. He did rather miss them, though. He continued with the last of Teresa's novels.

As he was making for the smoking room, the physician accosted him. He was a burly yet neat fellow, with understanding eyes. Whether that was duty or natural inclination, it was impossible to know. Harry apologised for missing his appointment and mumbled that he'd make another. For this afternoon? Having no excuse ready, he accepted.

When the time they'd set—the amorphous half past three—arrived, he was glad to have somewhere to go. He descended to the basement, reporting to the room where he had lukewarmly visited the physician twice since his arrival at the Hydro.

'I hope you are well?' the physician enquired.

'Oh, you know,' Harry said. 'Yes, pretty well.'

His pulse was taken, and he was appraised.

'Last week it seemed as if your vitality was coming back. I'd thought we were making good progress.' The professional man smiled delicately. 'I don't suppose you've been—let's say, living in rather a high fashion? I often see that here. Enjoying oneself is one thing, but we must be careful of excess.'

Harry protested that his living had been tolerably low, except for a little drinking of an evening.

The physician raised his eyebrows, but appeared not unamused.

'My sleep *has* been irregular. But then that's quite regular for me. Actually, last night I had a particularly good rest.'

'Hmm. Gratified to hear it.' He uncapped a handsome fountain pen. 'I think I shall recommend the Chalybeate waters. Just the thing for brain fag and debility.'

'Splendid.'

'You *are* taking the sulphur water?'

'Oh yes. Maybe not with the greatest consistency.'

The physician sighed. 'You know, we don't advise self-treatment. The guidance of a medical man *is* important.'

'I set no great store by my own guidance.'

'Well, we'll do our best,' the physician concluded lightly. 'Come and see me next week?'

Harry nodded—wondering whether he would, and at the queerness of this man's profession. Even in this territory of prosperous tranquillity, what a river of vulnerability he must daily watch passing.

•

The afternoon drifted into a wicked evening of waiting. He finished Teresa's novel, enjoying it. There was a ploy in it that she had handled dexterously, with cunning calm. Once he was out of the convivial enclosure of the book, he was on tenterhooks. It didn't suit him to be inactive.

Not wanting to go far, he wandered the hotel grounds and smoked. It wasn't especially cold. Though sundown had passed, two men of middle age, one very bald and the other endowed with a berserk chestnut mop, took to the tennis court. Harry watched them for twenty minutes or so, relieved at the diversion, but they were playing a haphazard, frustrating game not aided by the risibly poor visibility or any talent to speak of.

He was in one of the lounge's armchairs looking at the grandfather clock at a quarter to seven, the time at which, on a lightly snowy night, Valeria hadn't been lying on their sofa as usual with her feline companion, a book and a hoard of digestives, because her life had ended.

He hadn't eaten anything, knowing he couldn't have coped with the dining room, nor even with the Winter Garden Ballroom—that unseasonable conservatory ambience and would-be insouciance.

The grandfather clock was striking ten when Teresa passed quietly in. She didn't look discontented.

17

SEVENTH AND EIGHTH DAYS

On Thursday, Teresa had to take action regarding her finances, which were running low. The rather comfortable sum of pounds she'd had the foresight to be supplied with was naturally enough after a certain number of purchases depleted. Bothersome.

She'd noticed a sign in a jeweller's on James Street—with a tempting Pearl Salon—declaring that old items would be bought for cash. She directed herself there, after forsaking Mrs Jackman at the baths, and was able to bring off an adequate exchange for her wristwatch and a ring to which she refused to wonder if she might be attached. Both being respectable pieces, her funds were decently replenished. They'd last until her husband's arrival, which shouldn't be delayed much longer.

But the moment had come to accelerate proceedings with that message in a bottle.

An advertisement in *The Times*?

Yes, capital. More stylish than a letter. The kind of gesture required of one living under a pseudonym, clinically clean. But standing in the post office, preparing to deliver a line or two, blankness came over her. The fuzziness, the dental-surgery fog. Damn and blast this writing fiasco. She was positively unfit to combine words to set on paper. Senseless.

Somehow, she calmed herself down.

And finally, a miracle. *Friends and relatives of Teresa Neele,* she jotted messily but there it was, *late of South Africa, please communicate.* And a box number.

Ha! Clever, really. Was it?

Errands concluded, she returned to the Hydro with the itchy impression back that something was approaching. The day had felt ghost-thin. At dinner, there were the challenges of eluding the Russian, discouraging the Jackmans, who wanted her to go on their driving excursion, and ignoring Harry without seeming to. She felt observed. It could have been her imagination.

•

The next morning, waking from another heavy sleep, she found her mind veering into her elaborate romantic dream from two days before. She and Shy Thing were outside inhaling the stormy air.

Embarrassed by having almost slid over in the mud, she told him, 'You have the most *amazing* fruit here.' It came out sounding saucy. She hurried on: 'I've been terribly disappointed, however, to learn that pineapples grow on the ground. I was expecting grand trees offering them to you at a civilised height.'

'I know what you mean. When I first saw bananas growing as a child, I was aggrieved because I'd imagined they'd be yellow, not green. Where's the pleasure in something you can't enjoy immediately?' The Australian boy was speaking without his colonial accent, in deep, pleasantly hard-to-place English tones. Rather like Harry.

'You remind me of my mother. High expectations. Mummy had a terrible hunger for wonderful things and excitement, which makes it hard to be content for very long. You're always waiting for the next strong, decisive sensation. That's why she tried out so many religions, I suppose.'

'Greedy for the sublime . . . But *shouldn't* one want a lot from life?'

'I've lost my darling Mummy, you know.'

He looked at her for a lengthy interval, then exhorted, 'Listen carefully. We've no time to lose. Will you trust me? You must decide. I'm leaving now and you'll have to come with me, or I'll have to leave you behind. I'm engaged to marry. The daughter of a wealthy family. It's you I love—only you, darling. If you thought you could ever care for me in that way, well, we'd have to run off to elope before the others return.'

'My decision is made.' She laid her hand on his arm.

He led her to two very fine horses that were standing at the ready. They mounted and set off. Side-saddle, she rode with panache. It had never been so natural. At first they passed through Australian fields, untold dryness, then the terrain began to resemble the rough, bleakish beauty of Dartmoor in its autumn mauves. The immoderate Australian light diminished and rain was gathering.

A storm. Wild rivulets coursed beneath the horses' feet and Shy Thing, leading the way, fell, his horse appearing to lose its substance beneath him.

She jumped down from her own steed and rushed to his side. When she touched him, he sucked his breath in, smiling weakly. His leg was injured.

The horses had taken fright and fled. However, not long before she'd noticed an abandoned hut to which she now managed to guide him, much of his weight upon her.

She nursed him there for days, months perhaps, preparing ointments from medicinal herbs she collected on the moor. Her wartime training as a VAD and a dispenser came in handy, though she worried sometimes that in this wilderness she couldn't discern a poison.

She cared for him with such devotion that she tended to get badly overtired and delirious, fancying herself with numberless boys in her charge, arriving from France and Flanders and Gallipoli. How to accommodate them? The tone of it all was warm. She wasn't green now as she'd been in her VAD days, no longer as hesitant and self-regarding. 'Darling,' she'd say. 'Oh, darling.' Then slim dark roots would twine themselves around her wrists and ankles, binding her to something cold and perfectly still.

And lucidity would return.

Just as she brought back Shy Thing's health, they realised she was suffering from an overpowering frailty. He was desolate. When would they ever get themselves to a church and become man and wife?

One day there was something black on her leg. A growth on her fair skin, a horrifying spider-like filigree. Swamped by shame, she screamed, and wouldn't look at it. To soothe her, Shy Thing stroked it. He found beauty in it, somehow.

They thought her strength might return if she could bathe in the sea. Her secret hope was to be freed of the black growth. He carried her over one shoulder like a sack of coal for so long she lost track of time, or maybe she was passing in and out of consciousness. They reached a place similar if not identical to the ladies' bathing cove of her childhood. Torquay! However, mixed bathing being some years off, as distant as adolescence, Shy Thing shouldn't have been there. She told him so. Saddened, he waved to her as she entered one of the bathing machines operated by a wizened, testy old man.

The door bolted, she changed into her flattering little emerald-green bathing dress from Hawaii, feeling all the old exhilaration but also confusion, because she was already an adult, after all, and what she wanted was to be with Shy Thing. The contraption began its bumpy roll from the stony beach into the sea. Abruptly she knew that he *was* inside it with her. He'd made himself minute, and hidden inside the black growth on her leg. Rather original.

'Good heavens, you're here,' she said.

Do you mind?

She did not respond. The situation made her timid. As they could apparently now talk without speaking, she tried to avoid thinking. Like with Mummy.

Don't worry. No one will find out.

The bathing machine had travelled as far as it would on its straps. She'd liked the sense of close confinement, but she unbolted the door on the water side.

The sea, its smell intensifying. She descended into the softly repetitious waves. They were separate again and he had returned to normal size, though he was keeping beneath the surface.

Won't you have to come up for air?

Not so much.

My father says that *gentlemen* from the Torbay Yacht Club watch the ladies bathing or lying on that raft through opera glasses.

Dirty old devils. Seeing me would teach them!

He was taking care not to touch her. There were the faintest whispery movements against her, like ribbons of seaweed or fish quivering past. Her bathing dress was gone. She was sure, then, that the black growth on her leg had gone, too. She was no longer frail. It was a little like the release of urinating after a long time of holding in, tension leaving, a burning melting between pain and rapture. Feeling was finally accepted and owned.

She wasn't taking care not to touch him now. Delicious—so long as no one saw.

•

Bringing in tea, the chambermaid disrupted Teresa's reverie, as she was wont to do. All at once keyed up, Teresa petulantly refused a newspaper and asked for breakfast in bed, evading the sensitive eyes of that well-formed, faintly sapped girl.

Alone again, she attempted a new tack. There was a notepad by the bed. At times you could catch the artistic part of yourself off-guard. I couldn't care in the slightest how you pass your time, brain. This here is just in case you should need to make some list unrelated to work, to a train or anything like that. Shh, softly, softly. Thinking of nothing much, quite relaxed, thinking of nothing.

Now quick, hook through the throat: what horseplay might unfold on the Blue Train? Theft of expensive jewels? Don't struggle. A train. Some doubtful individuals. One at least a thoroughly bad lot, and the others have to seem as if they might be, too. And a girl with grey eyes. A woman, really, not terribly young anymore, but enchanting to men who know how to see it . . . And?

Very well, just a train carriage. Go from there.

Lord, how agreeable a train journey to the Riviera would be. Victoria Station, the deep blue cars and brown-liveried attendants. The exotic, regimented business of tickets and passports. Hurtling into the green tunnel of Kent, passengers good-humoured from champagne and pleasant prospects. Aromas of fish and Stilton in the dining car. The lament of the Westinghouse brake making you giddy with that intoxication of leaving, part sorrow, part ecstasy.

Enough procrastination! A train carriage . . . Baggage rack, windowsill, wooden panelling. The confounded wooden panelling! Maddening having your eyes frozen on the frame of a picture. Where was the grey-eyed woman?

There, there was Katherine, now, good . . . But just sitting smugly, a slightly unnerving doll. Stubborn, stubborn. You could throttle her. And the train itself remained *too* real . . .

There was nothing on her hook, *rien de rien*. She pitched the notebook across the room, seconds before the maid knocked. Coming in with the breakfast tray, the girl noticed the fallen object with its splayed pages, but did not comment on it.

Gorging herself on toothsome kippers, Teresa wondered if she shouldn't after all go on the Jackmans' pleasure tour. But no, better to be alone. She especially shouldn't run into

Harry—not with that deviant dream lingering. She ordered another pot of tea, and drank as she dressed, in the tweed skirt again, with a white blouse and the mauve cardigan.

A speedy departure after checking with the hall porter for letters and nodding taciturnly at Redhead, who accorded her a taciturn nod in return. Noting something in a ledger, this lady was a strengthening sight, a portrait of dedication to work. Her solid shape only made her appear more dependable and unflappable. She might have been taller but an assertive head of hair compensated for much.

Teresa passed through the crowd around the Pump Room, thinking sparingly, silky thoughts. She avoided the gardens clogged with water-drinkers taking their fifteen-minute turns between doses, and was soon confronting Montpellier Hill. It was the sort you leaned into, the way you leaned into Torquay hills—as if into a stiff wind, with dogged defiance. Prevailing over it, she gazed wistfully through the window of the Imperial Café, but just after breakfast had to be judged too early for cake (she *did* want to keep this improved figure for her husband), and the day would still have been wide open after that.

She had a great need for movement, a horror of inertia, which came on like a fear of asphyxiation. She knew this from her suburban life. From the worst days, when writing was difficult. A sense of slow drowning. Into her mind came the fine dark roots that had encircled her wrists and ankles at one point in her dream.

Go somewhere. Just go.

Adjusting her cloche hat and gripping her bag securely, she went on to the train station, where—stroke of chance—a train for Leeds was drawing in. That would do for now. Go from there.

•

Being in the new city, where absolutely no one knew who she was, released the pressure from her lungs. She was mollified.

Teresa ambled and shopped at Schofields, drawn to taupe-coloured items but eventually persuading herself in favour of a midnight-blue dress, a nice classic in light wool. Another pair of stockings. A restrainedly pink foulard. In the department store's restaurant at an appropriate hour—obliged to ask a thin, ancient deaf lady the time as she had no wristwatch now—she consumed leek and potato soup, and dryish roast chicken, neither noteworthy. Later, a similarly pedestrian scone. Usually deploring food that failed to live up to its potential, today she didn't much mind. (She may have been, as she had done during her married life, as she had always done, using food to plug any possible gap.)

It had been dark for some time when she returned to the station. She pondered the boards with the destinations on them, so infused with the atmosphere of departure. The muscular desire for travel persisted. Still, she didn't see how she could avoid going back to Harrogate, where her husband would soon arrive.

And where there was a room at the Hydro, with its bed and basin, a window regarding Swan Road and a wardrobe full of Teresa Neele's agreeable new clothes. Where Harry was. On the platform it was damply bitter and she tucked her chin into the fur ruff on the coat that had also become familiar, she realised.

No riveting train-related antics occurred to her during the return journey. On the notepad she'd brought along, just to be moving her hand in that way, she wrote: *Darling . . . My darling . . .*

It would be essential to keep track of money, so she made a list of recent acquisitions. She had no trouble recalling the price of each, but the days on which she'd purchased them weren't clear to her. During the first week or thereabouts of a trip, time was roomy, cavernous.

•

When she entered the Hydro—the grandfather clock recording ten—he was in the lounge, in an armchair by the fire. That was to say, Harry. Not her husband. A phlegmatic girl at the reception desk smiled noncommittally and went back to reading a newspaper.

'Teresa!' he said, standing.

She would sooner not have endangered her tentative self-command, but she could hardly recoil and turn around. She approached him. Its mussed appearance made you wonder if he'd been running his fingers through his hair, and his eyes, she let herself notice, were enervated and reddish. A forceful odour of tobacco reached her.

Remember, you aren't sure you can trust him.

'Where have you been?' he demanded, with the offended righteousness of a wife reproaching a husband for coming home tardily.

'Please lower your voice. I've been to Leeds shopping.'

'Leeds!' he retorted, as though finding this preposterous.

She made for the lift and he followed. She must have felt she owed him proof because she raised a hand to show him the shopping bags. They boarded the lift, and the ascent commenced.

'*Leeds*?' He was becoming more pliant. 'What did you buy? Can I carry those?'

'This and that. No thank you, they're quite light. Well, I'm tired, so I'll be saying goodnight.'

They'd alighted on the first floor. Harry accompanied her to her room. Awkward.

''Night, Teresa.' But he continued to stand sentry by the door. He laughed. 'God, I'm just relieved!'

He ran a hand through his hair. The compulsive gesture moved her. And some of the warmth of the queer dream returned—yet she was as apprehensive as she'd been that morning, waking. Steady, she said to herself. This man she had kissed knew who she was. She opened the door.

'Sorry,' he said, moving out of her way, only the length of a short step.

She could have gone in then without another word. 'Relieved? I don't see why you should be.' He was leaning against the wall by the door now. The pose seemed to reflect not false casualness but a frank requirement of support. There was a looseness to him tonight. 'Have you been drinking?'

'Not a drop.' He laughed again. 'I was imagining things, that's all.'

'Imagining things—about me?'

'I was afraid,' he murmured.

'Afraid? Whatever of?'

He exhaled heavily. 'Afraid you might . . . do something to yourself.'

She snapped, 'I don't know what the devil you mean.' Knowing, of course.

She had the irrational idea that he would hear her heart beating. She almost slammed the door but instead she looked at him. His eyes were frightfully dark and disordered in that face both slim and deep. She felt fatigue, then, the zing of her nerves, and a kind of fellowship.

'Well, we'd mentioned . . . Casablanca, and . . .' He shook

his head. 'I've been miserable these last days. And bushed. Though I did finally sleep last night.'

There was a silence that she fancied transparent, free of artifice or design. Two exhausted people occupying the same corner of space. Her resolve to resist him was softening. She was perilously close to inviting him in.

'I know I had no right to be—worried—you'd hurt yourself,' he was saying ramblingly.

'Because of a flippant conversation? Or because of who you suspect I am?' She felt something of a child's fury, rather directionless and passing. She dropped her voice, which had risen. 'You presume to know me?' She was attempting not to watch his mouth, with its full bottom lip. She would not reveal herself.

'No, listen. I don't mean to presume anything. And I don't *care* who you are. Officially, that is. I really don't. The newspapers—it's all a matter of perfect indifference to me.' His eyes were downcast. 'I shouldn't have told you I loved you, either. Precipitate, stupid. Which doesn't mean those aren't my feelings.' She remained mute. 'We don't have to discuss that. But I'd like you to know your welfare is important to me.'

'Why should my welfare be in danger?' she asked bumpily. She had inadvertently released the doorknob, which she had been holding.

The door swung open and they looked into her room. A fire had been laid but did not burn. His eyes travelled to the bedside table, and he seemed to blanch. Swiftly, she pulled the door to again.

'Look here. I owe you an explanation. Well, there's a story I'd like to tell you that might help you understand my . . . concern. If you'll hear it. I've never told it to anyone, you see, but I want to tell you.'

His voice had gained a heated intensity that scared her. I must close the door on him, she decided, though she could not bring herself to refuse this request. 'Very well, but you should go now. We can talk tomorrow. Perhaps not here at the hotel. Bettys? Eleven o'clock tea?' He would let her close the door on him, wouldn't he?

At last he nodded. 'Tomorrow, then. Thank you.'

His voice resembled the voice in her dream, as she was remembering it. She did not know if it was the voice of someone she could lean on. He had not yet turned to go when she closed the door.

18

1922
TSS *Aeneas*

One night during the long sea journey that conveyed them to Australia, her husband returned to their cabin at around ten. This was usual, the later entertainments not his cup of tea. She stayed on with the mission at the captain's table to listen to an after-dinner concert the Autumn Sighs had decided to bestow on them, despite being rather tight. Their stamina, considering, was admirable. Such silly evenings were no doubt so festive because by now it was dawning on them that the principal talent of the major, their director on the Empire Tour, lay in passing himself off as an expert through wild improvisation. This, along with his highly mutable humours, lent things a madcap tone that led one to wonder how successful they could possibly be in cultivating trade relations in the interests of the upcoming Empire Exhibition in London. Thoroughly amused by it all, she justified her enjoyment of the revelry by telling herself it was her job as the wife of the financial adviser to the mercurial major to be a good sport. Wanting to play her part that night, she'd even taken a glass of burgundy and, with heroic persistence, finished it. She supposed it was the very act of floating that made what happened on board a ship seem to flow with a peculiar current.

It was near on three am when she bade the company goodnight and rose to leave. Doing so, she caught her reflection in a looking-glass. Oh. Her colour had changed. The merriment or perhaps the wine had given a distinct light to her eyes. She lifted her hands to her face.

Beauty resuscitated.

She had always expected, when giving the matter any airy consideration, that the lapsing of her beauty would be awfully long and placid. A leisurely slide into a more sober handsomeness. Which in turn wouldn't so much be lost, at last, as kindly subdued like a beloved landscape by gathering dusk.

Well, it was not so. The truth was that her physical attractiveness—what a *lovely* girl she was, had been—had begun quite abruptly to leave her a few years before. No gradual picturesque nightfall. Nothing tranquil. The great, rude shock of that merciless dulling.

The secret padding and suspension of her face had grown flaccid. Just a little, but enough to show the direction in which things would go. There was a flattening of her mouth that made it appear broader. Her cheeks, too, appeared broader. Her eyelids looser and heavier. Her much-lauded fair skin had started to look patchy, humdrum. Where was the indefinable yet essential something that had energised her whole appearance when she was at her best? That sort of creamy inner blaze?

To be dispossessed of it was baffling, chilling. Was it gone for good?

She had discovered that there could be brief revivals of her former looks. Very good sleep, a beautiful outfit, a long peppy walk on a cold day, or delight, might afford some hours' grace. She appeared to have been awarded a little now, and it excited her to be pretty again for her husband, to whom her beauty had meant such a lot.

She rushed along the narrow corridor towards their cabin. The wine seemed to have rearranged weight in her, causing a leaning kind of propulsion and making rather a burden of her head. When she paused, she caught the roll of the ocean in her legs and hips. A distant tremor. She rode two seas, the enormous one beneath the boat and a smaller invisible one on which her body or soul was a vessel. She saw suddenly that she'd been waiting, throughout the years of their London life, for sensations this strong. Cramped rented flats and household economies had left her needing euphoria. She wouldn't have admitted it.

The door of their cabin. Could he be waiting up? She entered.

It was dark. A pity he wouldn't see the girlish contrast in her skin between rose and ivory, her adventurous eye. She moved blindly in the tight space, blundering mutedly out of her shoes. Smiling, she reflected, Marriage is a straitjacket, but who'd be free? She shed her shawl and stood in the satiny puddle of it, unfastening her dress. An awareness growing from the soles of her newly unshod feet, a diffuse goldenness. She distinguished his slender shape. Long flanks and bent knees: he lay on one side like a boy. She'd slip into the sweet conspiracy of conjugal repose, and at some juncture they might even awaken seeking one another. She could have been passionate that night.

But his breathing was not audible. He was *too* silent. A foot shifted. 'Hello, darling,' he drawled, utterly awake, as she jumped. 'Have a nice time?'

In her confusion she opened a cupboard and her hands struck against a hard, complicated object, long and repetitive, and full of empty space. Ladder. She foundered searching for a black joke about its usefulness on the high seas.

'It wasn't too bad.' The heat was draining from her face—no doubt returning her to plainness.

'You're loving this.'

'What?' she asked, breathless.

'The late nights.' His words were drawn out and sultry. 'All the gaiety.'

She tried to skirt his displeasure. 'Stomach's still bothering you?'

He rolled onto his back, sighing. 'Oh, much the same as before.'

'Shall I fetch you some sodium bicarbonate?' She was vigilant for any sign of an invitation to approach him. In the penumbra she detected none. They were powerless before a surly force.

He only sighed again. After a moment, he said, 'You're doing a splendid job.'

He meant that she was acting and pleased with herself. Not entirely wrong. He could be damnably perceptive, knowing she acted in company to avoid being tongue-tied. What else was she to do? The injustice! She was not unused to him insisting on socialising on his own terms, with a golf club in his hands. And well she knew him depressed and sulky, his needs becoming finicky. But she'd imagined that on this escapade, which *was* his work, he'd be jovial, mock-heroic and cocky. Instead, he appeared not to consider any of it even a little mythic. No, the odd small worlds of ships, the mandatory sociability and the foreign cuisine took a toll on him. The discomforts of travel riled, stupefied him. Well, she too had had to endure. This journey was not what she'd anticipated, either. And she was not the best sailor.

That lurking mechanical smell of ships—a horrid clammy cold—made her as morbid as a dog about to be bathed. She always clung to her bunk with the maudlin misery of seasickness, too like morning sickness, for the first half or so of a sea voyage. Though since she'd overcome the last bout, she'd been, she thought, staunch and valiant.

Her dress fell and she climbed into her bunk in her slip, nostalgic for the nights they had spent headed for South Africa on the *Kildonan Castle*, sleeping unclothed as it crossed the equator, the air whirled by the electric fan. She longed for him to touch her. To come to her, even in anger, so she might vent her own frustration. Being ruthless with each other, they could have found a path back to affection, or new forms of warmth.

'You resent me enjoying myself.'

'Oh, hardly. Let's sleep, shall we? I'm worn out.'

A temper rising. He refused to share her carnival spirits. Her comeliness and the flexible, racy feeling wasted. He'd encouraged her at times to try wine, and now that she had and it flattered her, she might have arrived at a rendezvous point from which her husband had departed, loath to wait. She had already been obliged to recognise that their curiosities rarely met. She'd learned long before how astoundingly little given he was to anything imaginatively daring. But from this time on, it became harder to make their differences into comedy. And in that floating moment—although it would take weeks more until she fully measured it during a Queensland afternoon storm—she perceived a fissure between them. The barrenness of her thwarted desire. A certain lack. Thereafter, the drinking of alcohol would put her in mind of a close and tippy place, like a ship's cabin, as sad and wanton and queasy as an imploding fantasy, as loneliness.

19

SAUDADE

En route for his appointment with Teresa at around ten forty-five the next morning, Saturday, Harry had reached the end of Swan Road, relieved at having got clear of the Hydro without waylaying encounters, when there was Mrs Jackman emerging alone from the Pump Room. Odd that she should be taking the waters without her husband. You always saw them together. Maybe on account of this, and because he was worked up over the prospect of meeting Teresa and telling her about Valeria, as well as hopefully learning something of her feelings for the Colonel, it had taken him a moment to place the older woman. Her face was already fixed on his and blossomed in a smile before he'd entirely made sense of it.

'Harry. What luck. I've been wanting a private word with you on the subject of Teresa.'

'Oh?' he said, as if he were not racing towards the very woman.

'I'm worried about her. I don't know if you've noticed, but she seems rather up and down. I don't mean to pry but I suppose I can't help seeing my daughter, Jane, in her. Jane lost a child, too, you know. It's the worst thing imaginable. They can appear perfectly well and not be well at all.'

He couldn't doubt her sincerity. The Jackmans remained convinced of Teresa's fabricated story. The comments at dinner about the missing lady novelist had been innocent chatter. Mrs Jackman drew nearer, bringing draped about her a soft old woman's scent that he found not distasteful but mournful. He wondered if Mr Jackman smelled it, or if *his* stole of age prevented him from noticing. Would you be aware that a fragrance of waning life was creeping into your habitual odour? Into your wife's? How could the realisation be borne?

'I saw what it does to a woman. And they might think they're better off on their own—but are they really? Should anyone be too much alone after such a thing?'

'But you can hardly force company on someone. I'm a solitary sort myself, and I must say it's a wily habit to break. People can be surprisingly content, too, left to their own devices.'

Her dubious smile took on something romantic, and suddenly he understood: she was trying to bring him and Teresa together! He felt a little burst of melancholy gratitude.

'Incidentally, Birk Crag was glorious. Oh, beautiful! The moss, the ferns. True, fresh mountain scenery . . . You'd both adore it.'

'I'm glad the outing was a success.'

'You might consider going together.' This was clearly no attempt at vicarious amusement, but a generous impulse. He was nearly inclined to bend and kiss her forehead, as he might have kissed his mother's, if he'd had a different relationship with his mother.

'You know, I like the idea. I'll suggest it to Teresa, if I happen to run into her.'

'Well, I'll leave you to your assignation,' she said, her expression telling him she knew he'd rather not be frittering away minutes conversing with one distanced from the real business of life.

She was less robust and blithe without Mr Jackman. He hoped they wouldn't die far apart in time.

•

Teresa was seated by a window. She wore a dark blue dress—perhaps purchased in Leeds—that looked fine-woven but warm. A pinkish foulard at her neck. You had to admire her upright carriage that unthinkingly accepted her place in a world of eminently agreeable things. She couldn't have chosen a better locale in which to disappear than Harrogate. She was a natural flowering of its self-pleasuring ambience.

Yet when she said, 'I've taken the liberty of ordering tea and cakes,' the words were unstable and a hello patently absent. 'Is that all right?'

'Cake is always all right.' His voice, too, was high-strung and somewhat breathless from his hurried march up Montpellier Hill. There was low piano music and the warm, heartening smell of good tea and coffee. 'I've seen Mrs Jackman just now. She's mad about Birk Crag and insists we take ourselves there at our soonest convenience.'

'I like the Jackmans. But I'm nervous with everyone.'

She had not looked at him, saying this. His own eyes fell to her hands that she had subdued upon the tabletop, to her gracile wrists.

'I understand. You don't want anyone asking too many questions about South Africa and so on . . .'

'No. That story will fall apart very quickly.' She laughed wearily. 'As stories do.'

He didn't ask what she meant, though he recalled something mentioned in that morning's *Daily Mail*—supposedly quoting her mother-in-law—to the effect that Teresa hadn't been able to complete a novel she was working on because she was mentally unstrung. Their cakes were brought, and he was pleased to see her apply herself to them with her usual enthusiasm for food.

'There was something you were going to tell me,' she reminded him, as if he needed reminding.

He ate a macaroon quickly and coughed. 'I know I said I would. How to come at it . . . in a café, in the light of day? It's not a light matter, you see. I'm afraid it will make you think badly of me.'

'Why should my opinion be important? Who am I? A shade. No one.'

'You're not no one,' he said carefully. And continued, confused, 'You are very far from being no one. Sometimes, travelling, one meets people by chance who one just knows instantly *are* important to one, however ephemeral the encounter.'

'True.'

Their tea arrived, and she poured.

'I failed my wife.'

She waited, but he added nothing.

'What if I were to tell you that I failed my husband, too?'

Tautness between them, the flexed muscle of secrecy, each tipped towards the other, yet pulling back.

'Would you talk to me a little about that? I promise I will try to explain myself, but I'll need some more time. It's harder than I thought.' He saw her considering doubtfully, registering what he was asking—disclosure that he had not yet provided himself. He went further. He pushed her: 'You've run away because he betrayed you?' While she covered her mouth with a serviette, he carried on, 'A sensible course of action, I'm sure.'

A spasmodic twitch of a smile. And then, her face going very neutral, she murmured, 'I know it looks bad and complicated from the newspapers. But that's all twisted. I didn't anticipate . . . In fact, it's quite simple.' Her hand fluttered in front of her face, and returned to the table. 'Yes, he betrayed me and I had to show him what he's done.'

Harry nodded. Her hand rose again fussily, as if to check her lips for crumbs. He sipped tea and scalded his tongue. She was now cutting a slice of strawberry sponge cake into segments.

'He doesn't realise. He can be such a boy.'

'I see.' He felt a sick sort of exhilaration. He glanced around the café. No one appeared to be paying them any special attention. Why should they? There was no reason to think that a missing novelist, maybe the most notorious woman in the country at that moment, was in their midst. All that would be observed, looking at Harry and Teresa, would be—what? The two of them would not look easy enough together for a married couple, or as hardened in uneasiness. Would their laboured exchange seem that of new lovers? He found in himself a perverse desire to draw attention, for what was occurring between him and Teresa to *exist* in the eyes of the world, because that might have made it less uncertain.

'He's asked for a divorce. He thinks it's that easy—snap your fingers and it's done. Fifteen years of life razed.'

'Ah.' He was inspirited by the word *divorce*, but disturbed by the tight cadence of her speech. It was vital he take the right tone. He'd have given a lot to be allowed to hold and quieten her hand, to fondle her wrist.

Having just bitten into a wedge of cake, she said through a screen of fingers, 'I threw a teapot at him.' She appeared to swallow with difficulty. 'The torte is excellent.'

'Did it hit him?'

She looked startled. Then they began to snicker, a naughty, lovely bridge of sound, feral notes in it that didn't belong to gaiety.

'No.'

Laughter abandoned them, and he asked, as insipidly as he could, 'Who's the other woman?'

'A friend of friends. A golfer.' She smiled caustically.

'Oh, for heaven's sake. And very young, I presume?'

'*Mais bien sûr.*'

'Won't you be so much better off without him?'

The extent of this miscalculation was immediately obvious. Her face fell from humour into the innocence of shock, a white wall. She forgot her cake.

So she hadn't run to escape him—but to bring him back. The cake plates had a look of ruin to them.

'You still love him?' Harry asked after a moment.

As if this made everything painfully evident: 'He's my husband.'

Her plummy accent that he'd somehow forgotten had come into relief with this declaration, obscurely impenetrable. He struggled not to be combative. 'You say you've failed him. But isn't it he who's failed you?' His smile felt sorrowful even as he tried to make it innocuous.

She shook her head wilfully. They had both lost their appetite. The cosy café had turned claustrophobic. Why had she kissed him? What had that signified? He remembered what Dickens had said about the freakishness of Harrogate and the lives lived there.

'Could we walk?'

She assented, and he saw to the bill while she stared out of the windows. He feared that the confidences were over.

They didn't speak again until they'd been strolling for some minutes by the stream in Valley Gardens. They were vaguely following the noble, leisurely progress of a swan. What an improbably graceful creature a swan is, he thought. You wouldn't reckon it would survive much longer than a flower. The sun had presented itself, brilliant and quite searing, as winter sun could abruptly be on occasion. He was almost able to forget the quirky situation and pretend they were sweethearts, for a minute or two.

'I left him alone too much. You see, my mother died and I couldn't think. I was at rather a low point. I was trying to get everything organised at Ashfield, all her things. My God, the endless furniture, the musty rooms, the pictures, photographs, letters, piles of papers done up in ribbons . . . drawers and boxes . . . You don't realise, all the drawers and boxes that go into a life. The weight of it. But I should have been at Sunningdale.' She gave him a somehow ferocious glance.

'Shouldn't *he* have been with *you*? Standing by you through all that?'

'No, you don't understand. He's never been good with suffering. Any kind of suffering, sickness, sadness. I knew that perfectly well. But I couldn't *remember*, I couldn't see for grief. I was blind with it, mucky, tacky—I positively *stank* of grief. That's how I failed him.' Her words were surprisingly acidic, self-hating.

He couldn't stop himself. He took her elbow and held it tightly. 'I do understand.'

A fleeting sense of her leaning into him, but just then the saxophonist from the Hydro Boys passed them, close enough for Harry to find the pinkish-white hue of his skin quite boyish in daylight. The saxophonist saw and recognised them, and made only an ironical little gesture at his hat, his usual stagy chumminess evaporated. He suspected her? Harry released Teresa at once.

'The saxophonist,' he breathed.

'Seemed a bit queer,' she said in an undertone.

'Yes, I don't like it.' They were gazing around them now and, picking up their pace, they moved towards Bogs Field. 'We probably shouldn't be seen together too much. You know, in case. In case they discover . . .'

'You don't think they will, do you? The papers have to quieten down. Anyway, he'll come for me soon.' The Colonel. 'Look.'

She'd taken a copy of *The Times* from her bag and was offering him a page from it. It took Harry a moment. *Friends of Teresa Neele, please direct themselves* . . . She was hoping to convey a backstairs message with this? For the first time, it truly occurred to him to wonder about the balance of her mind.

'How will he know this is you?' he challenged.

'It's *her* name—Neele. The golfer's.'

'Ah.' So she'd taken her rival's name as pseudonym. An odd transposition—with revenge as its motive? Or was there only a sad, private kind of violence in it? He sneaked a look at her face. She was studying the peaty, spongy ground. The small, triangular field they were standing in was dotted with scores of mineral springs marked with iron and stone lids. 'You really think he'll decipher this?'

'He has to. All wells, are they?'

In a flash he decided that if she was mad, it was simply the ordinary madness of heartbreak. He despised the man who had inflicted it on her. 'I take it. What a naturally *opulent* area this is. Liquid wealth in its earth. Seems rather arbitrary, the way such riches are distributed, even unfair.'

'Maybe. But you have to know to look for them, and be very organised and professional in how you use them.'

The Quality's style of thinking, he mused. Or the Successful Person's.

She went on, almost babbling, 'Wouldn't it be nice to live underground? Be like a badger, the king of your own labyrinth? The dark would be customary. It'd never matter how you looked. You could get as fat as you liked. There'd be no newspapers. You'd miss the crosswords, but you might be a simpleton anyway. Things like the opinions of others wouldn't worry you.'

Her voice had turned plaintive, and he'd have gladly taken her far away from the aboveground world of newspapers and human judgement, if he could have. 'Will you satisfy Mrs Jackman and let me accompany you to Birk Crag tomorrow, for some fresh air? It really might be good for you to avoid the hotel a little, you know.'

She hesitated.

'Until he comes for you,' Harry added, biting the inside of his cheek until the pain brought a queer answering convulsion in his groin.

'It couldn't hurt, could it?' she seemed to ask herself.

Perhaps she was already sorry for the titbits of information she had tossed to him that day, a few relics from her former life. He was wolfish for these, while wanting her to remain safely hidden from others. He wished he knew more and could be confident that she wouldn't try to hide in the conclusive way.

She met his eyes. 'What you had intended to tell me . . . you'll get to that? Because today I find that I have been the one unburdening herself.'

'Yes, I promise. It might take me a while to work up to it, but I will.'

She continued to observe him. 'It's good to have a friend.'

Again, this sounded like a question. He weighed the word *friend* and found it light. Could she truly still love the Colonel? She was definitely right to doubt that Harry could be a friend to her. He wasn't sure of it himself. He agreed with her misgivings: the threat embedded in any bond between them was clear. Yet he was intensely drawn to her. 'Meet here at lunchtime? One thirty, say? I could bring a picnic.'

'*I* will bring the picnic,' she said, showing that she was not conceding to him and remained on her guard.

'Capital. You should go on ahead now. We shouldn't arrive at the Hydro together.'

He watched her leave the gardens. As she did her head tilted back and he interpreted this as an admiring appraisal of the Grand Hotel, surely the town's most sumptuous lodgings. She would fantasise, he imagined, about staying there, seeing herself fulfilled in that deluxe turreted vision, glamorously sated, in the same way he fantasised about the sombre quietude he'd enjoy as an inmate of the Bath Hospital—also, admittedly, a magnificent structure—further along the road. How laughably different they were, despite his inherited money and passably English accent.

He lingered awhile on the marshy ground, taking what he could from the winter sun while it lasted, knowing now with certainty what he'd as good as known since he'd met Teresa: his feelings for her were doomed. Perhaps it was the transient heat that brought back a memory of the immense summer sky above his parents' farm. More than usual, he felt deracinated, an exile.

•

He dined late, at ten, to avoid Teresa and the Jackmans. After, he took himself to the smoking room. The Russian was there alone, the air possessed by cigar smoke like a pungent, virtually material spirit. Harry considered about-facing and politeness be damned, but the Russian's meditative expression stopped him. Incongruous—however, who was Harry to tell what in that face was in tune? He was hardly even acquainted with the man.

The Russian nodded as if welcoming the intrusion and said, not at all unctuously, but rather forlornly, 'I'm leaving in a few days.'

Harry guessed that he'd hoped for an adventure he'd not found. He sat in the armchair opposite the Russian's—a hefty, well-sprung thing—and set about preparing a pipe of cherry tobacco. Valeria had claimed to like the smell of it on his clothes. She had inhaled these sometimes after he'd undressed and hung them up, reminding him of his family's blond mutt, Roger, who given half a chance would bury his head in dropped items of their underwear. There had seemed in the dog's obsession to be a profound attachment to the family combined with an instinctive animal enjoyment, an incentive somewhere between sentiment and sex. It had caused uncomfortable giggles in the household, where neither senti-ment nor sex, nor even laughter, were really acknowledged. Valeria's habit had touched and aroused him.

'Back to Russia?'

'Oh no.' He smiled. 'Back to Knightsbridge.'

Harry wondered if he'd fled the revolution, and if life seemed pale to him here at this distance from his more vibrant homeland. Or did he feel calmer, more at ease? It was companionable to be sitting smoking together. In this setting the Russian's poise—or charisma, or whatever it was—wasn't threatening. He seemed to embody that French concept of being well in one's skin, contentedly, fully occupying one's body. Harry realised he'd not been so relaxed in another person's presence in some time. They were, after all, he discovered himself thinking, fellow émigrés, as well as sharing an appreciation of Teresa's magnetism. That brio behind frosted glass.

'I'm Australian.'

'Ah,' the other man reacted simply, without remarking on any accent or outlandish fauna. Harry did not ask about Russia or his reasons for leaving it, either. That was his business. After a while, into the conversational spaciousness that had formed and which now appeared to permit them to speak frankly, the Russian said, 'Sometimes I get homesick, or—the Portuguese have a term, *saudade*. It can refer, I believe, to missing a place, but also just to nostalgia, to longing *tout court*. To something perhaps less precise, more fundamental than wishing you were somewhere in particular. A pretty, haunting word.'

'You're a linguist.'

Yes, why shouldn't he be a man of culture and feeling? Why should he have to be dangerously seductive, fascinatingly repulsive, louche? He wasn't really a rival. Harry didn't have to dislike him or find evidence of baseness in his words and physiognomy, making him into the slightest fiction of a fellow, a foreign villain such as might machinate in one of Teresa's books. *They* were jaunty dreams, and what Harry was living now did have something of the unanchored bizarreness of a dream—but also the murkiness that tailed waking reality.

'*Vous parlez français, alors?*' Harry was always willing to have a shot at translating himself into this language.

'*Naturellement.*'

They chatted amiably for a quarter of an hour or so more. Harry noticed, with mild angst, what possibly were widening gaps in his French vocabulary, dwindling resources. It occurred to him that one might apprehend something similar on entering the new mental landscape of one's dotage. Eventually, he left his companion to go for a breath of night air.

Hearing Yorkshire voices coming from the drive that didn't strike him as belonging to guests, he moved into the shadows of a tree. A moment of eavesdropping confirmed that he'd surprised a conversation between the saxophonist and the drummer. They were a little way from the front entrance, smoking. Harry recalled the saxophonist's wry expression as he'd avoided raising his hat in Valley Gardens, and he intuited, feeling a cold inevitability, what they were talking about. Teresa.

'Wouldn't do that for a poor woman, would they?' the drummer said. 'They just wouldn't. Would they look like that for you or me?'

'No,' agreed the saxophonist.

They meant mount such an expensive and thorough search. Make such a fuss.

'Yours.' The drummer—older, shorter, and thicker in the waist—handed over what must have been the saxophonist's share of their evening's wage.

'Thanks. I'll be off to get some petrol for my bike. Wouldn't fancy walking home.'

It had indeed grown cold and breezy. Harry tried to imagine what it was like for such a young man to ride his motorbike through winter nights to a posh establishment where for a few hours he entertained the affluent by making the more responsive tap their feet or dance, before tucking a scarf down into his coat against the wind's whims and climbing back on the motorbike to return to—what sort of home? Listening to the two men, so much more substantial there in the moonlight than himself in the shadows, it seemed to him that since he'd become a widower and ludicrously wealthy, money had been cushioning him with a layer of deadness, like pillows strapped about him. He'd barely had a thought for politics. Of course, some months previously it had been impossible to avoid hearing on the street and in hotel lounges inflamed talk of the General Strike, and being aware of the tides of nervousness and righteous indignation surging through the newspapers, but it had all remained pretty abstract to him, in the way of the plot of an implausible drama. The debate would have been real to these men. He envied them the dignity of their workingmen's contact with life.

'All that money.' They were talking about her again.

He missed something, and then heard from the drummer, 'I'm just saying it's interesting, is all.'

'A coincidence.'

The tone now was knowing, wasn't it? He could under-stand their resentment of the missing woman. How desirable and grotesque, like high fashion, would seem the existence of one like her to them. How vaporous, forbidden. Laughable. Maybe they were right.

He moved along the front of the Hydro until he got to Ripon Road, where he began a night-time walk, knowing it would be a long while before sleep found him. When the entrance to Valley Gardens came into view, he remembered ambling there with Teresa at the speed of a ghosting swan. He continued on, wanting the Stray's open monotony. It was no doubt true that if one of the bandsmen or he himself were to go missing, far less money and effort would be spent on a search. But they'd not become a spectacle as she had, either. A well-to-do female novelist, for all her easy privilege and confidence in her right to live in perfect happiness and style, wasn't allowed to go a little demented from heartache in privacy. She didn't have the privilege of coming apart quietly. And perhaps her type of privilege had been a layer of cushioning that, if anything, encouraged risky naivety, a belief in her entitlement to love and joy, forces over which money's sway was questionable.

His exhalations were visible, rifted escort clouds. He walked faster, blurring streetlamps and the largish moon that sat at the edge of his sight, and wondered if he should move back to Paris—if that would strip the pillows from *him*, help him to really live. Or to come properly, privately apart.

20

TENTH DAY

She was feeling nothing of the neuritis, she realised in the dressing hall at the baths. Moreover, if everything was rather addling, she wasn't on the whole passing an unpleasant time. It had been all right. Indeed, it had been a reviving change from the plain horror of before. A spa town was a fine thing: it was sometimes necessary to be taken care of. And admired. Perhaps the air of sanatorium romance that bathed these places was curative. It certainly affected the imagination, at least of one who already as a girl had been stimulated by the idea of nursing pale languishing men.

She slipped into that peach-house-in-the-summertime heat, passing other robed or towel-draped women adorning deckchairs. The French word for those seats was *trans-atlantiques*. Where were they all headed on this odd ocean liner? The oriental sensation of walking over tiles in bare feet pleased her. She had become an initiate. How beautiful the female shoulder could be, proud and full, marbly. You did *see* why men went silly and primitive over women. (In some way you understood.) Her state of mind was still drawing on the wellspring of the romantic dream and it was a labour to be logical, though she was doing her best to keep her musing light. Her husband had to respond to her message. Nonetheless, she wasn't feeling—she had to acknowledge—like his wife. She had begun to feel like another man's lover. And such excitement had its troubling way of overruling caution.

She was ready for the cold plunge bath. Lovers are audacious, not needing or able to hold themselves back from more extreme experiences. The small pool was at that moment empty. She disrobed.

The metal rail icy to touch. The first step down—and the second. Oh! Feet and ankles crying out. Knees. Skin uncomprehending, lungs registering alarm. Pausing, breathing. Here we go now, move—immobility was thought and suffering.

White-hot ice burn. Gasps. The work of gasping.

And she swam, appalled mind cast off somewhere behind dumb body. A few strokes, turn around, back again.

Harsh purity. Her skin finally opening, as if to seawater, the door to a new compartment of her mind sliding across, she saw her.

The Neele girl.

They've come from lunch at the Savoy and will have drunk wine, because she'll know how to. She likes the taste. She's on a bed in the curtained, nectarine-coloured light of a hotel afternoon. Any shadow in that luxurious hideout is fabulously unreal. Silk bloomers reveal slim golf-adept thighs. Slight silk like something molten washing over the fine-grained young skin. Her small hand on her intact stomach that never had to house a child or comfort itself through the slow going of marriage. Those neat thighs clench and slacken, slacken and clench, a kind of swarthy shine upon them. Her eyes are widening as if in fear as he approaches the bed. Her stifled grin. The shame in it makes him so aware of sensation. His heart is smarting, because when the sex impulse is strong, how can the heart resist the flame? Nerves humming like lies. Their perfection disfigured by abandonment.

He underestimated his wife if he thought she couldn't see the appeal of all this. She was hardly blind to beauty. Hadn't she chosen him?

She had imagined such things before, hadn't ceased imagining them for months—but not like this. Now her point of view was . . . almost conspiratorial. Not quite. However, her jellied understanding was setting. She swam around the tiny pool, a few strokes, turn around, a few strokes, until the cold wasn't cold anymore, just something she was passing through, held up by. There was a pulse in it—her own heart's.

•

Later, Teresa went about the town in a state of anticipation, buying picnic things. Apples. A bottle of cider. Liver pâté. A block of orange cheddar, a wedge of Stilton. A cushiony white loaf of bread. Two sweet buns glossy with sugar glaze, their paper bag almost immediately mottled with oil.

•

'You wouldn't think there'd be any mountain scenery around here,' she said as they were setting out.

'You wouldn't. We'll have to pass through a crevice in the universe. But don't be alarmed. I'm equipped with a guidebook.' His voice was a little unsteady as he added, 'So you're in safe hands. I gather we go down here a bit, and then we'll come to the footpath, see?'

'Oh yes.' Despite glancing at the map, she didn't, really. It was hard to concentrate on it, maybe because the plunge bath had left her elated.

From Bogs Field they made for Cornwall Road.

On the far shore of what seemed a substantial pool of silence, he said, 'Those, I gather, are the Harrogate Corporation's reservoirs. They supply the town.'

'Ah?'

He went on some minutes after, 'Apparently, if the day were clear, we'd see mountains off over there.'

There was nothing to be seen in the distance. It had rained in the early hours of the morning and a light lingering mist veiled any prospect. They laughed sheepishly. It was cold, a fresh Yorkshire cold.

They followed Cornwall Road to the right till they reached the brow of the hill, then turned left onto what they figured must be the footpath leading to the Birk Crag Quarry.

'That range of rock there—or millstone grit, against the side of the hill—is the result of volcanic action,' he said, reading from his guidebook.

She thought he was using it as something of a shield or a diversionary tactic. What had he wanted to tell her? Walking with a person of the opposite sex in a civilised garden full of well-dressed ladies and gentlemen wasn't at all the same as rambling alone together over more open country. True, he had kissed her at the hotel (and she him, astonishingly, something it was better not to think of), where there had been people close by, but outdoors with hardly a soul around they were unable to look one another in the eye. Other than his late wife, Valeria, would he have had much experience of women? Not that *they* were courting, of course. What was this? Nothing. She didn't even answer to her name here.

'*Birk* is birch, you know, in Scottish.'

'Oh? I met my husband at a ball near Exeter. We danced. He impertinently insisted I cut some of the other men from my dance card in order to dance with him twice more.' Why discuss him? 'The evening ended and I thought that was the end of that. I was, after all, engaged to another boy at the time.'

'You were? Be careful of the path—it's muddy in places. Then what happened?'

The twang of curiosity in his voice. So congenial to inspire interest, to have a man intent on tunnelling with a lamp into the dark of your mind. 'He came to Ashfield on his motorbike. I wasn't at home when he called. I was across at a neighbour's house, dancing again.'

'You were quite the dancer.'

'I was. A tango, if memory serves me.'

'One last tango . . .'

'Yes, something like that. Hard not to wonder what would have happened if one had gone on dancing. But that's not possible, is it? One gets older and at some point the dancing stops.'

'Hmm. *I* never really danced—as you no doubt concluded from my recent performances. Of course you mean settle down, put away childish things, and so on. And in that sense, maybe I never did stop dancing. I've never been much good at feeling like an adult. To my dishonour.'

She glanced at him. 'Nor I. Though you do find yourself having to accept being bored a lot.'

She may have reddened. Should she have been talking so? Was Harry her ally? Chatting while moving through the trees—right now, some lithe, glitteringly ashen birches—had the fatalism of sleepwalking. Hearing herself speak of her other life terrified and relieved her. They walked side by side, one of them sometimes passing ahead if the way narrowed. When it was his turn, she had the opportunity to observe his slenderness and slightly asymmetrical gait, one arm around the parcel of their picnic provisions and the fingers of the other cradling the guidebook.

'How swiftly the foliage changes,' he commented. 'Notice all these ferns suddenly, and the heath and gorse.'

There was a sound of falling water, and soon they saw a small waterfall coursing down the side of the ridge to their left. The gentleness of their fluid progress through the wood and Harry's reserve, now that he had finally stopped referring to the guidebook, were working on her. She wanted to ask him what it was that he had promised to tell her, but she sensed it growing in him. Meanwhile, the agreeable disorientation of having him for a confidant was tempting. 'You know I'm a writer, I think. Not a renowned one—not very—but I've done some little things.' He wouldn't have read anything of hers, would he?

He stared ahead. 'Yes.'

'Well, you asked how I failed my husband. It was in that area, too. I didn't just neglect him after my mother died—but also before, by writing. To write you have to leave people alone, you see. Absent yourself. And even when you're in company again afterwards you're different, no doubt quite unsatisfactory as a social creature. A bit exalted in an inward, probably very irritating way. Or thoroughly tired and cross. Absolutely beaten, at times.'

'I think I can imagine.' They were ascending, the gradient increasing quite rapidly. Perhaps both taking account of this at once, they gazed down into the valley. He was smiling ambiguously. 'But surely he absented himself from you every day, when he took himself off to work in the City? Surely on occasion he returned weary and peeved?'

'Oh, often. But men are excused for being like that, aren't they? We don't expect them to be constantly willing and sweet. Or even to be all that *with* you, when they are with you. In any case, he was working to maintain his wife and household. I was entertaining myself.'

'Not solely. Your books entertain others. They'd make some money, too?'

Having to accept this made her smile. 'I bought a Morris Cowley. It was one of the most exciting things that has ever happened to me. Like growing marvellous metal wings.'

'There, you see. You were earning.'

'You know, the writing was something to do in my wifely solitude and I don't know if I could—or should—have avoided it. I don't think I am truly remorseful about it.'

'I take off my hat to you. For a while, in my foolhardy youth, I thought I'd be a writer. In France. I fancied the idea of it. The problem was that I turned out to be quite good at avoiding actually doing it.'

'You were lucky, I'm sure. Yes, it's wonderful fun for a few seconds here and there—like driving a Morris Cowley. You career along through picturesque countryside. Mostly, though, you're a wretched foot passenger trudging in inferior shoes through indifferent scenery. And it's mizzling. For hours and hours on end. The next day you'll have to set off again. The tedium deranges you.' She reached out to caress the trunk of a birch, her hand falling short of it. 'One day you might even discover you haven't the slightest notion of where you are. You recognise nothing, and you can't walk anymore. You have no legs.'

'You've felt that?'

'Yes. I'm legless at present.' She could tell that her attempt at a smile was failing. 'I'll probably never publish another word. There's a trifle I was working on, but I can't go on with it. I can't.'

'Would you hate it if I asked what it's about?'

'Yes. The answers always sound so stupid. It was about a woman having a spot of bad luck on the *train bleu*.'

'She was going to Nice!'

'Alas, she never arrived. She died. I despise everything about it. It fills me with pure revulsion. Can't we talk about something else?'

'Of course. I'm sorry. Insensitive of me to bring it up.'

'Most. But it's my fault for telling you things. I'm afraid it's rather easy to talk to you. You're dangerous.'

'I am?' He turned towards the valley, and when he faced her again she caught another ambivalent half-smile. 'Mrs J was right. It's very lovely here.'

'Proper countryside.'

'You're wrong about one thing.'

'Hmm?'

'You *are* a famous writer. You've become one over the last week.'

She stopped walking. He appeared to wish he could take the words back. She didn't know what her face showed but she gathered it alarmed him. The path rose ruggedly before them. The crag they were climbing towards was an almost perpendicular precipice, possibly one hundred and fifty feet high. Her light mood had knocked into foreboding, and mud's slippery possibilities started to concern her.

'We don't have to go up to the highest point.' His tone implied he thought it better they not do so.

'It's all right.' She entreated herself to keep her eyes on the ground.

'Take my arm, if you need it.'

'I'm all right.'

Presently, coming to the summit, they stood on a projecting rock covered with hoary lichen and searched for a view the guidebook had promised. Still not possible to see very far. In place of a view, a pleasant if vague impression of misted woods falling away towards other even hazier woods and farmland. She held her breath, listening, distinguishing the sedative strains of streaming water.

'How secluded and serene,' she said. 'I love this sort of position, high above water. From the road outside Ashfield, where I grew up, you could see the sea in the distance, down below. You get used to that. It ruins you. I've started to think that coming from Torquay on its seven hills is probably a curse for those of us who leave, because you expect you'll always be gazing at wonders from lofty vantage points, everything laid out before you. You can't imagine sameness. There, if you tire of one particular view, there are other hills to explore. It must make you—must have made me, at least—insufferably restless.'

'This is perhaps not so grand as Torquay, but it is very pretty in a tucked-away fashion.'

She agreed. Approaching the edge, she peered down.

'Don't stand too close,' he said.

She laughed and, without thinking, responded, 'Do you think I mean for this to be my end?'

He moved towards her rapidly. His eyes spooked her.

'I'd likely make a bosh of it and only break a few bones.' She tried to laugh again.

Before she could digest what was occurring, he had taken hold of her shoulders, with considerable strength. She heard the slap of his guidebook against the rock, the chink of the cider bottle and its brief rolling, the softer papery percussion of the other picnic things falling. 'How can you joke like that?' he almost shouted.

'What are you doing? Ouch!'

'What am *I* doing?' he asked, more quietly but with a sleepwalker's face—as if he were there and not there, only watching persuasive happenings unspool in his imagination.

A moment of truth had arrived. She flicked her head. 'If a body was found down there, it would be hard to know if there'd been any intention behind the fall, wouldn't it?' His grip tightened and her stomach flooded with fright. 'How easy it would be for you to throw me over.'

'Or for you to throw yourself.'

Attempting to wrench free, she pulled back as violently as she could. He held fast, but half stumbled forward. She endeavoured to take advantage of his loss of balance by raising her hands to his chest and shoving. Yet he was firmer on his feet now and they stayed locked in a strained embrace, a grim skirmish of a dance that seemed to have no conclusion.

In their struggle they had neared the rim of the rocky perch. She made the mistake of looking over her shoulder— the feeling of a great drop.

'No, Teresa,' he was saying. 'You don't understand . . .'

Vertigo.

She closed her eyes against the dizziness, seeing an alternative landscape: a small, profoundly still lake, sheltering box trees, dark intricate roots. The end point—was this it?

He had lifted her. She was cognisant of steps, the strange magic of moving as one, their volumes combined into a dual human. Like Harry, she was there and not. Her body had in some fashion been curtained off from her mind.

But he stopped walking. And, 'No!' she cried, thrashing.

His arms loosened, and she slid or fell out of them. She was in a crouch, rock beneath her. She dragged herself backwards until a little distance separated them.

He too dropped to sit on his haunches, and they regarded one another, animals poised mid-fight.

Her dizziness was subsiding, her mind returning to fully occupy the present. 'What don't I understand, Harry?'

'Teresa, do you think I could *hurt* you? That I . . .' His voice was low and clogged with emotion.

Her own breathing was jagged. She remembered her shoulders in his hands. 'Harry, you must tell me. Now!'

21

WHAT HARRY TOLD TERESA

It was at a quarter to seven on a snowy Friday evening in 1923 that he arrived home from work to find the sofa empty of Valeria. Flash lay there alone, wound tight and unresponsive. This was a sight he'd looked forward to, yearning for an end to his wife's lassitude, but found jarring, encountering it in reality. In the bedroom he was happy to see the shape of her in their bed, because she hadn't slept in it with him for weeks.

He loosened his tie and came to sit gently beside her, not yet realising that something had spoiled the air in the room. He had no inkling of catastrophe.

But it was there in their bed that, judging from the temperature and rigidity of her—of what remained—she had died some hours before.

On the bedside table were boxes of Veronal cachets, to which they both had recourse every so often when unable to sleep. However, this number of cachets, with their insides removed, was unreasonable. Inconceivable.

Deranged.

Harry stood up quickly. Sat down. He touched her, her face. He covered his mouth. Took in his hands the weight of her lifeless head.

Completely dumbfounded that all her sighs and gasps, disjointed stories and half-sentences, the shadows he'd contented himself to know from the corner of his eye, the entire universe of her, should have been extinguished.

He was babbling, apparently. Darling, *amore*, *bambina*, baby, my darling, sweetheart, dear heart, oh God, *amore*, love, Valeria.

Any name for her rang hollow. Any name for what she was—had been—to him was inadequate for such total feeling.

He looked for, but did not find, a note.

Briskly he went to the kitchen as though he might happen on a solution to the problem there. He picked up a tea towel and, after a hesitation, abandoned it. He retched a little. He returned to their bedroom.

Just *the* bedroom.

He recognised something in his confusion. He remembered waking as a very young child from an enforced nap, his mind bleary, time in disarray. A piece of the day, of the life he might have known, had been subtracted without his permission. What he was standing on had moved. Possibly nothing was trustworthy any longer. At around the same age he had sat marooned on a bed beneath a tented blanket, reflecting that death must have been like that blank blackness.

He had had—amazing luck—ten years with Valeria.

Outrage.

Harry searched again, still without success, for a note addressed to himself, an explanatory note. Its absence was conspicuous and unthinkably callous. Diabolical, this doubled silence.

•

During that depraved dilated night, the face of Giacomo Petri, Valeria's first lover, came before him as he'd seen it in the last moments at the Caffè degli Specchi, after she ended her liaison with him. Harry's sympathy for the man had always been theoretical, and it remained so. No, he did not exactly feel kinship with Giacomo, but he did give him a good deal of thought when he too learned what it was to lose her.

In a windy square, telling Harry why she wanted to be done with Giacomo, she had said, 'Because I'm not happy, of course.'

How so, 'of course'?

Had she been warning him, right at the beginning, that for her happiness was unsustainable, impossible? An unworkable ideal, a flawed proposition. A faulty promise.

22

TENTH DAY, AFTERNOON

She was absorbed as he told her about the night he had returned home to find that his wife had suicided. Much of the fear stirred in her vanished. When he reached Valeria in bed, she had seen her mother, also, expiring in the bed at her sister's house—a particular death having a way of sponging up the rank overflow of others. She thought of Mummy wondering whether her youngest daughter, still on the train from Manchester, would arrive in time, and later understanding she couldn't wait for her. Just as Valeria had decided she could not wait for Harry to come home *that* night, nor ever again face a night, nor the wait for anyone. Both women had finished with waiting. She'd perhaps have wept if she'd been alone.

Harry looked spent and glazed. It was safer not to go to him.

'I'm sorry,' she said.

'Thank you,' he replied. 'And I'm sorry for frightening you before. I . . .'

They added nothing for several minutes.

'You thought I was like her? That I'd do what she did?'

'I was afraid of that.'

He considered her interrogatingly, but she only shook her head slightly. 'Why? Why did Valeria . . . ?'

He raised his shoulders, and sighed when they lowered. 'Why indeed? Because I failed her, I expect. I certainly couldn't make her want to live.'

'Will you let me look at the view now? I promise . . .'

He hung his head. 'Yes.'

Near the edge, though not too near, she gazed down. After a moment the surroundings appeared to come closer, as if they'd been lurking back and abruptly stepped forward. In gaps between the alders, ferns and bracken were milky flashes of the small brook they could hear. There it was, travelling irrepressibly along the bottom of the glen, around the boulders that littered its bed. Lichen lying ghostly over rocks. Moss like sections of delicate Turkey carpets. Green! So unadulterated it poked at the eye—had it been a flavour it would have been acerbic, exhilarating. The air, too, became an insistent pressure against the skin, cold and very clean. Mountain air, old-world. Holly, white thorn, ashes, oaks, hazels. The birdsong, ringing within a parcel of crystalline silence, made her think of flutes played inside a church. What a life force there was in that mountain glen. It passed through her, subtle but clear and relentless. She had a sense, almost, of resurrection. She was happy then to be in that place in that instant that was so whole.

'I'm happy.'

'What did you say?'

She walked back to Harry, who had remained sitting where he had told his story. She was still wary, but mainly because of her desire for him. She did not say again that she was happy, or touch his shoulder, as she might have done. 'Let's go down somewhere nice and low and have what we can salvage of our picnic.'

They descended the way they had come. She was now unafraid of slipping.

Harry remarked, 'I sometimes wondered, not very often, if Valeria thought of other men. Married men, I think, tend not to imagine such things about their wives. Maybe we should. It might help us to see the other person better. Marriage can make you invisible to each other.'

'Yes. And I know what you mean—some men don't appear to imagine much at all.'

'Were *you* attracted to other men?'

She wouldn't look at him. 'It's a writer's business to picture alternatives.'

They settled on a pair of large broad rocks, and ate nearly without conversation. The Stilton was very nice, and the cheddar and pâté divine, earthy and sharp. Buns simple and enjoyable.

As they were munching apples and passing the bottle of cider back and forth, he said, 'Can't we play that we're going to send everything to the devil and go and live in Nice?'

'Together?' she enquired innocently. 'In the same house?' The horror of what he had evoked earlier seemed to push them into a light, slightly absurd tenor. It was the only reaction to it they could find. Grief made logic convulse.

'Only if you wanted. We could also be neighbours, if you'd prefer—or think it more the decent thing.'

'One of the qualities of the French is that they appear less preoccupied with decency than we are.' She was flushing.

'And that is very pleasant.' He gave her an open, delightful smile, and then looked away.

She stood and brushed off her skirt. He stood, too.

'Our home in Nice,' he went on. 'How shall it be?'

She composed a thoughtful face and they resumed walking. 'Of course, we must have a sea view. And a terrace overlooking it where we'll eat enormous resplendent meals.'

'Yes, won't we? What do you say to a little wrought-iron balcony, also? That could be charming, *n'est-ce pas?*'

'*Tout à fait.* Maybe I could learn to drink, at least champagne.'

'I'll do my very best to teach you.'

'We'll have an excellent French maid or two. Not too pretty. Old and haggard.' The shared pipe dream was intoxicating.

He hesitated. 'We could have Venus herself for a maid in our house in Nice and I'd be entirely indifferent to her charms.'

She sniggered. 'You wouldn't be.'

'I would. On my honour.'

'I'll hold you to that.'

'Please do.'

He tossed her a lasso of a look, from which she slid free, with some awkwardness, continuing, 'We won't welcome into our home anyone who likes golf.'

'That goes without saying. They'll be barred. Or we'll have a legend over the door to frighten them away: Abandon all hope golf players who enter here.'

She just wanted to think of fun. 'You realise that with our high-toned life we'll need plenty of money?'

'Well, there's my fortune,' he said.

'You know, I think I *could* earn my living,' she boasted on a little wave of jubilation, 'maybe even well, if I really set my mind to it.' For now, no need to consider never publishing again, having no legs to walk on, et cetera. The virtue of fantasies naturally being that disappointment and dullness didn't have to reside within them. They were making a splendid vision.

'I doubt it not. You'll make a princely living. When we first arrive in Nice, we can stay at the Negresco, while hunting for our perfect abode. I met my employer, Mr Ainsworth, there. In 1913. I associate that night with the lightness of things before the war. An ambience—balmy and frivolous—in which anything seemed possible.' He paused, and added quietly, 'It was just youth, too, I suppose. That right to frivolity . . . Not that I ever particularly felt I possessed it.'

Returning to a road full of people, motorcars and carriages was discordant. The day faded. They were like children who, having been left to their own devices playing at dress-ups, must take off the bright finery and face sullen adults. They concurred that in the interests of discretion they wouldn't dine together. Only Teresa would eat with the Jackmans. Passing the Grand Hotel, they nodded to a regally stout old lady being towed along by a bent-backed bath-chair man. Teresa tried not to think of the other Grand, where she had spent her wedding night.

'We'll meet tomorrow?' Harry enquired.

She nodded. She'd lost all judgement concerning her conduct with him, and though she did not know what they were to one another, she was inclined to go on feeling like a lover. 'Could we listen to the chamber ensemble together at the baths?'

'Mightn't it be injudicious—at this stage of affairs—to meet somewhere so public? How about the gardens opposite the Imperial Café? If we proceeded on across the Stray, we'd hopefully have some privacy.'

'Yes, of course. All right. Three o'clock?'

'I'll be looking forward to it. We can make further plans for Nice.'

She smiled and without further rejoinder hurried away from him. Her shoes were rimmed with the dark mud that appeared to ooze everywhere from the peaty northern earth.

23

TENTH DAY, EVENING

The Jackmans lamented Harry's absence and the headache Teresa claimed had obliged him to dine in his room. When she reported her impressions of Birk Crag, a hopeful glow came to Mrs Jackman's cheeks. Teresa had determined not to dilate on the excursion, but it was tempting to gush over the grace of that place. She noted a warning of inexplicable tearfulness, warmth and constriction, in her sinuses and throat. The roast pheasant was tender and she tried to engulf her mind in that savoury submission to her teeth.

'I don't suppose you'd find such country in South Africa?' Mr Jackman asked.

Mrs Jackman came to her aid. 'I think that in the matter of beauty—true beauty—no style of nature, no particular lovely place can be said to be superior to any other.'

'Well said, my dear.'

The Hydro Boys weren't playing that evening, and they were all intent on retiring early. By nine thirty they'd said their goodnights. Teresa checked with the night porter for letters. Not one.

About to mount the stairs, she was startled by a hand on her elbow. Recalling the fine roots of an elegant dwarf tree. Mrs Jackman. She was, Teresa thought, prettily old.

'It never seems right to bring this up before the men,' Mrs Jackman murmured. 'But I've been wanting to say . . .'

Teresa nodded, light-headed. There it was: she was discovered.

'About your little daughter you lost.'

'Ah. Yes.'

'I don't speak exactly from my own experience—still, I observed it with *my* daughter.' They moved to one side to let a young man pass. Mrs Jackman gazed at him, then appeared to make an effort to focus and brighten. 'You won't be as you were before, yet you will carry on. And you must remember that this is the case for us all, to a lesser extent. I mean, every day something is lost and we're a little changed, are we not? And onward we go. But destiny might reserve any number of surprises for us. New loves, even . . .'

Teresa assented dumbly. Though she was safe, her heart remained flustered. She was praying that Mrs Jackman, who was taking such an interest in her happiness, would never find out she'd lied to her, to them, that she wasn't the woman she masqueraded as. 'I'm terribly sorry for your daughter's loss. And for yours. It must have been dreadful. Is it a happy marriage, your daughter's? Impertinent question, I know.'

Mrs Jackman had lowered her eyes to the circular designs of the oriental rug they stood on, or to those of her memories. She looked up. 'Peaceful,' she replied, after a moment. 'Quite peaceful.'

They nodded at one another with a gravity that struck Teresa as feminine. On impulse, she pressed Mrs Jackman's small venerable hand and found both of hers clasped.

'Sleep well, my dear,' Mrs Jackman entreated her.

This brief exchange transformed her mood. Her tread was heavy as she ascended the stairs. She returned to her room feeling—not a wife, no, not that. But a mother.

Not exactly a mother. Certainly not a contented one. And yet, a mother.

She turned her key and entered the room in darkness. She stealthily approached the bedside table. She picked up a framed boyish photograph of a little girl that sat behind the barricade of books, barely able to distinguish it by the light journeying up through the undrawn curtains of the windows on the ground floor.

Just as her husband was not dead, nor was her daughter. Beautiful. Her girl.

With Mummy there had been meetings of a kind in a lush place of the imagination. She'd assumed she'd share similar encounters with her own daughter. Who, however, had turned out like her husband. Not much given to imagining. Or Teresa had not known how to encourage it in her—really not having expected any special effort would be required. Mother and daughter were too unalike for their love to be altogether natural. Even her guilt was sporadic and incomplete. She could never entirely get over the sense that *she* was the injured, ill-used party. The child was supposed to have been a miraculous gift, a great gladness. Difficult not to blame her, being honest, for the loss of youth and lightness.

When it was too late, after the interminable sick fatness and the bloody violence, you were shocked to see you'd signed a contract locking you in to mortal time. As she has begun today, I will end one day—quite so. (Was *she* the Gun Man, a pistol, a time bomb folded into the womb?) And with the same fatal gesture, you'd ceased to be the heroine of events in favour of a rather pathetic role as a disoriented survivor and a weary helpmeet. Your own childlike pleasure in life would not come so easily now. How hard you'd fight for it. Reality had firmed up, because indulging in fantasy, at least in the company of a child who didn't, was awkward. The ongoing war of ensuring you were left properly alone! To lose the command of one's solitude, the free run of one's inner realm . . . What a price. There was endless fancywork of words and sentimentality seeking to embellish motherhood.

But on most days, frankly, it was tatty and depleting. Being of service. Cumbersome slabs of boredom.

She abandoned the photograph and closed the curtains. Stumbling a little, she went over to turn up the lights. She took off her shoes, undressed down to her petticoat, in which she stood before the glass. Despite being thinner than she'd been for a long time, her figure nonetheless continued to suggest dumpiness. Mummy had berated herself for this and, incredibly, it had happened to her, also. The child had turned her into a frump of a matron. Just when she was coming through all the confusion, the discomforts, humiliations and suffering, the feeling so much an *animal*, she realised she'd produced a startlingly beautiful child—but this beauty had been in exchange for her own.

She'd kept waiting to see herself slender, if not emaciated, in the weeks after the child's arrival. She'd felt so hollowed by the shocking ejection, yet her figure appeared to have coarsened indefinitely. Things had moved and reassembled, changed irrevocably. Her hair and eyes were dulling. She'd not even had the consolation of seeing her own loveliness transmitted to the child. *Her* looks were her father's. She was dark, lithe, delicate in her features. Neat, symmetrical, flawless. As if refusing her mother credit for the tempestuous months she'd accommodated her. He might have produced their offspring without maternal help, as in some Greek myth. Father and daughter were playmates. *They* were both pragmatic, easily physical. Shunning and scorning dreamy eccentricity. Their love for each other was perfectly independent of her.

What were they doing now? Were they reassuring each other? Did they need reassurance? Was he learning to miss her? Was she? (The thought of her usually a little belated. It had been too easy to leave her behind for nearly a year to go on the Empire Tour.) As a child grew older you tried to go back to your normal mode of being, and at times you managed it. With a vague sense of peril, of having mislaid something that shouldn't be lost track of. Making it hard to think with any seriousness of Nice.

She took off her pearls and brushed her teeth. She washed her face, smoothed cream into it, and rinsed a little under her arms, dabbing some rose eau de cologne there afterwards. Mummy: how had she managed—and gracefully? Where had that love come from, that golden aura? Was it easier for Victorians, the ones as comfortably off as she, to create golden auras around their children? Did modern women go wrong in trying too much to steer their own course through life? To claim satisfaction? But Mummy, always on the watch for transcendence, had claimed satisfaction, oh yes.

She filled her new hot-water bottle at the basin, knowing that she should have asked for boiling water, that this wouldn't be hot enough. All the same, she got into bed with it quickly, appreciative of the rubbery smell.

Panicky sadness was rising as it had last spring and

summer during the days and weeks of her toil at Ashfield following Mummy's death.

•

The photograph of herself that she'd stumbled upon among Mummy's things—looking so grave, aware of sorrow's weight—had dismayed her. Where had such an expression come from? She'd had a marvellous childhood. Hadn't she? So how to explain that face?

All she could come up with was this: herself in bed in the nursery, watched over by Nursie. Nursie's supper tray was brought and perhaps she would get a little of that tasty meat. The villa was plunged in quiet, though wind breathing among leaves was a reminder of the encircling garden. By inconstant firelight she studied the motif of mauve irises ascending the wallpaper until it mutated into a shimmery dance, nearly animate.

Infuriatingly, she couldn't quite place this homey scene. But—could Nursie, in her frilled cambric cap, have been an anachronism, and what she actually remembered was lying in bed years *after* Nursie had returned to her family in Somerset, *missing* Nursie, one evening following Father's death? Perhaps during the weeks her mother and sister had been absent from Ashfield, resting in the south of France? If she strained, she could vaguely recall a notion from that interregnum of gigantic scope—as if space had acquired a new dimension. Something like the effect of an everyday room abruptly emptied of furniture, at once echoing and unknown. Or Mummy was back from France, but on the evening in question, still disoriented and grief-saturated, she had considered any company at all too fatiguing and so sent her young daughter early to bed.

With the fanciful reasoning that a mind in pain sometimes burrowed into, this daughter, become an adult woman, imagined Mummy's sadness flowing through their villa like ink in water, passing bluely through the walls of her bedroom.

An underground suspicion told her that Mummy's melancholy predated even her father's illness.

Then where *had* it started? Had Father himself been responsible? He adored you, darling Mummy, but lacked your intense sensitivity. Was he too quick to leave for his club of a morning, to host a dinner party or some amateur theatricals you wouldn't enjoy? Too complacent a lover, oblivious or unable to reach your deeper yearnings? So damnably hard to pinpoint the origin of sadness.

Was it simply an ocean lapping at babes in their mothers, leaking through the most immensely permeable walls, blueing the tunnels of infant veins? Was that where woe began?

She had stared at the photograph of her younger, weighted self, the air rife with crushed roses. She could have screamed till she had no voice left. And it was only days till he would come to see her at last, divorce on his mind.

24

NIGHT-TIME VISITATION

It was between two and three in the morning, but he wasn't asleep when a knocking sharpened his attention. Reclined on the narrow bed in his woollen dressing-gown, he had been nestled in a cave of Sibelius and sherry. He waited for a second knock to be sure he hadn't imagined it. It *had* been on his door.

In a befuddled fashion he rose, wondering if he should dress and for once regretting his tipsiness. He stopped the gramophone. He hesitated. He didn't call out to ask who it was. Some poor insomniac, most likely, wishing to insult him for his blasted music. It couldn't be her, though he was convinced it was. He deposited the glass he'd been drinking from on the writing desk, retrieved his slippers and stepped into them, fastening the belt of his dressing-gown. He straightened blankets, patted down pillows. He seized a shirt from the armchair and threw it into the bottom of the wardrobe. He did likewise with a towel.

Nervous that the knocker would desist and dematerialise into the strange indeterminate dark of hotel nights, Harry opened the door.

Teresa. In a mauve dressing-gown. She seemed a little confused.

'I'm sorry to disturb you,' she whispered. 'Wake you. It's unforgivable.'

He whispered, too. 'I was wide awake. Will you come in?'

'If you don't mind. There's something I feel I have to tell you.'

It was uncanny to have her in his room, where for days the atmosphere had been unquiet with thoughts of her. They stood facing one another in lamplight.

'Are you all right?'

Her hair was combed and her dressing-gown neat but there was something almost fevered in her appearance, perhaps in her pale eyes, which were extraordinarily elusive in the penumbra. She put a hand to her face, then folded her arms and half turned away from him.

'Oh,' she said. 'It's difficult. Living incognito and all that.'

He made a movement towards the light switch.

'No—don't put the lights up. The lamp is so much friendlier. I must be a mess.' She brought a hand to her face again.

'No, you're lovely, if you don't mind my saying so. Forgive my manners. Won't you sit down? Can I offer you something to drink?'

'No. I won't stay long—but you sit. Do.'

The armchair was too relaxed for the situation, so he turned the chair at the writing desk to face her, and settled self-consciously on it, rearranging his dressing-gown over his knees. When he looked up, she was taking in his room.

'I have a daughter,' she pronounced brusquely, harshly.

'I know.'

'You know?' She laughed a rattled sort of laugh. 'How slow I am. The papers.'

'Yes,' he admitted.

'People are nosy.'

'They are—we are. We can't help ourselves.'

A silence, and then she said feebly, 'You must think me a terrible mother, for leaving her like that.'

'No, life is wretchedly complicated. You had your reasons, I'm sure. I don't see why anyone should judge you.'

'I didn't want you to have a false idea of me.'

She was an unstable apparition in the quiver of the lamplight. Harry would have liked to say something about appreciating her books, but bringing them up seemed a delicate matter—like encouraging two people between whom there is some private history you haven't grasped to engage in conversation.

Before he found words, she went on, 'I don't think I was made to be a mother.' She smiled, her face richly shadowed.

'Why surely,' he said, 'not all women are. I don't think my mother was.'

'No?'

Harry shook his head.

'I'm sorry.'

He shrugged and turned his hands over on his knees. After a moment, he stood.

'The thing is,' she murmured wonderingly, 'it's more peaceful not to think of her. You really don't find me bad?'

He shook his head again and neared her a little. 'Thank you for telling me.' He held out a hand.

She took it, bobbed her head. The most rapid, skimming kiss. The lightness of her lips and hands, and the tenebrous slopes of her inner arms, bared by the sleeves of her dressing-gown that had fallen to her elbows, affected him. But before he knew it, his hand appeared to be levitating in space. She'd stepped back. This tentative approach, together with his own actions earlier in the day, and especially her fear of him that he'd felt with his own hands, all stopped him from reaching for her.

'I'll go now. I don't know that I trust myself to stay longer.'

'You know I'd like it, if you did stay longer? If you didn't—perhaps—trust yourself.'

She smiled. So soon the door was closing and Teresa had gone. His fugitive. He saw her still in the lamplight. The image jumping, coming close and vanishing. She'd been in Harry's room.

The smoky net of slight drunkenness had been jerked from his mind, leaving an acute transparency. Blatantly obvious that he wouldn't sleep. He smirked at the very idea. His wakefulness was so absolute it didn't distress him. If he was troubled it was by Teresa, who went on flickering before him. Offering, and withdrawing. He lay down on the bed to reflect, and did so for many hours, never quite dreaming. For some predawn time, he thought of Valeria.

His wife had seemed ideal to him, subtle and dramatic, blasé and sober. As unobtrusively superb as the city of her birth. Swanlike in her sliding through of existence, invisible, striking. If she'd lacked anything, it was surely nothing one needed.

But then Mrs Mortlake had passed away.

Before, though, when everything had appeared normal, would he have seen sadness if she'd been displaying it? With Harry's glum moods paraded around the house as brashly as peacock feathers, how would she have revealed her own? The idea mortified him.

If the unhappiness she'd confessed in passing all those years ago was larger than dissatisfaction with Giacomo, what could its true source have been?

When Mrs Mortlake took her last bad turn, the old thing had started talking a great deal, uneasily, about her childhood. She was very keen, rather feverishly intent, on clarifying something from 'when I was small'. Valeria did not often admit to possessing a tender heart, but Harry could tell she found the notion of Mrs Mortlake as small poignant because her voice stumbled in her throat when she recounted this.

'I try to help,' she said, 'listening, asking questions, but I can't give her the relief she is looking for. We never quite get to what troubled her. It might have something to do with fearing horses—or storms—or one particular storm that frightened some horses.'

This was possibly their last proper conversation, Valeria losing the inclination to talk at any length after Anne Mortlake's death. He wanted to see a clue in it. Could the old lady's obsession with childhood have caused Valeria to reflect on her own? He'd no reason to suspect that any of his wife's memories of her own smallness would have seriously unbalanced her. Valeria had visited her parents once after their marriage. Only her sister had come to them in London, twice. Maybe her family felt rejected by Valeria's choice of a colonial and London over newly Italian Trieste. Disappointed by the humbleness of her life. She wrote them long, impress- ively detailed letters each week with the martyrdom of a diligent schoolgirl. (Harry's parents received two or three unenthusiastic missives from him each year. With a clinging culpability, he imagined his mother reading them on the veranda in eucalypt-scented, coppery afternoon sun, while in his armchair in the sitting room his father glowered over something, perhaps missing his days of active work on the farm, when Roger was still at his side—the mutt who had long since passed on, not to be replaced.)

True, it was her father's profession to know humanity as distressed and secret. He wondered if the presence of such knowledge in a childhood home could spawn difficulties and a tendency to hide. If you accepted the existence of ghosts, wasn't it more likely you'd happen to see one? Fancy yourself one?

The only other thing that occurred to him was that mishap during carnival. Joy at the beautiful costume. Running forbidden, promising to obey. Forgetting, rebelling. Her mother's handiwork profaned. Beauty spoiled, bare legs and humiliation. But surely all normal enough and harmless. No, the unhappiness she had evoked in the square was her failure to be fulfilled by Giacomo, or some impulsive dolefulness tinged with sensuality that young people experiment with. Harry should know, having unpardonably indulged in such sulks long beyond youth. He didn't want to blame Valeria's childhood.

He was, in fact, most attracted to seeing the fault as his own. Giacomo hadn't satisfied her—but nor had he. (*He* was the origin of her melancholy. Flash had appeared to know this and hold it against him.) If Harry had managed to make himself a writer, or at least grasp the trick of contentment, their life would have been lighter. She might have painted. Blaming himself was the way to avoid blaming her (the great dark temptation) for betraying him with the lover with whom one could never compete. Yes, Harry's blue moods had to have been the culprit, seeping through their house like ink spilled on the most lush, corruptible paper. His magnum opus.

●

At around eight o'clock in the morning on Monday, the thirteenth of December, he took out a sheet of stationery with the legend *The Harrogate Hydropathic* across its top. He was going to write to Giacomo, his wife's first lover, whom he'd last seen thirteen years ago at the Caffè degli Specchi wearing a look not so much of despair as of dissolution. He didn't know how he'd find an address, or even if the man still lived, but with dawn entering the room, these were minor points for later consideration. He wrote a letter he might have written years before. However, there could be something unpredictably headstrong in the timing of one's actions, an impossibility quite suddenly turning into a possibility and even a necessity. Harry had long held Giacomo in his mind as a competitor, or at least as someone who had enjoyed experiences that he envied. He had begrudged Giacomo opportunities he had profited from—to feel the pressure of her hand, the temperature of her cheek or lips or neck, to regale himself with her scent, to watch her (vaguely ironic across a table, silently awaiting him in the corner of a room, intently crossing a public garden, drowsily rising from a sofa), to catch her mysterious shifts into total visibility. Harry seemed now to have no further need of resentment.

It was a short letter that took a long time to produce. He wasn't in any hurry. He informed Giacomo of Valeria's passing. He said he was sorry for what he must have gone through all those years ago. In plain words he stated that he understood and sympathised, because he also had loved Valeria very much. He also had been forced to let her go.

Sealing the envelope, Harry wondered how much this missive from England would surprise him, Giacomo Petri, teacher of classics. At this very instant could the man have been watching the sun lift whitely over that calm inlet of the Adriatic? Worn in his late middle age but turned out with consummate care, hands in the pockets of a long dark coat. Breathing in murky-sweet sea funk and purest Arabica coffee, and deriving a pleasure from these small things that made them as large as sacraments, primal enough to pacify desire, at least halfway. Harry hoped so.

•

When he finally drifted off, the corridors had been reson-ating hypnotically with footsteps for hours. He'd spoken to a chambermaid, asking that he not be disturbed as he'd been up through the night and now intended to have a little kip.

It was two fifteen in the afternoon when he woke—physically restored but with the old child's anguish at having been deprived against his will of participating in a key phase of the world's proceedings. His engagement with Teresa at three darted into his head, and he sat upright in bed like a corpse returning to life in a farce. He hurried through dressing and shave. He was starving. He requested that coffee and some bread and butter be brought up.

He ate and drank standing at the window, gazing down at the stone facades of proud, tastefully affluent houses and the more ostentatious dome of the Royal Pump Room. From behind glass the afternoon looked gentle, foggy.

He thought he detected a change in the lounge when he went down, but he couldn't put his finger on it. Everything appeared much as it always did. He noted a newspaper on the table by the armchairs and apprehension quickened in him. He had no time for it, however. Perhaps he just didn't want to know what it contained.

He wished the proprietress of the Hydro a good day, and she reciprocated. There might have been a new carefulness in her efficient manner. He'd suspected she was shrewd.

Beginning the climb of Montpellier Hill, he saw the saxophonist and the drummer sitting together on an easy seat in the adjoining gardens, conversing vehemently. Seeing Harry, the saxophonist hesitated in mid disquisition. He indicated the hotel guest to his companion, and they both waved and smiled. Though the saxophonist's smile was insistently familiar—like those he'd bestowed on Harry before, no doubt a manifestation of his artistic persona—it made Harry anxious. Hatless, the gawky angles of his pale ears made him seem very young and impressionable, especially alongside the drummer, whose pose on the other hand suggested braggadocio. On stage with the Hydro Boys, the latter had never really come to Harry's attention. He waved back and hastened on.

He arrived a few minutes early at the rendezvous opposite the Imperial Café. She wasn't there. Would she come? Their arrangement had been made before her late-night visit. He observed sartorially confident ladies coming and going from the café. Furs imperious, hats perky. The temperature was agreeable enough but a cooler wind roused itself from time to time. He fastened the buttons of his coat. By twenty minutes past three she had not arrived and he began to seriously fear she wouldn't. He lit a cigarette. The day was closing in. He recalled her teasing chiaroscuro form in his room in the early hours of the morning, her weight in his arms as he'd carried her from the edge of the crag.

Five minutes later, he ran frantically to W.H. Smith. With great impatience, he waited behind a soft-spoken boy, who was methodically purchasing some letter papers and a pencil. Finally, Harry bought his *Times* and jogged back to his post.

No Teresa. He couldn't see her approaching from any direction. He considered the sky. It was the blue hour, which usually encouraged a soothing elongation in his mind. Tonight it did not.

On page sixteen of the paper he found it: *The Missing Woman Novelist*. Search by two thousand people. He read in jagged bursts, looking wildly up at intervals in case he should somehow miss her.

An arresting scene was evoked. Heavy mist. A force of fifty police officers leading search parties of volunteers and bloodhounds. The roads around the plateau at Newlands Corner, where her motorcar had been abandoned, congested with more than four hundred cars and many motorcycles. The Silent Pool searched. No trace of the novelist uncovered. Grand effort, in vain.

The sky's blue had very nearly been usurped by black when she arrived at three forty-five. Her cheeks were pink— from the baths? Or from knowing herself the object of an awesome manhunt?

'I'm so sorry!'

Harry gave her his hand, and she briefly took it.

'I thought you wouldn't come.' If he hadn't known her better, he might have wondered if she were inebriated.

'I was leaving the baths and in the reading room I saw . . . that.' She'd noticed the paper under his arm. 'A mix-up. Such a mix-up . . .'

'I know. Shall we go somewhere quieter?'

She appeared to have trouble concentrating, so he took her elbow, but only for a second or two. Once they were on the Stray, she placed her feet surely.

'This whole belt of land,' he said spinelessly, 'which goes for over two hundred acres, I believe, was set apart by the legislature in 1770 as a free common for all people.'

'Ah? . . . I'd no idea I'd cause this, honestly.'

'Of course you didn't. How could you?'

'What will I do? I can't go back now, not like this.' Her lovely distant eyes were stunned, gleaming. 'What a debacle. And here, will people start to . . . ?'

They were moving more slowly over the open ground. The fog and gloom gave the parkland a velour soft-ness. Not wanting to alarm her, he didn't mention his intuition of something being wrong at the Hydro. Nor the apparently intense conversation he'd just witnessed between the bandsmen, or the other he'd overheard some days before.

'I don't know. It might be best to think of moving on.'

'Yes.' Her face remained abstracted.

'We just need to stay calm and think this through.'

'Make a plan,' she said. 'It will be all right, won't it?'

Streetlamps came on along the perimeter of the common. Low on the horizon the moon was already visible. Even sheathed in mist, its shape was generous enough to make him speculate about its fullness. If it wasn't at its roundest, then it was only a hair away—to what side, just before or just beyond? It disturbed him not to know. 'Yes, it will be all right. And . . . will you go back to him?' He refrained from referring to her daughter.

'I can't divorce.'

'Oh, no? You love him?' He had asked this before and not received a reply. His eyes stayed on the moon's veiled girth. So long ago, his father had taught him the name for such a moon: *gibbous*. But waxing, or waning?

'It would be wrong,' was all she said. And after a pause, 'I was sure he'd come. That he'd understand. But he's taken too long and it's all got so out of hand, so muddied.' She glanced at him and away. 'I could go somewhere for a few days. Clear my head.' It had begun, very lightly, to drizzle. 'That might help me to start writing, too. I tried again today. Absolutely nothing. And I must—I really *must* earn my living, don't you see?' The idea appeared to obsess her.

'Be patient with yourself,' he said, suffering from atrocious impatience. 'But I do think moving on would be wise. Would you like me to help, perhaps to look into travel arrangements?'

'I don't know. I'm so on edge.'

'What about . . . Edinburgh?'

'Edinburgh. Would be nice. A city to get lost in. But just leaving all of a sudden would look odd—like fleeing.'

He agreed. Neither of them wore raincoats or had thought to equip themselves with an umbrella, but the fine moisture was reinvigorating. He felt he could have used a real dousing. 'What if tomorrow you were to tell Mrs Jackman, say, that you've had a letter asking you to join a relation in London? A female relation unexpectedly arrived from Cape Town, or something like that. Then you could go the following morning.'

'That might work.'

They continued a little in silence, and she offered him a sidelong smile, grateful—but it wasn't gratitude that interested him. The fog was growing thicker, the rain more decided.

'You know, I really would like to help however I can. To come with you, even, if you wanted.'

'Wouldn't it look suspicious?'

'We wouldn't depart together. I could wait a day or two before joining you. That would give you time, too—to think in peace.'

'You *are* kind.' She went on quickly, 'I'll have to think about it.'

His heart had gone a little silly. It was gnawing at him that she'd just slip away. Like in his dream in which she'd turned to sand, a woman who couldn't be held. 'How will we meet next?' he asked desperately. 'To talk, I mean.'

'Shall I come to your room again?' she suggested. 'Late?'

'Yes,' he said, overeager. But he was also aware of the need to protect her. 'Be careful no one sees you. And perhaps in general you could avoid the bandsmen. Tonight you might consider dining at Bettys. If you left a message for Mrs J saying you had an engagement, they wouldn't worry. It can be my turn to eat with them.'

'They'll be pleased. They've been chagrined by your absence. They're going to be shocked, you know, when they find out.'

'Yes. But they're warm-hearted. I think they'll understand.'

'You believe so?'

There were few things he was sure of believing. He nodded, realising that having walked in a loop they were arriving back at the corner opposite the Imperial Café. Her face, he saw by the cloudy golden light of a streetlamp, shone with water. She allowed him to put his hand to the brim of her hat to gather a beading of raindrops before they fell.

Reluctantly, he proposed, 'You should go back. You'll catch cold.'

'Yes. I must think.'

'*À ce soir, alors?*'

'*À ce soir. Et merci.*'

Her company, Harry felt as she went off into the damp dark, was like that of the sea. Gentle, powerful. A commanding undertone telling him he could not do without it. Some twenty minutes later it was a drenched man who returned to the Hydro.

25

LAMENT OF THE NYMPH

The hours leading to her knock on his door were freakishly drawn out. After retiring to his room he found he was incapable of reading—it might have been different if he'd had more of Teresa's airy yet firmly delineated novels, but those he had with him by other authors proved unsuitable—and he'd no patience even for music. He pulled out his suitcase from under the bed, with an idea of packing. Of course, even if she agreed to let him join her somewhere, he'd promised to stay on at the Hydro for a little longer after her departure, so as not to give the impression they were travelling companions. He was, notwithstanding, aching to launch himself into the gestures of leaving, to convince himself that they'd really made a shared plan. She had seemed to assent to it, but she was evidently flurried, shaky. And she possessed great determination. A part of her still hoped for a reunion with the Colonel.

To calm his nerves, Harry pictured himself in a room with this blighter. There he was, foolishly debonair, slouched against a wall. Harry beckoned to him to approach. When the Colonel was close enough to hear a whispered secret, it was with a zippy little knife that Harry took the bloke off-guard. Just holding it up to his face, just to undo his self-congratulatory look. To teach him not to feel quite so unassailable, to have some imagination. Naturally, Harry had never wielded a weapon in such a way, though this didn't interfere with his enjoyment of the fantasy. Smiling, he opened the suitcase.

In the bottom of it was a small sheaf of pages that he'd quite forgotten. He sat on his haunches considering them. Then he took them out and carried them over to the writing desk.

Next he looked around the room, assessing his other belongings. He gathered what little there was onto the bed. Clothes. His few gramophone records. A handful of novels. An electric flashlight (he always travelled with this, never using it, nor having any clear notion of what he expected to illuminate by night). A half-full bottle of port wine and one, almost finished, of sherry. The residue of a life. Indeed, he was struck by how this might have been a collection of last effects. Laid out, it all appeared both rather irrelevant and poignant, somehow embarrassing evidence of personality, of need.

He shook himself out of this meditation, trying various arrangements for the items in the suitcase. He worked as though the order he was creating was of consequence. He made some calculations as to the clothes he would require for his remaining days in Harrogate, and left these out, together with the wet things he'd changed out of after returning from meeting Teresa. He refolded trousers so that they hung more satisfactorily in the wardrobe. He drew closer to the fireplace the chair over which hung his sodden coat. He fancied a smell of pure Yorkshire rain was rising from it, and this brought him a vision of Teresa's pale, slick face. He tidied his shaving kit. For once relishing its statement of impermanence, he'd have preferred to keep the suitcase in view, but it was impractical manoeuvring around it there on the floor. He lowered the lid without fastening it and pushed it once more under the bed. In all the travels of his itinerant life since Valeria's death, he'd not experienced this anticipation. This hunger for adventure.

Waiting was more arduous after it turned idle. He was flighty. He stared a good deal at the moon through the window, tracking its slow, unavoidable ascent. When it freed itself of the mist, he was certain it was full. At around eleven a light rain set in once more. The humidity lifting off his drying coat, scented with the outdoors, kept her pallid, potent presence with him. The furnishings of that room he was soon to vacate wore as much as ever their aspect of affected cosy familiarity. But all furnishings, he reflected, not just those of hotels and inns, were unsettling. Like the objects one travelled with, just on a grander scale. Decor was a kind of memento mori of the person who'd assembled or dwelled amid it. Such objects were so naked, so brightly, hopelessly possessed by aspiration.

Harry didn't know what he'd have done had she not arrived at midnight. She wasn't obliged to knock twice, this time.

Her entrance was silent, quick. She was more composed than earlier.

'Are you all right?'

She nodded like a child displaying stoicism.

'Good food at Bettys?'

'Yes. I was very greedy.'

It pleased him to hear of her appetite. 'Excellent. I was just deciding that the decor of rooms depresses me.'

'Oh?'

'Why, I don't know, it seems so much trouble to go to— *decorating*. A distraction. Endeavouring to make ourselves happy with pretty things . . . When one day someone will have the job of getting rid of it all, anyway. Clearing it out and starting anew.'

'How morbid you are. I *adore* furnishings. I've spent so many amusing hours decorating. It's one of my favourite pastimes. You don't find it agreeable, coming into a well-furnished house?'

She herself had described the oppression of going through the contents of her late mother's house, but her mind was elsewhere, and of course he didn't wish to remark on that. It cheered him to be called morbid. 'And how practical *you* are.'

'I've never been accused of being practical before.'

'Teresa, last night you told me about your daughter, and tonight there's something more that I want to tell you.'

'Only fair.'

'It's the rest of the story—of my past.'

'Go ahead.'

'Perhaps you could sit?'

She looked at him more carefully, then said, 'Very well,' and complied.

He liked watching her long body arrange itself in his armchair. He moved to the hearthrug and stood facing the fireplace.

'One other person knows what I'm about to tell you. Mr Vaughan—fine chap.' He cleared his throat. 'After Valeria,' he began with a wavering voice that bolstered itself as he speeded up, 'I wasn't well. I wasn't looking after myself much.' He swallowed. 'I'd resigned from my work. I hardly went out. Sleep was . . . a problem. I couldn't have gone on like that, see?' He turned to her. She was listening, expressionlessly. He'd drawn the curtains when she arrived, but he gazed at them now as if the moon were still on show there. 'I went to my doctor and asked him for a prescription of sleeping draught. He considered me warily. I pitched myself into a furious speech about how I'd lose my mind if I had to endure another night without rest. He capitulated, at last, and gave me what I asked for. I got the stuff from the druggist and took it home.

'I left it for days in a wooden box in the bottom drawer of the dresser in the bedroom. There were some of Valeria's summer things in that drawer. Blouses and skirts. A dress so old and ratty she'd deemed it fit only for wearing about home in heat waves. She used to move light things down to the bottom drawer in winter when she didn't need them. Anyhow, for a week or so I ignored the box remarkably well. Maybe it was my final effort at being a man of substance for Valeria. Or the opposite. Maybe I was trying to reject the path she'd shown me. In any case, I sat in our sitting room with Valeria's cat Flash, who was growing churlish—she scratched me once quite badly, I have the scar—and willed myself to forget that box among the light things whose season wouldn't come again. I avoided the bedroom. I slept on the sofa—I *was* the sofa.' The fire crackled and they both jumped. 'There's nothing to say about it. One day I stopped ignoring the box. I opened the drawer, moved her soft old frock, and took it out. I prepared a tray, putting the poison on a plate. Filled a glass with water. Brought it all into the sitting room. The scene of the crime.' He laughed.

'What happened?'

'I tell you I would have done it, but I was interrupted. Mr Vaughan came calling.'

'He saved you?'

'He did. At the time I couldn't see it that way. I'd botched yet another thing. Couldn't even murder myself!' He turned awkwardly back to the fire. He heard her standing.

'Harry.' Her hand on his arm. He turned again and their gazes ran together, more freely than they ever had before. The perfume of roses. 'Grief,' she sighed, her eyes long corridors of it. 'I'm sorry.'

Her hand falling away, her warmth reached him nonetheless, like it had when they'd danced the first night, and when they'd kissed. No kiss now, only a holding of eyes. The unearthly idea struck him that ghosts would embrace so, nearness in place of touch. And weren't they ghosts? She going by an assumed name, a fugitive from her former life. He drifting through some vagabond's afterlife, some twilight sleep that did not spare him memory. Yet, as drained as they each were, a force moved between them. It had been there from the beginning, jittery, building into this vigorous electricity. It was elating, and sad. It frightened him. Excited him. Teresa made a throaty sound resembling truncated laughter, which caused his knees to tremble. Then she moved away.

'I told you because I want you to know me,' he said rather breathlessly. 'And to understand why I was afraid for you. I was seeing *myself* in you.'

After a moment, she mused, 'There were several times, maybe once in particular, when I considered—that. When I thought it might be a road to take. Do you think we should have a drink? Start with those drinking lessons?'

'Heavens, yes. Let's.'

Rain on the roof could suddenly be heard and her eyes lifted towards it.

'Rain,' he said, serving the last measures of sherry from the bottle.

'You've tidied?'

'Oh, a little, yes. Mending my bad bachelor ways.' He smiled bravely.

Nodding at the glass she took from him, she said, 'I never fancied losing control. I was arrogant enough to think I could entertain myself with my ordinary mind. I'd no trouble intoxicating myself. I always felt rather invincible, which may have been dear Mummy's fault, I suppose.' She sipped, coughed a little, and bowed her head. Her voice was disconsolate when she spoke again. 'Is love where we go wrong? Where the grief comes from? I've been thinking that it might be too much of a burden to impose on someone—loving them, I mean, and expecting anything at all in return. I've always thought of my childhood as blissful, but I wonder now if Mummy didn't love me *too* much. If, in such love, there wasn't a demand too large for a child to fulfil. And she had to know I'd desire such love from others, also, and lose her, eventually.'

He pondered this at some length. 'I wasn't particularly aware of love, growing up. Or I was, though it was rather threadbare.' He thought of his own mother's austere ways, the greyish, subdued look of her on the days when she'd slept poorly, her lemon-coloured apron. The very occasional weak antique jokes resuscitated from her childhood they'd shared, as he helped her to make preserves, and that heady atmosphere of stewing fruit and sugar. He asked himself whether she had hoped for another child but thought that probably she hadn't. His father might have—in a selfish, unreal sort of way. Harry found that tears were nudging at him, and forced himself to breathe deeply. '*I* never felt invincible, yet you and I have both suffered. Then take Valeria. I thought she was perfect, so nonchalant. And look . . .'

'Quite,' Teresa said pensively. 'I've been wondering how far back we have to go to discover the origin of sadness. For example, after she was widowed, Grannie, Mummy's mother, gave Mummy to her sister, Auntie-Grannie, to raise, and it seems to me that being sent away from her true home left a mark on Mummy. But is that far enough back to go? Must I look to earlier generations?'

'Do a post-mortem on the childhood of all of one's ancestors, right back . . . to the garden? I follow you, and I do it, too: try to explain sadness to myself. I've been doing it lately, actually I do it all the time, but we can torture ourselves that way. And then again there may *be* no reason for sadness.

There certainly seems to be no motive. No one has anything to gain by it, do they? What possible logic . . . ?' He noticed she was unsettled and emptying her glass quickly.

'What if it were simply *in* one's character? Heartache. Without any real beginning. So there was no preventing or escaping it . . .'

'In the blood? But we must believe that we can be as we decide to be,' he said. 'Otherwise . . .'

'Otherwise it's unbearable.' With each sip she was grimacing a little or smiling strangely. 'I lost everything. My mother, my husband. I had to get away from that house in that banal suburb. I drove to a place called the Silent Pool. The road you almost took—I saw it in front of me there.'

He sipped his sherry. 'You're much stronger than I am. A woman of courage and daring. Maybe you *are* invincible, part god. Your mother was right.'

'Hardly.' She flushed. They listened to the rain. 'This isn't like me, to just say what's in my mind, private things—it's very against character. It's really incredibly easy to talk to you.'

'That's how it is for me, with you. While we're at it, you'd better know the *very* worst of me. Here on the table is my magnum opus. All twelve pages of it.' He gave the thin stack a derisory tap with his fist. 'I thought it might lighten your spirits, show you that the Blue Train isn't such a disaster. But my aim is also more egotistical than that. I want to show it to someone, finally. I want to show you. I never did to

Valeria.' She made as if to speak. He added, 'I'll still love you if you don't like it. I do love you. Don't feel you have to say anything. I know the situation is . . . unusual. All this is so sudden and far-fetched. Like something one would invent.'

She went to the curtained window. He thought he saw her sway on her feet.

'Did you see the moon?' she asked.

'Magnificent. You're tired?'

'Or drunk. Is this what blotto is? You expect . . . I don't know. My thoughts feel *less* slurred to me than usual, almost as if they were growing too distinct. I might not sleep tonight. I'm afraid. I feel something bad will happen, something is coming for me.'

'You could lie down here for a bit.' She looked at him questioningly. 'All strictly honourable—I'll sit in a chair, of course.' They tried to laugh. 'If you fall asleep, I can wake you before dawn so you'll have time to return to your room before anyone is up.'

She finished her glass. Her colour had risen, it seemed to him even in the lamp shadows.

'And what if *you* fall asleep?'

'I'm a high-class professional when it comes to insomnia.'

'I might, you know. If you're sure you don't mind—for a little. For some reason, the idea of being alone makes me nervous.'

While she settled herself, he turned down the lights, leaving only the lamp on the writing desk burning. He sat in the armchair. His hands shook.

'Have you decided anything about where to go?'

'I've thought about it constantly but haven't been able to make up my mind.'

'Well, there'll be time for that tomorrow,' he said uncertainly.

'I'm wide awake.'

He laughed. 'Tell me something.'

'Mummy encouraged me to go to a hotel on Dartmoor to see if I could finish my first novel there. It worked.'

'Edinburgh might be like that. For the Blue Train.'

She groaned theatrically. 'You *are* an awful man, bringing that up.' But she went on, 'Visions of trains plague me. It's chillingly lifelike, exhausting. I sit in one compartment, I pass down the hall, go into the dining car. If I can see my characters at all, they only sit there regarding me with horrid placid stares. Katherine . . .'

'Katherine?' he asked, when she faltered. 'What's she like?'

'Oh, not quite young anymore and not a flashy beauty, but she has something—in an autumnal sort of way. You'd like her. Grey-eyed. Very acceptable figure. Very English, level-headed, determined. And yet she won't do anything. It's galling!'

'And . . . the little Belgian, does he appear in this one?'

There was a silence. Had he made a mistake? He thought she was striving not to smile.

'You've read me.'

'I confess, yes.'

'Did you like him?'

'Very much—coming across as so comically vain and irrelevant, while being as sharp as a mean knife. He's good company.'

'Ah . . . thank you.'

'One is sorry to put you down.'

'Oh. Harry, I went to Australia once, some years ago. In a new country, trees and hills always catch my attention. There, neither was as I'd imagined. All those white-barked gums seem . . . reversed. Like the negatives of photographs of trees.'

'Yes,' Harry said, surprised. 'Spirits of trees.'

'And we glimpsed some low mountains in the distance one day, the Blue Mountains. Indeed, they weren't the grey-blue of *our* far-off hills—but really blue, cobalt. You rather have trouble forgetting Australia.'

'Yes. You rather do.'

A longer silence established itself. Thinking she was falling asleep, he savoured the altered mood in his room, the tenacious rain and the drink, whose flavour at the outset was slight: cool and lemony. After which came the alcoholic heat and toasted, walnutty roundness, with notions of wood, caramel and salt, while you held it in your mouth.

•

He heard something. He was disoriented for a moment, so he must have dozed off. Teresa was weeping. 'Darling,' she was saying softly. 'Mummy darling.'

He roused himself and went over to her. He kneeled by the bed. Her face was turned away. 'Teresa, I . . . I'm here.' He touched her hair. She was hot. Rose fragrance, lightly peppery.

'Darling, oh God, darling . . .'

It was painfully excluding, the darling being her mother. But he continued to stroke her hair, and gradually she ceased crying. Emerging from his blankets, her neck seemed staggeringly innocent and undefended, like an armpit laid open. He'd have liked to feel for the tremor of her pulse and, by a stronger light, to find the almost imperceptible creases in that skin, to smooth them with his thumbs. She turned her face. Her breathing was erratic.

'You aren't afraid of feeling,' she said, measuring him up with liquefied eyes. 'You remind me of things, of myself. It's chaotic. But you're so attentive and sweet.'

'I used to be afraid of feeling. And I haven't always been . . . kind.'

'You are with me. You are now. Trust me, I'm a good judge of character, usually. Harry, I'm so very sorry for what happened with Valeria. And afterwards.'

'Since I've met you'—he went on caressing her hair—'I'm more alive. I almost feel as if the broken parts of me were starting to knit back together.'

Teresa smiled, growing calmer under his hand. It appeared to him that he could comfort her in a way he hadn't been able to comfort Valeria. Whether because Teresa's suffering mirrored his own, because she chose to show it to him, or because he was finally able to share the distress of a woman he loved, Harry wasn't sure.

'Couldn't we consider Nice, really?'

His heart beat hard awaiting her response—but this came with the playful flavour of make-believe, of a floaty kind of collusion.

'Perhaps we'll just decamp. Cut and run. It *would* be lovely.'

Difficult to know if her eyes had brightened with mirth, or new tears.

'We will, won't we? Give them the slip.'

'It wasn't all a colossal bluff, you know.'

'I know.'

'I've made the most utter fool of myself. I'd never have caused all that drama.'

'Don't worry. After Edinburgh—when we're living in Nice—such dramatics won't touch us. We won't care about them a jot.'

Her mouth went serious. 'Could I be a good mother in Nice?'

What to say? He'd no idea how one went about being an adequate parent. He hadn't even made a success of himself as a husband, a childless adult. Was she contemplating a life with him? 'There'd be so much tenderness in our home . . . And I'd help in all the ways I could.'

'It might be easier to love her there.'

'Yes, because we'll be very happy. Teresa?'

'Yes?'

'You wouldn't even think, ever, of doing what Valeria did, would you—not in Nice? I mean, one of us would never make a decision like that without the other. Of course, it'd be out of the question because we'll be so happy, but . . . if for any reason it wasn't, if it came to that, to Casablanca, we'd do it together, wouldn't we? Will you promise? Like you described, swim out into the ocean on one of those hot days. The important thing is we'd never leave the other alone, would we, darling?' He permitted himself the luxury of that *darling*, knowing he might not get another chance to say it. Her eyelids fluttered. He might have been going on excessively but his words seemed necessary for warding off a dark presentiment. And he wanted to offer her something absolute. He sensed that only a truly excessive love would soothe her.

She said, 'I promise.' And continued, 'I think I'll tell you now about the night I ran away from home. I'll make my deposition to you.' She smiled a little. 'I might fall asleep after, if you stay here by me.' She took the hand that had been touching her, making a mesh of their fingers. 'Is this where the naughty cat scratched you?' She stroked the dainty bulge of the scar on his palm, and then released his hand. 'I'll always prefer a dog. They adore you completely.'

Harry brought the chair over, to sit by her. It was good to be there and to listen to her voice. At last, she went quiet.

He kept telling himself he was awake.

He and Teresa were in two trains bound in opposite directions, which slowed as they passed one another, so that he was able to make out clearly, heart-wrenchingly, her dear lost face.

•

Daylight. The sentinel had slept. He woke as if receiving an electric shock. Twitching like the fish discovering a hook has tethered him by a taut line to doom. He recalled waking in this way often after Valeria's death, only then it had seemed to occur while he was scarcely at the lip of sleep. This sleep had been prolonged. The last vivid dream had involved bits of houses, some reworking of his parents' farm, funny staircases abutting closet-like rooms that had never quite existed.

He was folded in two and sore. He sat up. The bed was empty. He stretched, observing the play of sensitivities created by the contorted night. An odd irrational energy, too. His yearning for her.

He got to his feet and looked about. His magnum opus had disappeared from the writing desk. He reassured himself that a doubtful, denuded feeling was common before a journey.

26

FIRST DAY
Berkshire

Archie had not come home. She had waited until late and he had not come home. He had chosen to be with the girl. After promising to try again, after giving it all lengthy consideration, he wanted a different woman, a girl, and a different home.

Agatha left the house, with her wedding ring in it, with the child in it, and drove away.

•

Her only plan was to find some stillness and give herself over to it. She knew that she was warped: all of her limp, sunken, molested, infirm. Logic had derailed and sleep no longer answered exhaustion. But for the first time in weeks, it seemed possible that the flustered fluttering of her heart might have been fading a little, that sinister prelude to an ear infection receding. She sat in her snub-nosed Morris Cowley by the Silent Pool, the beefy darkness of the countryside drawing at her motorcar. It was a magnetic pull, a centripetal gathering in.

Almost supernaturally, energy and purpose returned, and she got out to look at the lakes she'd never before stopped to visit.

It was dark, the moon flimsy. There was an odour of slack water, strangely familiar. Sweetish, verging on moribund, but too vegetable to be quite distasteful.

She passed the smaller of the two pools, making for the larger. They were enclosed by box trees and leaf-covered pathways. On one of these, as her vision honed itself against the night, she was startled by the exposed roots of a yew, like a thick mad plotting of entangled ideas.

She retreated to the edge of the Silent Pool. Water as composed as glass. Was it the perfect immobility that caused this singular quietude? That bit of nature had a depth, a stature unusual in those parts, and it had attracted the folklore about Prince John and the woodcutter's daughter. It was said that the maiden, who had been bathing there, drowned when he forced her into deep water, and that her ghost made midnight appearances. It could have been around that hour now.

But no sign of the maiden. Alongside or fused with the turbid smell, which was growing in some manner syrupy, she fancied she distinguished that of pondweed and even saw splotches of this in places on the surface, verdant, lush.

•

A gap, as if she'd been overtaken by a short formless sleep. It was a confounding sensation and for an instant she wondered what murky forest she was stranded in. Where? Why? How had she lost her way? What had her sins been? The surface of the small pond, scarcely lit by the attenuated moon, was so unmoving it resembled an impeccable sheet of pearl silk. A pellucid eye, without an iris, blank but not unseeing. She stared long and deeply into it.

She was submerged in vastness, in fright. She recoiled and stumbled.

She half ran back towards the Morris. Where was she, and how had she strayed?

By not loving her husband as he'd required? By dulling, sullying herself with grief for Mummy? And so she must undertake a journey of expiation. What a trial, hellish, and now! When she'd comfortably assumed herself as safe in marriage as a beloved pet in a snug domestic haven. Cast out at thirty-six, possibly the halfway point of her life, from all that was normal and kind.

But it wouldn't make sense to get back into the motorcar, because she didn't know where to go. She wasn't prepared for being confined in there once more. She needed to linger in the open air. She wasn't cold on that lenient winter night in her fur coat—the sort of coat in which you could take on all weather. How bad could things be in such a coat?

She gravitated back towards the larger pool. Stars, bright and timeless. Not a breath of wind, the air becalmed. Her terror appeared to be abating. It was curious, but on a dim arboreal path she was taken by an imperious desire to lie down in that box-tree bower. Were she to sleep, though, would she encounter the Gun Man? She had no choice. If she couldn't rest a little, she might collapse. She sat and then stretched out, her head by the base of a tree, the coat like a silky languorous animal she was entwined with. She was also entwined with the possibility of death.

That nacreous eye, watching over her. If she chose to, she could stare into it again, drift towards the magnet of a watery end. The end would come about by her own hand. In her own hand she would write a carnal full stop.

Getting anything to happen meant proposing something. Knowing it *could* be so. Then deciding, making it so. Why was this decision so chilling? Like giving in to a terrifyingly powerful desire, or its opposite. The desire for nothing.

•

But she did not desire nothing. She woke in the box-tree bower, not paining anywhere or cold, aside from her feet. She had not dreamed of the Gun Man. As peculiar as it was to find herself there, it was also natural, like taking up a piece of familiar piano music midstream. She was stiff and her bones slightly creaky as she stood, but she felt fitter than before. Less bruised, less diaphanous. Rather at home in the night, her heart more resolved. She didn't start when some small creature shifted by her. A bird uttered a sliding note or two. Could it be a nightingale? Her wristwatch held up to her face appeared to tell her that, extraordinarily, it was twenty-five minutes past five. Hours of sleep and she was unspeakably grateful for the reprieve, for some respite, finally.

Saturday.

She was aware of the anchored peace of the still waters, of their open, silken invitation. Yes—but.

But no.

No, not now.

Now—no.

She had lost everything. However, there was still a lot that she desired badly, and what took root in her mind was getting to some higher ground with a view. Had Mummy's spirit come to guide her? God? She couldn't detect the presence of God, but as she got into the Morris this wasn't too pressing a concern.

She drove cool-headedly, expertly, back up towards Newlands Corner. She'd turn in for that vantage point over the North Downs. Motoring by night had become as smooth as cream.

No one about as she arrived at Newlands Corner and parked.

The dark she emerged into had a live quality. She stood gazing over the drop of the Downs, recalling the restless blackness that had been the sea beyond the suite at the Grand Hotel, Torquay, where she had spent her first night as a wife. Beginning the journey of married life.

And so many years later, considering the slanting land that appeared more and more solid, the sky above it higher, softer and less material, she could not have said if she was continuing a journey or, having terminated one, was commencing another.

There was a surge in the air, a light gust of earthy fresh-ness. The flicker of something: eagerness, if not joy. Wobbly inspiration. She'd never entirely believed in this country as *country*, though she had to recognise that it possessed something. She'd brought Peter here recently for a walk—let him not be fretting—and they'd rambled down that pathway. It passed a small quarry.

She began to follow their footsteps, making her way down to the quarry cautiously in her silly shoes, not the best for the occasion, yet how could she have known what to dress for? At last, the chalk pit was before her. Peter had nosed in those bushes at the edge of it, bemused.

This just might do to bring her husband back to her. To show him the vast romance in her that she could scarcely believe he failed to see. You were stifled by not being ambitious, by fixating on whether something owed more to fancy than common sense. It could be the outlandish schemes that had a chance of saving you.

Odd, chalky luminescence.

•

From the quarry, uphill, alas, back to the Morris. She wasn't moaning.

But the motorcar wouldn't start. It *must*.

It was ten minutes after six and the morning had acquired a quivery tension, although the begrudging winter sunrise was a distance off yet. She climbed out and got busy with the crank. No good. Hot and awkward work in a fur coat, furthermore. She doffed the coat and laid it like a child's body in the motorcar. A breeze demonstrated that she was sweating. Her throat was dry, too. She'd have welcomed a glass of water, and what she'd have done for a gallon of milky tea. Another impassioned effort with the crank and—just as despair might have poisoned things—a man's voice.

'Are you having trouble with your car, ma'am? Can I help?'

The freeze, and shudder, of shock.

A man on a bicycle. Not aggressive-seeming. Stout, athletic. Young, quiet sort of face. Farm worker, most likely. Her heart growing more reasonable, she understood that his arrival was fortuitous.

'Oh, would you start it for me?' Bizarre to be speaking,

as if she had stopped doing so years ago. She smiled, aiming for neighbourly, run-of-the-mill. 'I'd be so grateful.'

It was twenty minutes after six. He had it going in a jiffy, and was readjusting his cap and mounting his bicycle once more.

'Thank you, thank you so much.' She felt an imprudent emotion—people could be so simply good. He was possibly envisioning a wild scenario. Lone woman out in the dark and so on. Ha.

She gave him as sober a farewell as she could manage, got into the motor again, and drove off, because she couldn't have him observing her. No sooner had she gone a few minutes towards Guilford than she about-faced and returned to Newlands Corner. Arriving, she was careful to make sure she had no company. Not a soul.

Her senses were fantastically alert, each move having to be true and efficient. The motor seemed very loud and the headlamps to blaze inordinately. She drove gingerly down the path that passed the quarry. It was a little bumpy and this made her short of breath. The headlamps caught the quarry's white glow, and then the Morris was facing that smouldering bareness. She stopped.

Brakes off and the gear in neutral, she got out. Took her handbag that had all her money in it, as she wasn't remotely lured by the thought of privation. Her shoes slipped, found traction. She staggered a little, recovered herself. Her shoulders and back leaning into the Morris's heft, she pushed, gave everything she had. Something not worrying occurred in a muscle or a conjoining of them in the vicinity of her right shoulder. She felt both very light, liable to be blown away by the breeze, and awfully strong. The exultation of writing one's own fate! The car went the last extra distance, reaching and lodging in the bushes that had engrossed Peter. She waited. It stayed there, perfect magnificent beast, on the brink. Amazing how revitalising physical exertion was when it came to the forefront of your attention.

Twenty to seven. Almost time to sit back and regard with satisfaction what she'd done, seeing that it was good. She admired her own temerity. She'd worked hard and the results were pleasing, on first impressions. Resting on the seventh day would be nice. She took a certain pride in the details. The headlamps still burning. The items left behind: dressing-case, old driving licence (identifying documents striking her in present circumstances as in some way quaint), coat. She was warm and an abandoned coat was more affecting, insinuating fragility. While she wasn't, in fact, overly delicate, was she? That sleep had been nothing short of magic. How little one needed, after all.

•

So:

What kind of hypothesis would be formed? Well, the Morris had gone out of control, because she was so tired and distraught, et cetera, and she'd had an accident. Knocked her head? After which she'd got out of the motorcar and—disoriented, not knowing quite who she was even . . . yes, suffering from amnesia, she'd wandered off across the Downs without her coat, into the night. Where anything might have occurred. Or someone had done away with her hours before, about the time she was lying down by the Silent Pool, and then done this to her poor Morris to make it appear that there'd been an accident. Something like that. They wouldn't find a body, of course. But by then the necessary initial impression would have been created. She wouldn't leave him to suffer long, just enough to wake him up. She'd send a letter soon, maybe today, to her brother-in-law, who valued her and had a sense of justice, letting him know where she'd be, once she'd decided. And she would write to her husband again. It wouldn't take him long to come for her, half raving with worry and remorse and remembered love. Something like that. Go from there.

•

One last look behind to see that she'd done all she needed to do. A fond goodbye to her Morris, not an adieu—though life showed you that beauty belonged to you only in the loosest manner. Agatha couldn't tell whether her puzzle was lacking, or pretty ingenious. You never could. She must believe her intuition was a faithful compass and she was operating in complete secrecy. She would not let herself be distracted by the oddly luminous chalk quarry. Would she be sick? No, she thought not. Now she must go down, down the hill. She needed the weighted flow, the ease of a descent.

It was somehow medieval to be setting out on foot, marching between those dewy fields. The box trees on either side of the pathway made her feel protected. Coatless she still wasn't cold. The morning was exceedingly mild, tepid even, and the odour of earth and foliage was alluring, if less fulsome than it would have been in spring. Onwards, down, down. Everything had been so stuck and rotten, but at last she was in transit. Had the sky taken on the faintest, whey-tinged phosphorescence? On the path before her were patches of moss, and a thistle flower abruptly filled her hand. When the sun hit them, these would be purple flares.

The first houses, and she turned right at the end of what she learned was Water Lane, sucking refreshment from the words. She knew how to get to Chilworth station from here, through Albury. It wasn't too far. What a shocking relief it would be to have London swallow her for a little, to drink tea in the buffet at Waterloo, while settling on her next destination. To board a train that would travel through the quiet rapture of sunrise. Her mind in that moment was limpid: she'd had to push through a wall—and enter a place with more give.

27

TWELFTH DAY

The presentiment of a fateful incident had intensified. Half awake, Teresa observed softened darkness: the sun hadn't risen yet but would soon. She remembered dreaming of the desert, of lands bare and inhospitable while also in some occult fashion attractive, luscious. She understood where she was. Her first instinct was to locate Harry, and she had only to turn her head to the left to do this. He was very near. He had slumped so far forward on his chair that his head rested on the bed by her chest. She could have pushed her fingers into his silvered sable hair. But she knew—as Mummy had known certain things by reading the currents in a room—that their *aventure*, if such a curious, fragile thing could be labelled so, was drawing to its close. A course was set. Too late for Edinburgh. Let alone Nice. It had always been too late for Nice.

The nightmare she'd run from, and her true name, were returning. She opened her mouth to the cotton of his pillow, breathing its faintest perfumes, sweet skin and breath, a faded smokiness. The fleeting well-being this inundated her with was nearly worse than what she'd fled. Then she'd been a worn-out, unloved sleepwalker in godforsaken Berkshire. Now she was refreshed and susceptible to tenderness. Devastating not to touch him.

As she forced herself to rise, a part of her remained low and safe in the bed beside which her secret lover slept. The female figure getting to her feet, pausing, a hand by his face, was gauzy. A spectre.

Her eyes fell on the writing desk and she recalled the pages waiting there in the shadows. Writers dreaded this sort of business, but with *his* manuscript it would be different, no imposition. In fact, having a piece of him with her would help her to leave the room. A final hesitation. Feeling danger approach, the last minutes of anonymity ticking sickeningly over, she went.

In her own room, she admonished herself, Be calm. Normal behaviour was the ticket. She managed to dress, and go downstairs. She took some newspapers from the hallstand and proceeded into the dining room for an early breakfast. No Jackmans, good. She buttressed herself with poached eggs, pork sausages and black pudding, handling the *Daily Mail* gently.

A former policeman was stating that, given the missing novelist's talent, she would have a remarkably elastic mind. Smiling into her tea, she rather enjoyed this. She paid less attention to a plan for divers to search the pools in the area of Newlands Corner, and moved on to *The Times*. More about divers and a 'comb-out'.

She jumped to the following story, also about a missing woman, a different one, a student of just twenty. She was taken with the description of her. A sensitive girl, and the death of her father two years before had hit her so hard it had harmed her health. Her nose was a little turned up and she was given to be pale. Her underclothing was marked with her name—an endearing particular, though how frightfully ashamed you'd be to know it had been made public—and she had disappeared carrying a yellow leather bag with some Chelsea Library receipts in it. You had to have a bad feeling about the girl. A gloomy feeling, indeed. But don't get upset. Have a little more toast and jam, sweet-tart cherry jam, and look, the weather for the health resorts. Harrogate: fog, then drizzle. And it was Unsettled Generally in the whole country. How gladdening.

She went up in the lift for *her* library books. The bedside table looked bereft once cleared of them. The photograph of her daughter came into view. Beautiful.

She listened for Harry's music, but of course it was too early for that. Had a floorboard creaked? Was he stirring?

Before she had time to decide to go up to him, she dashed out, down the stairs, through the lounge, and out of the hotel. The whole operation completed without her being buttonholed.

She passed some quiet enough hours on the streets of Harrogate, of which she'd grown fond. It seemed as if the air were growing a little harder to breathe, however. The invisibility she'd known here was compromised.

She returned the books to the lending library, without borrowing more. She sat awhile on an easy seat in Crescent Gardens. The sky was overcast and promised more misty rain, but it wasn't cold. Clement, for the season. She walked through Valley Gardens, past Bogs Field's curious dotting of wells. She slowed to observe the swans on the little brook.

Lunch was an apple and scones that she ate idling along James Street, mesmerised by window displays. Lucent jewellery, warm-toned carpets. On a whim, she bought the sheet music for 'Angels Ever Guard Thee' for Mr Bolitho, who'd accompanied her on the piano the night she sang it in the Winter Garden Ballroom. Agreeable idea, guarding angels. By three she was at the Hydro and under the hands of the masseuse. The woman reported that her back was much improved.

'And I haven't really felt the neuritis in days,' she remembered. 'The arm is just a little funny. The powers of the cure, no doubt. I'm afraid my appetite is restored, too. I've put on weight.'

'You've a fine figure. If you can't enjoy your food, ma'am, what can you enjoy?' The masseuse's figure was hearty, bountifully proportioned, her glorious sleep-inducing hands muscular.

'Yes,' Teresa said. 'What else is there?'

•

To fill every last spare moment, any possible gap—to avoid imagining what was coming, or going to Harry—she ate apples in the bath. She had always considered this one of the finer ways to pass time or hatch a crime scene. But when her three apples were gone and her hands could only press into porcelain curves, her thoughts would not be corralled, and there was Mummy's absence.

That she was no longer a fellow inhabitant of life was a fact that had to be grappled with. An event that went on recurring.

She rescued herself with a vision of Peter. She could rustle this up, as he'd kept her company countless times while she bathed. She saw his firm little body and noble eyes. He would have preferred she desist from loafing in that obnoxious pond made from volatile rain. On guard by the door, he was committed to the job of protecting her. Surely one of the most delightful things about dogs was their breath-taking absence of self-doubt. How did they achieve it—embrace life so unreservedly? Peter wandered over to press his cool nose into her hand. *Dear* faithful Peter. He met his mistress's foibles and whimsy with indulgence, always knowing how to draw her gently back to reality. Her little one. Her child.

After the bath, she went to check for letters and messages. Nothing, but Redhead looked at her curiously for a second or two.

Teresa chatted with a Mrs Robson of Harrogate. She'd sidestepped her before, knowing she was friendly with the Lady Entertainer. Like the Jackmans, Teresa found being forcibly entertained of limited interest. She was informed that a hotel party was going that night to a dance at the Prospect Hotel. Fatalistically, she announced she might come along. She shouldn't have been dallying in the public rooms but she felt careless and detached. What was there to lose? Night had set in.

In the hall outside the reading room, she heard Harry's voice. He must have just come in from a walk. Before she could distinguish more than scraps of words, she opened the door quickly and passed in.

Mr Jackman was there, alone. Maybe she could prepare him for her possible expeditious departure.

'Oh, Teresa. How are you?' He laid a newspaper aside.

It was very warm close to the lusty fire. 'Well, I guess.'

'Please sit. Henrietta has abandoned me for the pleasures of York and I'm sick of newspapers.' He gazed at her.

'I am, too. What a comfortable room.' She approved of the hardwearing bookshelves and armchairs, and the large windows grandly showcasing the felty winter night as though it was a series of muted masterpieces at a picture gallery. 'I like this hotel.'

'So do I. No more falls?'

It took an interlude of groping about in her memory to recollect the day he'd come to her aid on the slippery cobblestones behind the Pump Room. *He knows,* she realised. *There is no need to tell him.*

'No more. And how are you sleeping?'

'It's up and down. You haven't seen Harry today?' he asked sadly.

'I . . .' She looked into the flames. 'I shouldn't.'

After a moment, he asked, 'What's today? I never know what day it is here.'

'Nor I—holidays are like that. Which is energising. Time usually seems so iron-fisted. But I gather it's Tuesday. The fourteenth of December.'

'Already? We come here for Henrietta's health, you know.'

'Oh?'

'Yes. She appears well, but—she told you about our daughter, Jane?'

'She did.'

'Who lost her baby?'

'Yes.'

'It wasn't Jane's but Henrietta's—ours. *Our* baby who died.' He rubbed his hands together. 'Jane died when she was a baby. Shocking thing. I was an automaton myself for a time.'

He wasn't asking for succour, so the confidence didn't weigh on her. 'Terrible.'

'Yes. That was when sleep became precarious for me. Anyhow, we talk of her as if she'd grown up. It's our little fiction. It makes it easier for Henrietta. And for me also, maybe.'

'I'm so sorry.'

'Thank you, my dear.'

The door opened to admit a waiter with a tray of coffee things. The disruption startled them. Voices from the corridor gave an idea of purposeful movement going on out there.

'Teresa, can I trouble this good man for another cup for you?'

'No, thank you. I should be going.'

When the waiter had closed the door behind him, Mr Jackman added, 'I sometimes manage to sleep by resolving not to feel impotent. Acceptance is important but so is not seeing yourself as helpless, at the mercy of misfortune. One should believe one is the author of one's fate, of one's happiness, if only in small ways, through small actions.'

'Yes.' They listened to the vivacious fire for a little, and then she told him, 'I must go.'

They stood simultaneously, he with the physical sureness she'd noticed that day of her fall, when he'd escorted her back to the hotel. She went over and gave him her hand, detecting an odour—a version of it, with a masculine inflection—that she in some way knew. From her Grannies? A melding of soap, cologne and older skin. She remembered being intrigued and reassured by this. She thought now that it was very human, in a slightly dusty way.

They held one another's hands until he pressed hers and said, 'Teresa, I've betrayed you.'

'How?' But she asked it slowly, extracting her hand.

'I was talking with a couple of the bandsmen about the story, *that* story in the papers . . . about the lady . . .' He looked woodenly into the fire.

She was much more equable than she would have expected. 'Yes.'

'And we concluded . . . that certain details corresponded . . .'

'Ah.'

He advanced, 'All I can say for myself is that when you aren't sleeping, you aren't quite yourself. You tend not to be your best self. It was a small action of which I am not proud. It gave me no happiness, none.' The hand that he'd continued to offer sank now to his side, fatigued and knowing. 'I couldn't hold my tongue. It was probably senility, senile jealousy. I had been imagining things about you, I am embarrassed to say, imagining . . . that we might be coming to care for one another . . .'

'You love your wife! Anyone can see that! *Don't* you?'

'Very much. Though what anyone can see is far from everything. And love is . . . a house of multiple rooms, rooms that look different on different days, in different lights. I don't need to tell you this.' He tried, with eyes that she had only then observed to be of a moist aqueous blue, to interrogate her. She wouldn't allow it. 'Rather late, I noticed it wasn't me you were coming to care for. It was Harry. How petty I am—do you detest me?'

'Heavens, why *is* love so mixed up?' She backed towards the door.

'Should it be simple?'

'I don't know if I forgive you.' She was withdrawing from the reading room. 'I don't detest you. I think I do understand.'

She needed air. The side door led her into the hotel grounds. Still not cold enough for her to miss a coat, not after roasting by a fire, yet the rarefied, restless atmosphere she had been conscious of all day encouraged speed. Her presentiment was confirmed. It was just a matter of time. When was it not a matter of time?

Circling the Hydro, she passed a golden-haired youth relying heavily on a cane, his progress lead-footed. Her head reeled, reflecting on what it would be like having to walk thus, on Mr Jackman's insomniac illusions and the inventions of his gracious, wounded wife. Even keeping to the less obvious suffering, there were so many sparks of pain burning in any one life and this multiplied across the population of a hotel, a spa town, ordinary towns, the island of Great Britain, the Continent, the Subcontinent, and so on. It wasn't a picture that could be sustained for long, such fireworks. And really, how little was made of it all, considering. How quietly it was for the most part borne.

When she came back in, it was only five minutes after five. The arms of the grandfather clock were advancing with exaggerated sluggardliness. Two hours more till dinner. The dragging of winter nights. About to go upstairs, she heard a group of new arrivals—an older man, a younger, and an elegant woman of rather fuzzy age—asking if anyone fancied a billiard match. Supremely indifferent to the scheme, she fell in with it merrily. She lasted only one game, the luck from her previous game not holding, in the way of luck, before inviting them all to the dance at the Prospect Hotel and excusing herself.

As she was entering the lounge, the Jackmans' voices stopped her. Harry's, too. They had to be by the reception desk.

'You haven't seen Teresa, have you?' His tone had two parts to it, a buoyant and a grave.

'I've been in York all day, I'm just back,' Mrs Jackman declared. 'I have never seen anything like the Minster's grisaille windows. The *greyness* of them—they are surprisingly dark—but all shot through with light.'

'I think she was going out,' Mr Jackman contributed.

Teresa waited.

'I might go out myself. See what's playing at the picture house.'

'Good idea,' Mr Jackman said flatly.

Harry seemed to leave immediately after. The Jackmans began a softer conversation that wafted out of earshot. She hesitated for another few seconds, and then made a bolt for the stairs.

In her room, she considered the bedside table emptied of books. Oh dear. A curse on her for not having borrowed anything else. She caught sight of Harry's manuscript on the armchair. She took it to the bed.

Curled on her side, she read his pages through twice. His protagonist was a maudlin would-be aristocrat of humble rural origins. She felt her mouth moving into a smile. Not much happened. It was all rather lugubrious, not her kind of thing.

Strident laughter rose from the drive and she went to the window. A number of cars and taxicabs were arriving. The troops mustering for the dance? There was more than the usual amount of activity on the stairs, also, but then the dinner hour had to be approaching. Silence, of course, from Harry's room.

28

1914
Torquay

She smelled the water as soon as they stepped down from the train. But the distance from the station to the hotel was only a few yards and their time in the outdoors so short, too short. It would have been better to linger in the open air, yet she crossed the ridiculously small space beside him to whom she, as of that afternoon, belonged.

And would belong for ever after.

It was late and they were overtired, while also far too excited to be sleepy. Taking possession of the first rooms that would be really theirs, they laid down their few pieces of baggage. Furtively they regarded one another, incredulous at the day's happenings. Was it just the previous night that he'd awoken her in his mother's house, urging her so rashly to marry him? After all their doubts and dithering, after her long wait for him, could this really be the Wedding Night?

She went out onto the balcony, where she felt more sensible. The sea in a reflective mood.

'Can you believe it's Christmas Eve?' she asked, hearing him behind her.

'Your mother will never forgive me for marrying you without her there, you know.'

'Oh, I daresay she will, eventually.' She laughed. 'She did warn me against you. She said you were ruthless.'

He laughed, too, his teeth disconcerting in the obscurity when she turned to see him. 'Well, I suppose I am if I want something. I wanted you. And I've got you, haven't I?'

How completely she knew that view, a lower variant on the one she had from the road outside Ashfield whenever she needed it, there throughout childhood. Her cherished Torbay. She squinted at the headland on its journey towards Brixham, the lighthouse at Berry Head pulsing like a slightly otherworldly greeting. She had a strange feeling of being inside something which, though familiar, she had until then known only from the outside. Numberless times, considering the Grand from Princess Pier or the Strand, or studying its distinguished shape on the seafront from the Imperial, whose lights glinted now beyond Beacon Hill, she'd had a thought for the ladies and gentlemen staying within it. On occasion, as she wandered along the beach below, she'd observed a soignée lady on her balcony, and daydreamed about the interior of the room behind those glass doors and the chic travels that lady was poised to embark on. Yet abruptly the vantage point of the grown-up on her hotel balcony was hers. She found herself searching for a girl down on the beach.

'Do be careful.' These words or their tone possibly not what she'd have preferred to hear. She was leaning over the balustrade, savouring a faint giddiness. 'You could fall down there and kill yourself.'

She straightened up. 'Says the pilot.' He didn't appreciate the joke and a disgruntlement ensued. He'd leave her absurdly soon to go back to all that. The things he wasn't inclined to discuss, not—beyond chipper, clipped sorts of résumés—in any interesting way, made him tense. This unpredictable balance between obstinate bravery and something less sturdy was fascinating. She'd mother, nurse, dote on, entrance him. They'd be absolutely everything to one another.

'Come inside.'

'But isn't it lovely?' It was possible that her special relationship with Devon disturbed him.

'Yes,' he said. 'Yes.' Awfully good-looking when he was exasperating. His hand came to her waist. She was readying herself for compliancy as he murmured, 'Forgiven me finally, darling, for the dressing-case?'

She went inside, husband on her heels. They'd laughed already over the row provoked by his Christmas present to her—somehow not what she'd expected, too workaday, though undoubtedly handsome and practical—but she remained nonplussed at her own warlike display. Both embarrassed and righteous. She'd not imagined there was such a virago in her. A pugnacious might folded into her timidity.

He trailed her laxly while she reconnoitred the charming rooms, drawing curtains. They hadn't yet taken off coats and hats, and maybe it was this that suggested they were travellers propelled by chance into the same railway waiting room. Acquaintances who'd never before found themselves so casually together.

'Come and get that off, will you?' He'd taken off his own coat and hat.

Having been shivery all day, she was sweating lightly, prowling around. If she didn't keep reminding herself of what was occurring with the drama and the levity of some party trick in the dark, it was difficult to believe. Today she was a bride, tonight was her wedding night, tomorrow they'd go home to Mummy for Christmas, and the day after that she'd accompany this remarkably attractive young man—*her* man, her *husband*—to London. From there he'd depart for France. She surrendered her coat obediently, and began to tease off gloves.

He leaned over and snatched her hat from her head. She was startled by this impatience. By air moving on her bared skin. She recalled the guarded winter-afternoon light that had suffused the church. After he'd hung their coats in the wardrobe, their eyes met. The blue of his: the heady shade of water traversed by sunbeams, of fabled jewels. Somewhat troubling that at night you could only guess at it. He looked rather as if he might cry.

'Lucky to get this room,' he muttered.

'On such late notice.'

Their gazes struck against one another again and he was smiling. She'd been mistaken, or his humour had taken a sharp turn. This was an adventure to him. Impressive— but sport. She wasn't vexed to see him go from delicate to incorrigible. His impetuousness had drawn her to him from the start. She could hardly credit her luck. Oh, she could, though, and she looked forward to a long career in wonder. (Should she have known that they'd never be so exotic to one another again? That only a beginning wears such a high polish?) She'd have liked to be free of shoes, yet was unsure how to proceed.

She said, 'I'll open the window so we can hear the waves.'

'Let me.'

Waiting, six months of aeroplanes flying, lists of dead coming back like splintered, unbelievably reticent love letters, while she attended the harmed and faded men encumbering long lines of beds at Torquay Hospital. Thinking of him, she would walk home in the clean air, after her duties, uphill.

Death was not real, and then real, real and then not, a legend, numbers, anecdotes, Father. Blood was the departing vital fluid of a man. And just something red to be washed from a white uniform, from hands. You couldn't hold the truths in your mind too long, not without life covering itself in a pall. Stories were the other side of the moon, but helped to lift the dreary cloth.

Like death, her husband was outright alien and wedded to her. Astounding. She clung to the tableau of the travellers in the waiting room—and to the dark screen that was a pending journey, awaiting the images that would flicker over it. She went to fill her lungs at the open window.

He seized her slippery hand and yanked her back. 'Darling, I do love you so.'

She might have suddenly arrived, a hopeless provincial, wisps of hay in her hair, at a daunting metropolis. She was willing but lost. Much was at stake. What was it, exactly, this formidable thing? Paralysed and tingling, she smiled. Bright child that she was, she knew disguise—so, sophisticate or ingénue? She wanted to be intrepid, wanted to be duly retiring. Both were seemingly demanded of her and they erased each other. She was idiotically, shatteringly romantic.

'We only have tonight.' She sounded reproachful.

He bent his knees a little, so that they looked eye to eye, as if he would jocularly deliver a stern lesson. This stirred hilarity in her. An off-balance moment during which he looked younger, adolescent. She swiftly relived her outrage over the dressing-case, the disappointment.

He kissed her cheek and she closed her eyes, seeing him impulsive at the controls of an aircraft, herself drifting between lines of hospital cots in her white uniform, a version of a nun, though aware of admiring eyes. She was in her first youth, her zestful beauty giving her a certain nerve.

With a new haste he finally found her lips, the journey begun. Man and wife. They'd melt together, somehow. Make an eternal shining oneness that would fill every gap.

29

TWELFTH DAY, EVENING

She came downstairs at around seven thirty, presentable, she thought, in the salmon-pink georgette, and with a rampant appetite. At once, she registered a suffocated perturbation in the lounge.

The epicentre of it was a man seated in an armchair, his face curtained by a newspaper. The air had grown very thin and sly. It was just as well, after all, she hadn't borrowed any more books, because whatever had been coming had arrived.

The newspaper shifted. And she recognised—her husband.

One last capacious holiday moment before time went faster. She had leisure to study his features, to observe him identifying her—quickly, his eyes, unwilling to linger or attach themselves, shot next, with insistence, to a man. A policeman, presumably. This was to be no warm reunion. There were to be no apologies on his part, no pleas for the future of their marriage. She absorbed all this, together with the pile of newspapers on the low table and a general stirring in the wings, as it were. And she mused that growing up was having disenchantment make plain that what you'd always taken for granted was yourself—the true dreaming-feeling part, the violent-loving part—didn't necessarily have a place in daily life. So there was to be no being whole. Living was passing between a series of compartments in which you took up different roles. Wife in that one. Mother in this. Daughter-in-law. Daughter. Your husband's lover. Lady being attractive and charming. Lady shopping. Lady lunching out. Lady vacationing alone. By and large the roles wouldn't come as easily or be as diverting as those you had played as a solitary child on the lawn at Ashfield. The deeper waters hardly flowed into them. Was the most fiendish truth that you were called on to be your own Gun Man, anaesthetising your dreams—as they were resistant to being killed? After which the only thing for it was to get on, hoping not to seem too disrupted, or dead.

'Hullo,' she said, going over.

He gave her a small frightful smile contaminated with irony. 'Well.'

She sat down opposite him, not too close. His jaw was hard, as happens when you've been in the public eye, in an intolerable role, with your fixed countenance, for much too long. He was an inferior actor. Maybe that was why she'd loved him, because he was so poor at pretending. She'd thought there was something pure and savage in that. He *was* pure and savage. He had a black-and-white, one-track will—essential in those who are mad about golf?—and perhaps this was admirable. Foul but probable that she'd go on loving him. Danged handsome in a new, well-tailored black suit. That infuriating show of self-assurance that got her blood up. Clearest blue eyes . . . obtuse, false. Cowardly. The control in his youthful face betraying a terror of showing himself shaken. She recalled him in that rare moment of open fear and romance under the beech the night she gave the day—as the French would say—to his child. She'd been almost more worried for him than for herself. Now, if there'd been a tidy, untraceable way of doing it, she might have murdered him.

Mr Bolitho, her accompanist on the evening she'd sung in the Winter Garden Ballroom, was passing slowly through the lounge and it would have been rude not to acknowledge him. 'Hello, forgive my speedy escape after our performance,' she said. 'You're an accomplished pianist.'

He stopped by her. 'And you could be a professional singer, Mrs Neele. But you've heard that before.'

'Not true—but thank you. My brother has just arrived,' she explained, nodding at the so-called brother, who looked quite at a loss.

He greeted Mr Bolitho curtly, making it evident that there was to be no conversation. 'We should really go in to dinner,' he intoned, blatantly only to her.

'In a minute.' She'd remembered the sheet music, 'Angels Ever Guard Thee'. It was protruding from her handbag in a neat role. 'A souvenir,' she told Mr Bolitho, taking it out and dashing off a signature.

Teresa Neele. A name light and filmy on the page.

Mr Bolitho blushed, with the blend of regret and enjoyment he displayed at the piano, and accepted the offering with a bow from a more gentlemanly era.

She was standing when the man who had to be a policeman —she thought she'd noticed him in the lounge the day before, a broad, inoffensive-looking fellow—was suddenly addressing her. He asked if she could tell him what had happened to her during the past eleven days.

She was unequal to his intent solemnity. His eyes were a depthless grey and in them she saw her importance to him, his longing for a great unveiling. She was almost sorry not to oblige, to have to present him at the end of his steeplechase with a white wall.

'Eleven days?' She smiled vaguely for the benefit of those around them and tried not to breathe too deeply of the thin air. 'So long?' She wasn't sure if the hiatus had felt less or more. 'I . . . I seem to have lost my memory.'

'Lost your memory?'

'Yes, it's only starting to come back now.'

'That's right,' her husband said, relieved at how this might exonerate him. 'She remembers nothing at all. We might continue this conversation later? My wife and I were going in to dinner.'

She nodded demurely at the policeman, who seemed not to have planned his next move. Mrs Robson, also dinner-bound, met her eye.

In a discreet but firm voice suggesting some sensitive family matter upon which it would be impossible to elaborate, Teresa said, 'My brother has arrived, so, you see, unfortunately I won't be able to come to the dance tonight. And I was so looking forward to it.' She didn't dare glance around for Harry.

•

There was a baleful peace at their table. How normal barely mastered tension felt between them—she took this in. She'd ordered the sole and was behaving nicely, restrained and mildly amused. Do remember, though, that the roles should be played adequately well, by all means, but not *too* well. A virtuoso rendition might make you forget what lay lower, desires biding their time. Out of the corner of her eye she caught the Jackmans settling themselves at a table and observing her, Mrs Jackman probably in puzzlement. She turned towards them for long enough to transmit a smile and have it good-naturedly returned. It wasn't all horrid and barren up here on the surface. There were bits of kindness.

One morsel of kindness sent you hunting for others, however. In the man opposite you. You didn't care for the rage so tightly laced inside his badly done coolness, though he'd have been through a lot, too—must have been quite humiliated—and was his jaw softening a little? Yes, there, and now you glimpsed the sanguine boy in the stony man, and would the boy see that you were graceful in your salmon-pink georgette? Mightn't he understand how sorry you were to have caused such a cock-up, the press and all those atrocities? That a broken heart had been the culprit? If he'd been suspected of doing away with her—well, wasn't there some truth to it? If he could see any of this, there might be generous moments to come with the child, also.

'Our daughter is well,' he sneered. One of his erratic instances of perceptiveness.

'Is she? Oh, thank heavens. I feel absolutely awful about leaving her.'

'I daresay you do. She doesn't know anything. We've kept it from her. Carlo has been marvellous.'

As she'd known Carlo would be, bless her, in her secretary's fabulously dependable Scottish way. Dear Carlo. She'd be glad to see her again. 'And . . . how is Peter?'

He knew she'd have asked this without delay. 'Pining for you,' he spat.

She was too composed and mature to say she imagined his lover, the bona fide Miss Neele, was pining for *him* at this moment. Silk-enveloped golfing thighs in a hotel room's nectarine-tinted light. The sole had no taste at all, its texture discomfortingly fleshy. The question was: were morsels of kindness enough?

'One of the chaps in the band recognised you from the newspapers.' It wasn't her message in *The Times* that had brought him. Had he ever been interested in decoding her messages? 'I was thinking I should give them all some little memento, a thankyou for the service rendered.' Expertly unfeeling, he went on, 'I'll have the car waiting for us in London. We'll drive back from there.' He wasn't able to bring himself to say 'home'. Swallowing his beef bourguignon must have been uncomfortable with his teeth set like that. He'd suffer from indigestion later. 'The only problem is the press. The bloody circus. Other thing we could do is get your sister here under wraps, take the train to Manchester and hole up at the hall. They won't expect that.'

Clever Sister would be a brick, of course, but how wearisome to have to justify herself to her. Clever Sister would be moderately appalled at the public display, faintly alarmed at the possibility that her younger sister had lost her mind, gone to pieces, something unseemly of that sort (and *was* this something of that sort?). Although being inclined to adventure and originality, she'd be stimulated by the cloak-and-dagger flavour of it all. Hadn't she gone to Torquay railway station disguised as a Greek priest? Brought off her number at the finishing school, that leap onto the table laden with tea things? She might rather welcome a spicy diversion from the stolid routines of the hall. She'd think the amnesia line was bosh. Would she be hurt that her little sister hadn't gone to her?

'Have you finished? I'll have to attend to the police now. Maybe even to the blasted journalists. I'll escort you upstairs.'

He hadn't asked if she wanted dessert. Maybe she did. Hadn't asked her to account for herself. Having no taste for the answer, and petrified she'd make a scene. How very little he knew her. She found she wasn't surprised that he had no wish to be alone with her, or even to know if she were well. He hadn't said her name. What had been coming was the opposite of desire—this death, the stone-cold cadaver of their love. She had known it, and stubbornly not known it, until then.

The chatter in the lounge was insistently loud. Mounting the stairs, she had the impression that the walls had grown closer from the pushing, from all sides, of a massive force. She would *not* look around.

'Quick now,' breathed the man who—the world would soon be informed of it—couldn't bear to be her husband any longer.

One step, two. Another. Good girl, like that. And another.

The last steps were easy, because Harry was on the first-floor landing. What a heavenly unthinkable disaster it would have been to walk into his arms. Coming down the stairs, he showed no sign of recognising her or acknowledging her companion. *He* could act. To an insensitive onlooker, to her unwilling Other Half behind her on the stairs, the profound brown-eyed glance would no doubt have seemed entirely random and insignificant.

She reached down into its low sorrowful heart, hoping that he too could discern what was buried in her for safekeeping. And they'd passed him and were approaching her room.

'Right,' her husband was saying in hushed tones, 'I'm in number ten, on the other side of the staircase. Go in quickly.'

Her actions would be supervised now. She remembered something, searched desperately in her handbag and retrieved it. 'Wait here. I just have to return an item to that man.'

'Who? Well, hurry.'

Harry was still on the first flight of stairs.

'Mr McKenna, I've kept forgetting to give you this back.' As he stepped up towards her, she stepped down into the warmth of cherry tobacco, sugared alcoholic sharpness, his rueful maleness. Standing over him, she offered his handkerchief. 'I've been carrying it around.'

'Why, thank you, Mrs Neele,' he said, without taking it. He whispered, 'I looked for you all day.'

They were barely out of sight in that slim parenthesis of the stairs. 'I couldn't see you,' she whispered back.

'You won't come away with me? We can leave this awfulness behind.' His eyes were languid.

'My daughter,' she said, gesturing at the sticky, sickly congealing of events the dummy-woman she had to be belonged to. 'I must go.' She thought suddenly that it was probably not even possible, or at least not fair, to make of another person your safe haven.

A brief hesitation she'd not forget.

'Thank you again, Mrs Neele,' he said loudly, clasping her hand in his, closing her fingers so tightly on his handkerchief that it was painful. Then Harry nodded and gave her a sad little half-smile whose message was comfort. And adieu. These last words almost soundless: 'See you in Nice?'

She turned.

And went back to her husband, who stopped his pacing to say, 'Don't worry—I'll take care of things. Explain that you've lost your memory. That you don't know me. You don't,' he added, 'even know you have a child.'

Harry appeared to have changed his mind, coming into their view before exiting it to ascend the stairs. Her husband darted him an irritated look.

'Very well,' she replied with a new strength, seeing repressed turmoil unfold in the only face more familiar to her than her own. 'Though just so you understand—I'll do what you wish, for now. Go along with it. But when all this is over, I'll do whatever I please. Count on that.'

He was livid, hardly breathing. 'Is that a threat?'

'If you think it one, then most certainly. Goodnight.'

'Agatha,' he implored, far too late, and she didn't turn back.

Once she was finally alone, panic gleamed like the shiny lining of a coat flapping open in a gale. Oh God. Such scrutiny. She was notorious! A seedy, dreadful incarnation of the dream of promenading down the high street in a state of undress.

Harry's music saved her. It was faint, trickling jerkily through floorboards and walls, over the increased noise bloating the Hydro. And her mind slowly began to dilate.

•

After some minutes, a soft channel down to a lower place was opening, and she drew on it. Everything would be all right, she told herself, if only she could do this, take periodic doses of this like sulphur water. She'd always done it, hadn't she? Didn't she know she always could? It would be possible when she was alone. When she was taking a walk in the country, or in a city throng. Perhaps even a little, much more surreptitiously, when she was in society?

Press on.

But being greedy, given to disquiet, the petted child peckish for splendour, she'd wait and wonder if she mightn't get more than these modest measures. And if there wasn't somewhere waiting for her a person who wouldn't blink to see her in the high street *en déshabillé*, her imagination rippling over her skin.

•

Remembering his maudlin would-be aristocrat was like having an unobtrusive friend sidle into the room. A surprise. Harry's protagonist, Henry, was not striking. But he was slender and rather agile from constant walking, and his eyes were melancholy in a gentle face. In those few pages, his life was fearfully unadventurous and something of a failure. He was bent on being urbane, a flawlessly *comme il faut* old-fashioned gentleman. He didn't entirely manage it. That breed was dying, in any case. He did appear to have a considerable capacity for affection—he was always falling in love, with strangers who accidentally brushed his arm in the street, hopeful window boxes, queer architecture and all manner of foolish notions. Though he never travelled, only moped around London, picture galleries, parks and the banks of the Thames, he came across as a nomad. This despite the fact that he'd occupied unprepossessing lodgings in Bayswater for many years. Notwithstanding his despair over always losing what he loved, he had a way of making a thing that took his fancy into his heart's one desire, a sacred home. The more she thought about Henry, the more she confused him with herself, this happening with people you cared for. With art, she supposed. Her eyes were wet. Elgar rather had that effect. *Elgar.*

Presuming Harry finished his book and published it, something she was afraid he wouldn't find easy, it was unlikely anyone much would read it—not unless it got a good deal more straightforward and eventful. She couldn't see that happening. But you never knew. Harry's prose read like a translation, somehow, the result of a filtration process she couldn't comprehend. What sieve had it passed through? It was fortunate he had an inheritance. She established herself at the writing desk To Give An Opinion.

> *Dear Harry,*
>
> *This is capital. You must carry on with it because I find myself becoming attached to Henry Jacobson and curious about his Fate. I do hope you'll give him some satisfactory romance. Otherwise, how can we bear it? Mind you're not afraid of being cheerful. People do like to be amused. A bit of a lark is pleasant and plausibility isn't terribly important, all said and done. Some restoring of order in the denouement is desirable, too—don't you agree?*
>
> *I think you are a fine writer* (a sound judgement, or her fondness for him talking? Having received a similar endorsement from a Respected Author as a young girl, she knew what such sentiments could mean to one). *Now*

understand that it will be a shocking amount of most tiring work and at times you'll be quite fed up and reasonably expect to go insane. But I know you wouldn't take any desperate action. You and I have an agreement on that score, do we not? Actually, I suspect we are beyond it, or aren't cut out for it. That road we saw before us didn't seem interesting enough. Wasn't it like that, for you? Was it Mr Vaughan who saved you? Why did you wait so long to take the poison? Was the sadness not great enough after all? Anyhow, mostly you'll detest or half detest and half adore your scribblings with a mad defensive passion. But stay entertained. We are told art is second to life—are we to believe it? Does art stop life from beating the art out of us? Is that enough to go on with? I don't know, honestly. Though I don't know that it isn't, either. And that is something, I guess. A start.

Thank you for being a warm friend, just what I needed. I will miss our funny conversations. Until Nice, that is.

Yours,

(She hesitated, and chose) *Katherine Grey.*

She vowed to leave it under his door very early the next morning.

•

She had just assembled a quantity of written lines without any terrible effort. The task had felt simple. It occurred to her that she might try a little work. Could she feel some industriousness coming on? Was the silence finally crumbling? She *would* work. It would not be a wifely pastime. She'd need money if she were to be alone. Her hundred pounds a year wouldn't go far. But it was all right: she would become a successful working divorcée. (Don't give yourself time to wonder if he'll change his mind.) She felt burgeoning in herself a true professional's obstinacy. Yes, she'd work, scrambling over the white walls of pages till the Wretched Book was conquered. And she'd sold books, had she not? Quite a number of the one that had had people talking. She'd been taken advantage of as a young writer—and as a woman—with dishonourable contracts, but she'd a new publisher now and herself to rely on. She could force herself to write whether she felt like it or not, whether or not it came naturally. What was natural? There could be pleasure in subjugation, in being a little rough with oneself, an autocrat, pushing the spirit into a cage, closing it into a strongbox. Quietening it down. And sometimes a channel opened, leading down to a lower place. What you drew up could be fun and could rinse your spirit clean. Save you. The sleeping dreams.

So:

A grey-eyed girl.

Intelligent, sensible, yet ravenous for adventure. Not everyone saw her subtle beauty. Those who did were captivated. Attired in a light grey *tailleur* with a look of Paris about it, she sat in her train compartment.

She was the surviving kind. It was the other one who'd die on the *train bleu* . . .

Was the dream beginning to stir, to awaken? She had a swift certainty that if she went on mulishly visiting the scene, something thrilling and nasty would suggest itself. The insufferable looseness would tighten, her body firm with urgency, because everything negligible, everything pointless, had been sharpened to a point.

She had to believe that it would again be as it was on the rambling, never-ending afternoons in the garden at Ashfield. Grassy warmth. Regal gulls swinging aloofly over. Clean brightness, woodsy shadows. A soft rushing in her ears of sea winds through infinite leaves. The expanse of salt water just beyond sight.

And she there in that complete solitude, that deepest privacy, but also jumping free. Off, away.

30

CONUNDRUM

On Wednesday morning, oblivious guests proceeded peacefully about invisible doings, lying abed, dripping egg yolk
onto sheets (those not confining themselves to the slimming
diet of grapefruit and split toast), dawdling over toilettes and
cups of milky tea, awaiting the effects of the cure on their
digestion, and reading chronically. Common runaways taking
for granted their right to the dusky pleasures of privacy.

Meanwhile, an unnaturally quiet hubbub simmered in the
Harrogate Hydropathic. All the telephones were engaged,
the employees as self-conscious as new actors. The lounge was
thick with shifty policemen and murmuring journalists. The
mood in the public rooms was incredulous and rather histri-
onic, with something of the rowdy funeral, or the constrained
party. Louder, more excitable voices could be heard from
outside. A landaulette was parked at the front entrance,

journalists thrust indecently against it. Photographers adorned the bonnet and the wings, but the landaulette was a decoy.

The missing novelist who had been going by the name of Teresa Neele was no longer missing. Nor was she, strictly speaking, incognito anymore. And celebrity was after her.

A man returning from a stroll designed to ease the damage of a night of dazzling insomnia saw her at a side door. He recognised her black cloche hat with its pale pink stripe and the coat trimmed at the collar, cuffs and hem with reassuring fur. For further reinforcement, she had chosen double-stranded pearls, champagne-hued stockings and dark gloves. Her eyes were on far too short a leash for her to remark him. She had no long-distance vision at all.

She paused as she tucked what might have been a folded handkerchief into her sleeve, gathering herself, and then gave a little gallant toss of the head. It may have been a pose or one of those gestures made almost without thinking, for survival.

Harry thought Teresa did not seem the quarry they wanted her to be, nor the woman who'd arrived there eleven days before, a queen brought to her knees. He noticed the clandestine taxi that would remove her from him, a buttons boy already holding open the door, a competent and staunch-looking middle-aged woman—sister?—standing by. And now moving towards Teresa, though with something like unwillingness, like aversion, was the Colonel. Dapper in Norfolk jacket and plus fours, damn him to hell.

When she strode briskly onto the path, her reserved, august deportment was that of a reinstated monarch. It was as she stepped off the hotel's grounds, reaching for the footpath with her left foot clad in its black-strapped shoe, that the one astute photographer who'd not been fooled by the ruse of the landaulette, the *Mail's* man, captured her. Doing so, he decided her legs were shapely.

Also preserved in the photograph would be shoulders that were a little hunched, and a head a little too far forward. A face in profile, clear enough. Gazing dead ahead. Eyes shaded by the hat's brim. Long, imposing nose. An expression obdurately blithe, as bland as a spy's. There would appear to be no one residing behind it.

At nine fifteen Harry observed Teresa (he'd persevere in calling her by the name she'd entered his life with) climb into the taxi, followed by the Colonel. He was transfixed as the motor bound for the station started its glide along Swan Drive. Other motors were in pursuit. A sense of betrayal hovered, or sacrifice. His eyes followed only what interested him as she sailed by the Pump Room. No mist, that morning, the weather remaining temperate for the season.

He watched until there was nothing more to be seen. Then he pushed through the press of trumped men and ran up the stairs to a room in which a packed suitcase waited under the bed, and on the writing desk, a small sheaf of papers, with a letter. His mind leaned towards the Riviera.

Heaven only knew why Valeria had kept secret the money that would pay for his passage there, if he so desired it. To punish, or to challenge him? To punish herself? So he would have something to smooth his way, once she had left him? To care for him? He hardly bothered asking himself this question anymore. It seemed a mystery to which the solution was beside the point. Despite his losses, and his not knowing where, if anywhere, he belonged, he was amazed at what a rich man he was.

What sense did it make to try to penetrate the secrets of a loved one? To question her most intimate choices? A woman had the right to be a conundrum that no one could resolve, perhaps not even herself. As slow-witted as Harry had been, he had learned this, after all. He had not attempted to convince Teresa to leave the Colonel, once he had seen that her mind was made up. Some choices were made in darkness and should not be forced to face the light. But turning in on oneself did not have to be a cold turning away. It could be full of feeling, part of love's repertoire. It could be all one could do for the time being, silence the only translation, while waiting for the Muse.

ACKNOWLEDGEMENTS

This is very much a work of the imagination, mixing facts and fantasy, though it was sparked by Agatha Christie's 'disappearance' and draws on the author's life and writings. A number of books and materials provided useful information and nourished my invention of a character, notably: *Agatha Christie: An Autobiography* by Agatha Christie; *Agatha Christie: A Biography* by Janet Morgan; *Agatha Christie: An English Mystery* by Laura Thompson; *The Grand Tour: Around the World with the Queen of Mystery* by Agatha Christie, edited by Mathew Prichard; and the Christie archive at the University of Exeter (to which Christine Faunch and Gemma Poulton facilitated my access). I have several times cited or paraphrased *The Times* and the *Daily Mail* from the days of the search for Christie. Christie's novels—especially *The Mystery of the Blue Train*, those written before it, and the Mary Westmacott books—were presences at the edge of my work. The letter to Harry includes echoes of letters Christie received from Eden Phillpotts, and I borrowed 'a little gallant toss of the head' from *The Secret of Chimneys*.

This novel was made possible by the invaluable Australia Council for the Arts. I am also extremely grateful for the assistance of Annette Barlow, Siobhán Cantrill, Ali Lavau, Clara Finlay and Emily O'Neill at Allen & Unwin; and of the staff at the British Library Newspapers at Collindale.